CINCO D' MOJAVE

NASH RUNNING BEAR MYSTERY
BOOK FIVE

BAER CHARLTON

MORDANT MEDIA ™©®
A Division of Charlton Productions

Cover design by Roslyn McFarland, Far Lands Publishing

Sketch artist Kelly Eamon

Rogena Mitchell-Jones, Literary Editor
RMJ Manuscript Service, www.rogenamitchell.com

Published by Mordant Media, Portland, Oregon

ISBN: 978-1-949316-41-4 [paperback]
ISBN: 978-1-949316-40-7 [ebook]

10 9 8 7 6 5 4 3 2 1

CONTENTS

Powder

1
COMPOUND

CERTAIN CHEMICALS, minerals, herbs, or spices are harmless when taken alone. But when taken in together...

Cooking has always been an art. Day-to-day cooking is, at its best, boring. At its worst, it is tedious. Jana sprinkled the rolled-out dough with the ground lavender, cardamom, sage, and deadly nightshade. The limited use of the scopolamine she had used before. Enough to block the nervous system in the lungs and gastrointestinal tract, but not enough to kill. But it would mask the other herbs as they worked. Her soft brioche rolls were universally popular among the group.

The turkey breasts cooking in the brick oven contained their sleep-inducing tryptophan. The calming nature of the lavender in the dry rub helped. Being vacuum marinated for the day in a stew of alcohol-infused Italian plums and tart cherries added to the juice and flavor guarantees seconds.

She had added the desiccated hollyhock for its kick to the tryptophan. But reduced the hemlock or water chestnut, as it was better in a hard alcoholic drink. But she could count on only a few who would imbibe the alcohol. Some drank nothing besides the water they harvested from the air, even though the water from the well was just as pure after filtering it.

She glanced over at the sound of the front door. The man walked past the door to the large commercial kitchen. "Hey, Peter."

The bald man stepped back into the doorway, drawing a long sniff. "That smells great. Italian chicken?"

She shook her head as she cut the dough into squares for the rolls. "Turkey. How was the traffic?"

His eyes rolled large. "I couldn't believe the congestion as I came up Boundary Road. There must have been at least seven rabbits. I think the temperature has triggered their sex drive over the heat. I had to drive around two in the middle of the road." He winked.

Her head and face jerked her short blond hair in a violent twitch as her tongue stuck out in a fat sausage to lick her lips. "I don't think they take that long."

He laughed as he turned to leave. "Either way, it was a hare-raising experience."

She groaned. "Terrible pun. In fact, it wasn't even bunny."

She could hear him in the hall. "Hey, do you know if Mitchel and Gomez finished last night's water capture?"

"I know they were out at the array this morning, but I think there's a problem with the solar collectors. They were working on them."

"Okay, I'll get with Steve and Amy before dinner."

2
POUNDING SAND

NASH ROUNDED the large outcropping of boulders. The wet faces strewn with decades of ocean abuse and love. The grassy seaweed clung to the barnacles as tiny crabs made their way slowly from crevice to hole to empty barnacle shell. Sea fleas and small beetles played their millennia-old game of tag. A lone bird wheeled overhead, tracking the runner splashing through the shallows around the headlands. The water was refreshing and meant there were only two miles of pink sand left to run.

Nash touched the tip of the one rock as she passed from splashing in the shallow water, creating tracks on the wet sand. The narrow trace of darker pink separated the water from the dry sand.

She could feel the depth of the shoe print as she jogged. Feeling the depth was a habit she remembered in boot camp and Basic Underwater Demolition or SEAL (BUD/S) school. She just hadn't remembered choosing the firmer path in the wet sand because it was part of the wet instead of the hotter, dry sand. Most just ran the path because it was less tiring. It was more like running on dirt paths—until the sergeants took pleasure in hosing down random areas of the dirt courses until the mud was ankle-deep.

Not for the first time, she glanced back to her right. The dog wasn't there. She had gotten used to glimpsing Powder's pink tongue lolling to the right side of her mouth as she shadowed her partner.

But after the surgery, only a brief potty or food break would separate her from Mina's side. Even when Nash packed her Go bag and laid out the tactical harness—the dog refused. Nash never pushed. She just left the harness on the couch and went to work like in the old days. She understood. Duty comes in different ways to different people, even when one of those people has four feet and fur.

Nash focused on the two sets of landing lights from a Boeing seven forty-seven. The owners had bid on the lights as part of a salvage operation. They mounted them under the restaurant's overhang at the top of the cliff. Without the high winds of a plane to cool the intense lights, they had rigged up a water-cooling system, drawing water from the ocean.

Early sunrise behind her reflected off the light's lenses. The four white dots were Nash's guiding lights for the last mile of her morning run she had started in the night's cool air. The daily half marathon had a calming effect on her. But when she could feel her blood pressure, she started earlier and ended later. Her longest run and toughest day had resulted in a forty-mile loop through the middle of the island.

But a crappy day in Barbados was better than the nicest day in D.C. She had started in a moderate storm at midnight. The weather had turned into one of the island's rare tropical storms. Tripping over a wobbly rock in the surf and hitting a cluster of other rocks was hard enough to require a few stitches. She wore a long-sleeved caftan around her wife. She thought it would cover the bandages and not worry Mina. Nash hadn't counted on her wife being such an eagle-eyed clotheshorse.

Mina hadn't mentioned it until Nash took the bandages off. Mina's only comment was the sleeves fit smoother, but she still limped like she had a knife stuck in her right buttocks. She made

Nash strip and come clean before dinner, after which she threatened to fire the nurse, Lele if Nash ever tried to hide an injury again.

Lele, who had seen worse with the two, only ruffled her special copy of the New York Times Barbados edition. She skimmed the news and pecked at the crossword puzzle throughout the day. She would often leave the finished puzzle around the hotel's rooms. She had cajoled magnets out of Chester or the boys in Washington and hung them on the refrigerator. None of the women had ever had children or nieces and nephews to dote on... so Mina gushed over the crossword *art*.

Nash slowed in the deeper sand as she approached the long stairway cut centuries before into the side of the cliff. The steps were wide and graciously gentle. The hotel manager had explained they had been used to carry bounty gathered from the sea up to the lodgings above. A large crane had been used to lower man-boats. Then, the so-called pirates would row out over the many coral reefs to gather the flotsam left by the ships breaking up from a storm. The false mast erected in the curve above the beach gave the illusion of a safe, calm harbor in a storm. The pirate captain and landowner was the only successful sea scoundrel who had never owned a ship.

They stayed in the special apartment—the preserved private residence of the former pirate. The floor-to-ceiling windows were doors fitting back into the walls. Glass in one set was to turn the elements. Leaving only the louvered shutters provided a refreshing breeze and the sound of the waves crashing on the rocks eighty feet below. Nash and Mina viewed the hidden, majestic glass doors as an option—but never used them.

Midway up the stairs, Nash paused and looked back over the calm bay. Each reef showed in the early morning light. The lighter bands, separated by the darker troughs of sand, glowed through the water. She considered going back for a swim but decided to enjoy the saltwater pool above when Mina was ready to spend time in the cabana later.

———

MUNA SNUCK A QUICK LOOK AT THE TIME BLOCK ON THE screen and groaned. She had, once again, fallen down the rabbit hole of the dark web. Looking at her right hand as if it was some alien hanging in the air with two large orange bulging craniums, she shrugged and popped them in her mouth. The bubbles of deep-fried fat sizzled as they melted into molten lava. Her eyes rolled as she smiled them shut, and she leaned back into her chair in bliss—to have a mouth, consuming lava. Her one eye opened as she made an executive judgment not to hit the shooting range at the crack of dawn. In celebrations, she clicked on the small triangle symbol with the exclamation mark in the middle. The world news highlights booted on the screen as her hand found the bag in the drawer.

Germany and France ship more heavy field artillery into Ukraine. The riots in Paris are smaller but no less destructive. An EF-4 tornado cuts a swath twenty-eight miles long through Ohio with seven dead. The international Pacific Rim trade group has again cut off minerals trade with China. Japan's central bank cuts its prime rate by half a point as the recession has failed to take a stranglehold on the islands. Again, Congress is in a deadlock over the omnibus bill, and it looks like they will go on their fall break, leaving work undone, the same as last year. In the California Mojave Desert, authorities have found nineteen bodies in an apparent mass suicide. Walmart says they will cut another seven thousand jobs in the USA to raise their stock price. Walmart and Kroger missed their second-quarter earnings by a full percentage point. The Auto Clubs report the national cost of gasoline rose again by fourteen cents this last week, ahead of the fall holiday season.

"Good gosh. For once, can't we have a dragon sighting? Or maybe a confirmed UFO landing in midtown Chicago?" She stood as she rolled her eyes. Looking around the darkened office space, she grimaced. "At least we've gone a couple of days without a mass shooting or a child with a parent's gun shooting a sibling."

"Did you say something?"

She jumped and swung around. She had forgotten the guard had walked through a few minutes before. The young, slender man stood in the archway, still plagued by a face breaking out in zits. "Oh. Leon. I forgot you were here." She frowned. "How long were you in the lab?"

He rolled his eyes. "The light in the autopsy room was still on. It took me a couple of minutes to find the right switch. Also, there were two doors open a crack..."

She pushed her chin up in acknowledgment. "Yeah. The drawers two and four don't chill, so Mike keeps extra supplies there ... Wait. Did you find the light switch for the overhead light? Where?"

He pushed his finger into the air like a rocket and aimed it at the other room as he let it turn him around. They walked into the chilled room. The light spilling through the open door illuminated the stainless-steel tables and doors as if it were the set of a dreadful movie. The guard reached along the top of the bank of drawer fronts and pointed. A small white switch, half the size of a regular light switch, stood out from a metal plate with a darkened red light.

Muna squinted. Thinking. "Hmm... turn it back on. I'll ask Mike about it in the morning. I've never seen it turned off, and judging by its location and the monitor light, I'm not sure it's meant to be turned off. For all I know, it might be to turn the entire refrigeration wall off. And there are six bodies we don't want to smell."

The young man turned it on and curled his lip. "Eew. Not my favorite room, anyway."

As they walked out, Muna shrugged. "You get used to it. Dead bodies, crime scenes, burned cars, hospital beds, and holes in your body... It's all part of the job. And it beats sitting at a desk crunching numbers like my father thought I should be doing all day."

The young man ran his fingers through his hair. "Accounting?"

She shuddered her head with a sneer. "Nothing so droll. Stock analysis." She shook her body and arms in a horrified shiver.

His face pulled back in feigned disgust. "I'll take walking security in the death room over that, any day."

Muna swallowed and popped one eyebrow. "Well, I dodged the bullet there. And speaking of bullets. The range opens in five hours. I need to go grab my beauty sleep." She pointed at the next floor.

"Don't you ever go home?"

She shrugged as she grabbed her phone off her desk and logged out of her secure links. "Not unless I have to." She glanced back. "Too many roommates." She moved her cursor to her secure parking space. "I share with seven flight attendants. You never know whose bed you'll be sharing and with how many."

His face reeled in shock. "How big of a house?"

She smiled at knocking the kid off-kilter. "Two-bedroom apartment. But it has a larger community bathroom down the hall. You know... with gang showers like in high school, but it's coed."

She snickered as she climbed the stairs to the dormitory. His face told her he probably still lived at home and locked the bathroom door. He never stood a chance as date material.

3

SORTING INFORMATION

"YOU TOLD HIM WHAT?" Ming's face was shocked at the joke.

Muna rolled her eyes with a smile. "Sorry, not sorry. It stops any chance of him deciding to walk security on the dorm level. I'm unsure, but they probably have a master key to open rooms. Which is something I'm not interested in happening."

"Hearing you, girlfriend. I never understood the older girls' bitching until I had to stop dressing like a little kid. I still worship at the shrine of the Kitty, but around campus, Sesame Street sweats and ugly Crocs with enough of the charms to sink a whale were my friends." Ming reached over to a bowl and picked another carrot stick. She stuck it into the side of her mouth and crunched down loudly. They smiled together. Girls together, nobody could tell they were being gross or wrong. "Seeing you open your mouth is... Wait. Smile." Ming gripped her fist in the air as Muna smiled a large, toothy kid kind of smile. "Now wide open with a zinger on your tongue." Again, the fist.

Muna laughed. "You just took screenshots." Her laughter blossomed into a fully opened mouth with half-chewed orange pork rinds. She then turned into a hysterical squeal as she saw Ming take another series of shots. "You are so evil..."

Ming shot her a shy girl pose with a giggle. "Catch a flight down. We'll tear up the OC and get trashed on the beach."

Muna laughed as she shook her head. "I don't drink."

"Who said anything about alcohol? We can go down to the Surf Shack and have the cook and Danny rip us some spicy hot omelets. I think Jazz would even be up for tormenting Frank and Danny. For lunch, we can hit the food truck for habanero tacos. Find some entertainment for the afternoon and then ease into the evening with sea bass on the beach down in Crystal Cove and sunset. Then we can finish the night with frozen bananas rolled in everything, a ride on the ferry, and end with a fire on the beach. Even Tree can't resist the last three."

Muna leaned in with a squinted eye. "Is the frozen banana a euphemism for..."

Ming laughed. "Gurl, you have a nasty mind. Get back to great food. They freeze the bananas on a stick. Then they dip them in chocolate and roll them in sprinkles, crumbles, or a mix of everything. Decadent and fun all in one. Then you walk a half-mile or so to the ferry while you eat. The ferry goes over to the Newport peninsula and the beach. We can have the kids prep a fire pit for us. Maybe have a campfire songfest like when we were kids." Her smile was wonky. "Or what I think kids did..." She rolled her eyes.

Muna smirked with a single nod. "Yeah, the hijab was kind of mood killer for the Girl Scouts. And so a camp-out for me was overclocking a mainframe until it would halt and catch fire."

Ming's eyebrows got huge as she chewed. She flipped her index finger back and forth.

"But the rest sounds fun." She glanced back toward the lab, where the two men were talking. Probably cooking up more dad jokes. "It's not exactly our busy season right now, but you never know about the end of the summer. With the heat, people do freaky things. Mostly deadly, but then there's also the random bank robbery, grifters, smuggling of drugs and people... Just enough to keep us in a job. What about you guys?"

"It's slow on the dredging side, but summer vacation is when some of the biggest gaming happens. So the Deep Six team has free range with the jet. Sometimes, they slept on the jet between competitions."

"Why slow on the dredging? I would have thought with the nice weather that dredgers would work like mad to make up for lost time with winter storms."

Ming snorted softly. "Dredgers take vacations. Usually, they want to spend time with family for a holiday, so the Fourth starts the summer slump, and Labor Day wraps it up. But our end of things can happen anytime in the year. So, the end of summer is slow while we game like crazy. Besides, the guys split the winnings with us. We cover all the expenses and get the lion's share. They pocket the rest and buy toys for better gaming. It's kind of symbiotic that way. Heard anything from Nash?"

Muna furled her lips and softly shook her head. "They're still down in Barbados. Last we spoke, the surgery went well. They got good margins on Mina's tumor. The radiation was a bitch, as expected. And she's due back at the end of the week to start the chemo."

Ming nodded soberly. "Well, give her our love when you talk to her. We could use some happier news these days."

Muna frowned. "Why? What's going on?"

"Jeez. It's all the news wants to talk about. The cult out in the Mojave Desert that killed themselves. Even Jazz is talking about them."

Muna rattled her head. "Haven't heard..."

Ming rolled her eyes huge. "Just turn on the TV news. I gotta jet. I can hear that Tree and Slug just came in downstairs. They have another giant trophy for the growing forest along one wall."

Muna smiled as she popped a rind into her mouth. "Go get 'em tiger. And tell them congrats from me."

The screen blanked black and then returned to the usual FBI logo surrounded by icons.

Muna swung her desk sideways and tipped back, thinking.

Turning, she typed a few words into the search. She scanned the page full of hits and chose one of the major networks.

"This morning, authorities responded to a report of unusual circumstances. After responding to the remote compound, they discovered the bodies of nineteen people. It appears they had eaten a dinner laced with poison and then gone to bed. Here now is…"

She chose another station.

"Authorities now believe the cult had possibly made a suicide pact. The charismatic leader Anthony Alamo purchased the commune property a few years ago. Anthony is the nephew of a former religious cult leader, Tony Alamo, who ran a slave labor underground back in the 1970s. Anthony Alamo, a longtime celebrity in the Greenie movement…"

She backed out and looked for a streaming news channel's link.

"Mohave Valley is an unincorporated area of the Mojave Desert on the Nevada border. The Fort Mojave Reservation police were notified of an unusual response to the parcel delivery. Upon investigation, the authorities discovered nineteen people dead in their beds. Foul play might be suspected, but there was no evidence of a struggle."

Another click.

"Early this morning, authorities stumbled upon a gruesome scene: they found a group of individuals in the desert near the Nevada border dead in their beds. The eerie similarities to Heaven's Gate, a cult that committed mass suicide in nineteen ninety-seven just north of San Diego, are not lost on investigators. The search for connections continues."

Click.

"We're back now with former LAPD profiler Serena Romulus." Turning to the other person. "Is this another religious suicide cult like the one led by Marshal Applewhite in Rancho Santa Fe back in the nineties?"

"No. The Heaven's Gate cult was intent on suicide from the

start. They were waiting for the comet Hale-Bop to reach a certain closeness in the sky and then committed their mass suicide. This appears to be more random."

"Random how?"

"A charismatic leader leads most cults. The people who join are usually uneducated and easily led astray. But with the Mojave Movement, the leader is anything but charismatic. He was a known advocate in the solar energy movement but think in the way of an outstanding leader. As for the names of the others found dead, we connected many to universities or held college degrees in many fields."

Muna moved the cursor to an icon she rarely ever used. She had made the icon from one of the first streaming video channels in the original cable TV days. The cartoon television had bent antennas, and the screen simply read TV.

She scrolled down the list of local channels for the all-news station.

"In the early hours of the morning, authorities uncovered a grotesque scene. A suicide pact of over twenty individuals had taken place in the wild desert near the Nevada border. They were all found lifeless in their beds, with no clear trace or sign of struggle. Authorities are now searching for possible connections and clues to explain this tragedy. We're going now to our own Steve Taylor in the Mojave Desert. Steve?"

Muna felt more than heard Oz behind her. The man was quiet. She knew he was processing the information and running it through his many decades of experience. She turned to look up at him. Mike was quietly approaching through the archway. Only the low whine of his one leg gave him away.

Oz pursed his lips. His voice was slow and not consciously but just thinking out loud. "It's been…"

Muna nodded. For her, it was history. But history she had heard about through references to cults, black T-shirts, and popular running shoes. "Twenty-five years…"

He looked down with a frown of questioning.

She tossed her head to one side. "Heaven's Gate? The Hale-Bop comet?"

Mike cleared his throat. "How many?"

"Twenty."

Both men's mouths rolled into hard white bars. Oz looked back at his lab partner. "It could have been worse."

Mike bobbed a slow, gentle nod. "With Kool-Aid and children."

Muna frowned. "Kool-Aid? As in the happy kids' drink of sugar death?"

Oz's eyes narrowed as he looked at the air and somewhere in his past. "It must have been in seventy-eight. We were in Paris doing Christmas shopping. One of the Congressmen went down to South America..."

Mike scrunched his eyes. "Guyana?"

Oz flattened his finger on Mike's chest. "Guyana. And I can't remember if they killed the Congressman or not, but Jim Jones knew there would be more to come. So they poisoned big vats of Kool-Aid so the kids would think it was a party. They all took a glass and drank it together. Those who didn't were shot by Jones's henchmen. About nine hundred in all."

Muna's eyes opened wide as she stroked her hand on her long braid and slowly turned to the news report. The screen only showed the tranquil arrangement of cars crushed in a ball on some bridge. She didn't want to hear anymore. She stabbed at the delete button.

Oz grumbled to clear his throat, but it still sounded full of phlegm. "Every generation likes to think those tragedies are behind us. But they're not. But I'd trade those events if it meant the daily mass shootings stopped. In the scope of a year, all those in Jones's camp are only a dent in the number of kids shot in mass shootings. Schoolkids. Little ones who are the innocent of us all. All they knew was they were going to school to be with their friends." He turned back toward the laboratory and his next autopsy. "And then those who make it to adulthood go to a nightclub to be with their friends, and someone doesn't think they deserve to." He turned the corner into his sanctuary of the deceased with questions to be answered.

Mike pondered the sad look on Muna's face. His was no better. "As much as he celebrates Dia de los Muertos or the Day of the Dead, he is the most sensitive person I know about the death of others."

Muna rocked softly. "I've heard him talking to the cadavers."

Mike winced as he turned on his mechanical foot. "I think most medical examiners do. I have a hypothesis, but I'm not sure that talking to the dead comes before or because of the career. We all seem just to do it. And we don't know when it started."

4

HOME IS WHERE THE DOG IS

"WELCOME back to the land of the daily grind. Lightly scattered clouds to remind you of honey-do items you forgot to do before you left. Sunny skies, just like where you left your heart and suntan. And we have it all topped off with a pleasant eighty-seven degrees with ninety percent humidity. Please check your seat belts and secure small items like cell phones, laptops, or children. We don't want them flying about the cabin as we land. And on behalf of your sponsor, thank you for flying Corporate Air."

Nash glanced over at Powder lying next to Mina. Her head was in her mommy's lap. The two had been dozing for the last hour or more.

"I gave her a sedative before we took off. I think she was fighting it for the first half of the flight. But she'll be groggy, and when we get her home, she'll just sleep until tomorrow."

Nash looked over at the nurse. "And Mina?"

Lele chuckled softly. She was adjusting to the unorthodox humor of the two women. The dog even had her own sense of humor about food and where she curled up to sleep. The nurse looked out of the window of the small jet as they made a gentle curve over the Potomac River. She thought about the last three weeks resting and trying to stay out of Mina's way while also taking care of her post-surgery medical needs. She had seen the woman work in Colorado while looking after Nash's battered, assembled family or crew. *Gang* was such a derogatory word. But it put a smile on her lips.

She had expected both women to bring laptops and burn the local Wi-Fi to the ground. But the two wives had applied their workaholic natures to relaxing and enjoying the island's warmth. The chief of police for the attorney general's office didn't even call or appear until day three. Lele thought about their flying in on a borrowed corporate jet. They had almost gotten away with flying under the radar until the woman in uniform sauntered in, carrying an unmarked bottle of hundred-year-old scotch. With her other hand, she held out the three asked-for burner phones. They were only for communicating among themselves. They took apart their phones and put them in Ziplock bags wrapped in aluminum foil. To be safe, the three bags had spent the vacation time in the hotel's freezer.

She turned as Nash tapped her arm. The woman held out her reassembled phone. "The hotel charged the batteries for us last night."

Lele watched Nash pull the parts from each bag and reassemble the other two phones. Thumbing the one awake, Nash had checked a couple of screens. "How many missed calls?"

Nash shrugged. "Seven. About what I'd expect for a day. But if I didn't return a phone call by the end of the first day, everyone would assume I was dead or didn't want to talk." She smiled at the nurse and flinched her eyebrows and one shoulder. "Works for me." She woke up Mina's phone and hit mute as the tiny mass of plastic and aluminum shook in her hand. She put it on the small table, face up. It rattled and walked along the slick surface.

As Lele reached to stop it from falling off, Nash shook her hand. "It's not finished yet."

The phone convulsed off the table's edge, flipped, and jumped on the carpet as the plane flared. As the plane's wheels chirped softly on landing, the two watched the phone flip one last time and die. Lele snorted. "You brute! You killed it."

Nash chuffed as she unsnapped her seat belt and bent to pick up the now-silent phone. Thumbing it open, she opened the one screen to missed calls. She showed the phone to the nurse. "Washington is a cruel mistress." The count read nine hundred and ninety-nine. After that, it stops counting. "It will take her days to unravel this mess. But most of it, she will turn over to her team."

"She has a team? Like yours?"

"Not exactly. She pays for hers. But they aren't as fun. Mostly, they research her. But mine have much funner toys."

The nurse stood and laughed an airy breath. "Noisy too." She turned to Mina, hiding her head and Powder under the blanket. "Come on sunshine. Time to go pour you into your own bed."

Mina whined from under the blanket. "I don't wanna move. Just stay here in my fortress of fur baby." Powder moaned softly.

Lele glanced back at a laughing Nash. "I was talking to the dog."

Mina threw back the blanket and sat up. "In that case... I'm going with my daughter."

Nash looked out the window. "Limo is here." She peeked back at Mina and rolled her eyes. "I swear. Tony can smell the scotch from a hundred miles away."

Mina bent and gazed out the window at the FBI deputy director standing next to an armored SUV. "Well, after all, you wanted to get the bottles home safely, didn't you?"

Chester smiled as the SUV quietly slid to a stop in front of the building, and then he stepped to the door. As the door cracked, he gently opened it. His smile got warmer. "Good evening Ms. Lee. Good to have you home again. How was Barbados?"

"Restful, Chester. Exactly what we all needed. And how has everything been here?"

He took her hand and guided her out of the vehicle. "We got the order and have stocked the pantry, larder, and refrigerator. Some of the requested foods didn't all fit in your freezer, so we stashed them all in the building's freezer. Just call down, and we'll bring it up."

Mina hugged him and then pointed back. "Lele will do the calling." She rolled her eyes almost round. "We have someone who can cook and not have us end up in the hospital."

Powder stepped out and looked around.

Chester chuckled. "Go ahead, Powder. I'll clean it up later." He pointed toward the young tree surrounded by the lacy cast-iron ring set into the sidewalk. It wasn't a forest, but it was as close as it would get—within seven blocks. He glanced back at the sound of suitcases hitting the sidewalk. "Just leave them there, deputy director. We have people for them from here on out. And good to see you again, sir."

Tony waved a hand as he ducked back for a couple more suitcases.

Lele stepped out and shook Chester's hand. "Good to see you again, Chester. At least they didn't fire me, strand me on the beach, or bury my body in the sand."

"Yes, miss. Good to have you back. And if you need anything, don't hesitate to call us. If the commissary doesn't have it, we can order it for you."

Lele nodded. "If you fill the order, we're good for the next few weeks. Her diet isn't unusual, but the regimen is not good to vary from."

He nodded. "Thank you for looking after her. We're here for anything you need help with. Around the clock."

She smiled as she thought how different it was from some hospitals she had worked for. "Good to know." She looked him up and down and squinted one eye. "Chocolate chip or oatmeal raisin?"

He pushed his hands together, lacing his fingers. "Chocolate chip, oatmeal, raisin, and don't skimp on the ginger."

"And the rest of the crew?"

He smiled with a wink. "Snickerdoodles and tad foots."

She closed one eye and cocked her head. "Tad foots. Can I Google the recipe, or is it a family secret?"

He snorted. "I'll send up the recipe. It's Cajun Voodoo. Think of it as a test. My wife made them for three years before she finally passed. Clarence has a very educated and particular pallet."

Lele looked at Powder, following the two women to the elevator. "Have your wife call me. I don't think I have three years. But I'm willing to learn a new recipe. I love jerked gator tail."

"COLBY? VENTI SOY GLUTEN-FREE CARAMEL MACCHIATO."

The young woman put down her paper and got up. Retrieving her drink, she grabbed a couple of napkins. Turning, she found a gray-haired man leaning slightly over her table, reading the headlines of her paper. "May I help you?" She hoped there was just enough chill in her voice to drive him off.

He turned—embarrassed. "Sorry. I just caught the headline. I remember the comet people in the north county..."

She put her coffee on the table. "Comet people?"

He took in her age and waggled his hand in the air. "You're not old enough. But they were up like Encinitas' way. One night, they put on their black T-shirts and Nike sneakers and poisoned themselves. They were going to go catch a ride on..." He snapped his fingers and smiled. "Hale-Bop. The Hale-Bop comet." He pointed at the headline on the paper. "Same religious commune whacko kind of thing. Mass suicide stuff."

She turned the paper around toward her, glanced at the photo, and then looked back up at the older man. "Did you know any of these people? Where you ever there?"

He scoffed. "No. Of course not."

Her one eyebrow stood raised. "So, you have no personal reality to base a judgment on." She sat with a sigh. "I might suggest you reserve comment until all the facts come out. Not everything is always how it appears."

His voice turned slightly snarky. "And I suppose you'll tell me you were there and know better than all the news media."

She shook out the paper and sipped on her coffee. "As a matter of fact, yes, I was from the start. And no, it was not a commune of religious freaks. It was a collective of scientists, from electrical engineers to physicists. The only person with a bible was the mechanic, and he cut the center out to hold a small handgun. Now, if you don't mind…"

The man held up his hands. "Sheesh. Try to be civil, and you get burned these days." He backed up and walked away.

She studied the article. There still wasn't anything of substance or the mention of names. As she skimmed the rest of the paper, she drew her cell phone out of her purse.

Sipping from her coffee, she scrolled through her contacts. Finally, she thumbed the phone number.

"Sanity retreat."

The woman chuckled. "You goofball. How's the Silly Conehead Valley?"

The man's voice was wheezy but full-bodied. "Thankfully, about a hundred miles and hours south of here. They don't know we exist, and we won't tell them. Sally routes her connection through the Grand Caymans, so as far as work is concerned, we're island rats and never have to come to the office."

She laughed softly. "What happens when they make you come to the office, and you show up pasty white?"

"I've developed a spray tan that is browner than orange. I was going to ship some to Florida, but I figured I'd never get paid. So, screw the orange meatball." She could hear him sucking on an inhaler.

"It sounds like the new location hasn't helped your lungs. Has it?"

He coughed. "Nah, I shot the lungs to hell. Uncle Screw-you

keeps saying it had nothing to do with the radiation or depleted uranium on the ship. But the past crew... we talk. The ship has one of the highest concentrations of cancers of any cluster. Land clusters aren't even in our ballpark."

She sighed. "And the lawsuit?"

He coughed. "About as expected. The lawyers must petition the US Government to ask permission to petition the Department of Defense to sue them. Kind of like that thing you did with the school when we were kids."

She rolled her eyes as her finger wound into the one curl of hair hanging out of her bun. "That was a three-year nightmare runaround to make me go away."

"Whatever happened with that?"

She choked as she started to take a sip of her coffee. "They told me if I dropped the lawsuit, they would let me walk down the aisle with the rest of the class."

He laughed until it became a coughing fit. "So, you provisionally won...?"

"I thought so. It was three days before the ceremony. I told them good luck finding a new valedictorian with a speech. I heard later that a handful of other kids went to Disneyland instead. They had the march in, kind of. It was more like a mass mobbing, but no speech or valedictorian. The mayor was going to talk about careers and opportunities in our futures, but Mom convinced him just to turn it into a reelection campaign speech instead."

It jogged his memory. "Oh, oh. I remember that. She headed his campaign, and he got reelected. Go, Mom."

She chuckled. "Go, Mom. He's still mayor, and she's the comptroller now."

She could hear his inhaler. He coughed softer. "So, what are you up to now?"

"I'm homeless. I left the last project kind of suddenly. So, it's just me and the camper van, looking for a place to land..."

She could almost hear her brother's smile. "And you thought

where better, but an apple farm, upstate. I like how you're thinking. I'll blow up the mattress in the garage or something."

She smiled with relief. "Thanks. Counting on my big brother is a rock I need right now. I'll see you in a couple of days. I think I'd like to wander up the coast. Clear my head."

"Get here when you get here. Love ya, Mighty Mouse."

"Love you, Super Dog."

5

ROUTINE IS THE DEATH

THE AFTERNOON SUN beat hard through the unwashed windows, heating the stone floor. The air-conditioning struggled—barely keeping up. It wasn't enough to prevent the dampness from turning to sweat and creating a dark path down the middle of Nash's shirt. She wasn't alone.

Ticking the last box, she wrote the date and signed her name on the tracking form. Again. She leaned back with closed eyes as her hand shut the thick folder.

"Is that the report on missing girls?"

She didn't have to open her eyes. The voice was almost as constant in her hearing as her wife. "Kids. There are boys in there, as well." Nash rolled her head as she opened her eyes to look at the deputy director standing in the doorway of his office.

She didn't have to ask how he knew. Nash had only started the report a few years before, and this book was already one of a few hard copy reports exceeding four inches thick. The report had started on a few girls missing from the Paiute reservations of California and Nevada. As word spread, it ballooned into a growing mountain of missing children. Dozens of reservations spread over dozens of states and Indian nations had caused multiple books.

She rested her hand on the tomb. "This is now only the Paiute nations. But there are a few of the smaller California tribes who only have a few missing over the past half-century."

"How many books are you up to now?"

Nash glanced over at the wall of books and binders. "Seven. But I'm running out of space in the Oklahoma region. I'll break it up for the next report by the three major nations or by state."

Tony had read most of the reports and was gaining familiarity with the reach and scope of the First People nations. "When you do, I think it's time also to start a cyber set of folders." He held up his hands. "I know. There isn't a formal inquiry the FBI, or even the Bureau of Indian Affairs can lay claim to. But maybe it's time we lend a little weight and support. Work with Muna and determine where it would do the most good."

Nash smirked softly on one side of her face as she studied the white man. The man had spent less than a week on any reservation but was beginning to understand. "I'd appreciate it, sir."

He nodded. "Just keep me up to date. I can't ride point with you, but I've escorted a meaningful string of pack donkeys."

"Mules."

"Mules?"

She smiled. "Donkeys are burros. They're great by themselves or a bonded pair. But they fight a string. For that, they need the calm of a horse, so they use mules. That's why it was a twenty-mule team, not an anarchy of donkeys."

He frowned as he turned from his doorway. "Um… I don't think it's called anarchy. Wouldn't it be a herd?"

Nash snorted. "I worked a case where they were rounding up wild ones. It's called a *drove*."

"They drove them?"

She shook her head. "Nope. They rounded them up. The bunch of donkeys was called a *drove* of donkeys. Like a flock of sheep, a congress of baboons, and a murder of crows."

He paused with his knuckle on the doorjamb. His frown

furrowed deeper. "What's the term for a group of agents from different agencies raising hell in multiple states?"

She pointed her finger gun at him as her smile spread. "*That.* That would be an anarchy of agents."

He snorted softly and closed his door with a soft click. His secretary softly chuckled as she exchanged looks over the tops of her glasses with Nash.

MUNA BROUGHT THE WHITE FOAM BOX INTO THE LAB. Her face winced to one side. "Mike? Oz? We have a crash here."

The whirring cycled with the soft clink of his other mechanical leg. "What have you got, Muna?" His arm looked like he was grabbing the back of his head with his right arm. But she could tell he was trying to stretch his afternoon blood sugar drop.

She squinted. "What did you eat for lunch?"

He waved his hand wildly in the air and pointed at the box.

She picked up the box and turned so she was between the box and the man. "No. Not until you take care of your sugar. Hit the fridge."

"She's right. We forgot lunch." Oz pulled the cloth helmet off his head as he walked out of the lab. "There's a pound of lox I picked up yesterday. I think we have some bagels..." He paused as he walked behind Muna. "Hmm... Who do we know in San Diego?"

Muna snatched the box back around to the front of her. "Nobody. That's the problem. Nobody who would spend the nine hundred to air courier this up to us."

"Well then, open it up."

Muna forcefully set it down on the stainless-steel table. "Not until you two behave. And no, we do not have any bagels. I threw the last dozen out when it became a lab project—a week ago."

Oz's voice echoed in the open refrigerator. "Eggs. And we

have… nope." He dropped the two rotten onions and something else in the trash. He smiled bashfully. "We have eggs and lox."

Muna squinted. "Check the cheese drawer on the left. I think there's still a block of hard cheese and half a wheel of brie."

Oz held up the brie and smelled it. "This will pair nicely with the salmon." He looked at Muna.

She shrugged as she slapped at Mike's sneaking hand. "Sounds Halal enough to me."

Mike whined softly. "Just a peek?"

Muna gave him a hard, narrow-eyed look. "I will check the condition of the ice. You set the table while Oz cooks."

Her back pocket vibrated.

She pulled the phone out and thumbed it awake. "Go for Muna."

"Hi. This is Milton Bradley… Not that, Milton Bradley. I'm with the county coroner's office in San Diego…?"

Muna sensed a prank but wasn't sure. She eyed the two jokers in the office, busy making lunch. Neither was reacting to the phone call. "I don't know Milton… are you with the coroner's office? Should I call them and check for you?"

The man was flustered. "No. I'm calling from the county coroner's office. My name… oh hell." He hung up.

She looked at her silent phone. It rang. "Hello."

"Hello. This is Doctor Bradley with the San Diego County coroner's office. Doctor Philo Askari referred me. Is this FBI Special Agent Muna al-Faragi?"

"Speaking."

"Good. Well… this morning…"

Muna leaned her hip against the table. "You shipped a cold box to us. We gave it to the bomb control agents. They'll be detonating it within the hour." She didn't hang up but let it hang in silence. Waiting for the joker to laugh.

The voice was strained and quiet. "Oh, I certainly hope not. They're blood samples…"

She rolled her eyes. "Okay. I haven't spoken to Philo, the human breadstick, since Quantico. How is the walking skeleton doing, and why did he put you up to this joke? And how did you get this number?"

"Um... I can assure you this is no joke. You're welcome to call me back if you wish. My extension is three fifty-seven."

She thumbed the phone to silent as she stepped toward her desk. Stopping, she turned and picked up the white foam box as she snuck a peek at the two men. She returned to her desk with the box under her arm. Sitting, she typed one-handed.

She scanned the San Diego County web page and clicked on the coroner's office. Setting down the box on the floor, she turned to the second keyboard. The one attached by wire to a separate computer, connected to the dark side of the world. She relied more on the search engines of the black web than the usual family-friendly pabulum of Silicon Valley.

The doughy face and thinning hair boasted more of a tan from overhead autopsy lights than the sun. She scoffed softly at the irony of him living in the sunshine of San Diego.

She dialed the number on the screen. As the computer answered, she asked for his extension. The artificial intelligence hiccuped and connected her.

"Doctor Bradley."

"This is Muna. I apologize. I've received more than my fair share of practical and unpractical jokes recently. And yes. We received your package. It's on the docket for the first thing after lunch. We hit a blood sugar issue. We're remediating, and then it's full ahead with your... blood, did you say?"

"Yes. Blood. We sent you sample sets of the draws from the nineteen people out in the desert."

Muna frowned. "The religious commune who killed themselves?"

He stressed his emphasis on the specific words. "The *community* of nineteen people found *dead*."

She felt like she had been kicked back to evidence three-oh-one at Quantico. "Yes. Sorry. We've only been catching snippets here and there between work. And we all know how the media makes up their collective mind and then votes and labels using circle logic."

He sighed. "Be that as it may, we need your lab to process the samples for biologicals. We got a couple of hits, but none make much sense."

"Why us? I mean, we're fine with it... but Los Angeles is closer and bigger... And don't you have mass spectrometers in San Diego? I would think with the border so close..."

He cleared his throat from the corner she had painted him into. "Three. And they didn't agree with each other enough to arrive at a consensus. So we have outsourced for second opinions. We shipped one set to you, one to LA, and one to Quantico. But Quantico gave me your phone number and said to call you directly. You are the lead medical examiner there, are you not?"

She coughed slightly. "It's a long story. What types of biologicals?" She glanced back at the two men standing in the large archway between the lab and the office. They had three plates in their hands but were blatantly eavesdropping on her conversation. She lifted her knee, placed her boot on the foam box, and pointed toward the table by the windows. She poised her fingers to snap, but she resisted.

She could hear the exhaustion in the man's sigh. "Between the tests on the foodstuffs left over from their last meal and the blood, we are leaning floral."

Muna watched the two men sneaking peeks back as they set the lunch on the table. "Yeah, we've been there before. I've got your number, and we'll keep you posted."

The relief oozed from the phone. She wondered how the response had been from the Los Angeles lab. They were always overloaded and understaffed. "Thank you. I'll look forward to your report."

She shifted the box under her desk as she stood and slid the phone into her back pocket. "Did you get drinks?"

In the afternoon sunshine, the two statues exploded into action.

She held up her hand to a stop. "Stop. Sit. Obviously, you two are already over-caffeinated. I'll get my own." She peered in the mug at something left from the morning… or worse. She then noticed the six mugs scattered about her desk. *I need a maid.*

As she sat down at the head of the table, looking out the window at the distant ocean, she put down the three mugs of fresh coffee. "Sorry it took so long. I was making a new pot and wrestling with whatever had been in the pot before. Those caffeine giants are hard to kill when they're still young and strong." Her face was pure innocence as she took a bite of the omelet.

She opened her eyes, looking into the mirrored images of the two men, each holding a fork of food in their gaping mouths with curiosity written on their faces.

She slowly chewed as she patted the napkin on her lips. She waved the white napkin like a flag as she swallowed. "Oh. That was Doctor Bradley down in San Diego. It's nothing. I'll explain…" Her voice dropped to her mommy's growl. "… when you two have finished your lunch."

6

ALL AHEAD STOP

LELE PULLED a small carrot and checked the roasted vegetables. They were tender, with enough firm form left, but not crisp. She glanced through the glass lid at the skinless chicken breasts, slowly poaching in the white wine sauce.

Nash leaned over and smelled. "Smells like a satisfying restaurant should."

Lele laughed. "I can teach you…"

Mina snuggled behind Nash in a hug. She hooked her chin over Nash's shoulder. "Fat chance. The bird would never survive her nine-millimeter."

Nash growled with a chuckle. "You don't hunt birds with a pistol."

"Okay. But you don't have one of those shotgun things." She rolled her eyes to Lele for help.

The nurse crossed the wooden spoon with tongs. "Don't look at me. I only hunt chickens by the breast and in the meat department. If it isn't wheels on linoleum, I'm not your girl." She pulled the top off the chicken, and a wave of herbs, spices, and wine hit them. She stuck the meter in the fattest breast. The light turned yellow and then green. "We're ready."

As Lele turned off the burners, she grabbed the tongs. Mina pointed at the smallest breast. "That was going to be mine... but I guess I can force myself around the extra ounce." She spooned a larger portion of the vegetables onto the plate. "The carrots are the desert. We can all use a little less of the extra sugars."

Mina smirked softly. "I think I got my fill of sweets today. I snuck a sip of Nash's coffee this morning—thought my back teeth would rot out by lunchtime."

The nurse slumped her weight to one hip. "No wonder you didn't nap this morning." She slid a narrowed eye toward Nash. "I thought you were using the pink stuff?"

Nash rolled her eyes. "I am." She held her plate forward. "Besides, you're the cook. Have you found any sugar in this kitchen?"

Lele snorted. "I haven't sicced Powder on it—yet. But I also didn't order any."

"Well, before you, those cabinets only held restaurant menus and..." She frowned and stared at Mina. "What did we keep in those pantry cabinets?"

Mina hid her mouth with her napkin and turned red at being caught eating before everyone else. The food muffled her voice. "Faux uck gah yachts." She chewed and swallowed as the other two looked at her. Putting her napkin back in her lap, she slid the fork back onto the table. "Phone books and flower vases."

Nash leaned toward the nurse. "My wife is ravenous, with the etiquette of a wolf. She gets it from her daughter." They eyed the subject of conversation, dancing back and forth from front paw to paw at their feet.

Lele put the large breast on the cutting board and cut it in half. She cut the one half into thumb-sized pieces. She bent and slipped a piece within an inch of the super nose. Powder delicately sniffed and then inhaled the food. "Hmm. It's good to know it was worth cooking. The rest we will eat like a civilized member of society." She pointed at the table. The dog sashayed to the table and crawled up into her chair at the head of the round table. *How did I ever live without such a dog in my life?*

She filled her plate and took her place at the other end of the table. The four started together.

"While I was shopping, I was listening to the news." Lele peeked up at Nash. "Is the FBI involved in the mass suicide out in California?"

Nash's chewing slowed. Her eyes fixed on the small vase of silk flowers in the middle of the table, her hand frozen, gripping the fork at the edge of her plate.

Mina glanced up. "Nash…?"

Nash grimaced, glanced at her wife, and then looked at the nurse. "No. Not that I would think. At least, I've never heard of us getting involved with suicide. I don't think we were involved with the Heaven's Gate thing. We only got involved in Jonesborough because of the Treasury irregularities and the attempt on the Congressman's life."

"What do you get involved with?" Lele rested her fork on the side of her plate with the tines down. "I mean, what got you involved with all the crap out in Colorado?" She sipped on her water. "They blew you guys up and then shot up the place, but I never understood why you were there."

Nash dabbed at her lips. "It all started with a murder."

"But a guy got murdered on Fifth Avenue yesterday, but I don't see any people wearing those blue windbreakers stenciled FBI on the back. So what was different in Colorado?"

Nash pushed her empty plate forward as she stared at Mina. The woman looked up at the silence and collapsed in exasperation. "Oh, come on. We've been together for how long…? And now you're worried about explaining how the sausage gets made?"

Lele frowned. "Sausage?"

Mina pushed the last bite of chicken into her mouth. She covered her mouth with her napkin as she pointed at her chewing. "Before I forget. You can make this anytime."

The cook in the nurse snorted quietly. "Good to know. I don't get to cook very much. Cooking for yourself... well, it's a waste of time. By the time anything is cooked, you're not hungry anymore."

Nash reached out her hand at Lele's plate. "If you can't finish..."

The nurse feinted a stab with her fork at the hand. "That is not what I said. Now explain the sausage."

Nash sighed. "It started as a murder. They arranged the body on the Four Corners monument. It's called a pose. The killer is saying something by staging or posing the body in a certain way, how they're dressed, or where they are."

"And on the monument?"

"We think it was to send the message that they were in all four states, or their reach was large."

Lele gathered her fork and knife at the five of the plate and pushed it an inch forward. "How big?"

Mina growled. "International."

Lele's face fell into disbelief. "For murder?"

Mina ticked her head. "Worse." She waved her finger back at Nash as she leaned back and closed her eyes.

Lele frowned. "Are you okay?"

The Asian nodded. "Just reliving the chicken. Go ahead Nash."

Nash's smile pulled back on one side. She had seen the look on Mina's face a few times with a sumptuous meal. "We got the call because the body was, in fact, body parts of five people, which makes it a mass murder. I got the assignment because it was on the Southern Ute Reservation." Her hand fanned up and down next to her face. "The FBI thinks I might speak the language or something."

The nurse flopped out her hand, pointing at Mina. "Okay, a little worse... but the sausage?"

"The victims were from different areas of the United States. One was Japanese Yakuza or Mafia, one was Navy from the D.C. area, and one was from Oklahoma. Quite the spread."

Lele pushed back her chair and stood as she took up hers and Mina's plate. "Hence the international aspect."

Nash picked up her plate. "Almost. The international connection we found... Actually, Muna found it after we were in the hospital. Well, friends of Munas. It's a guy I dealt with a couple of years ago down in Barbados. He deals in slavery and sex trafficking of under-aged girls."

"And they connected him to those guys somehow?"

"In business with them. Soften the girls up as prostitutes in the massage parlors and the young attractive ones, drug them up, and ship them to the highest bidder."

Lele paused at the sink. "Where?"

Nash shrugged. "Middle East, Africa, Asia... take your pick. Or they stay domestic and move them from city to city as hookers, call girls, or massage tricks. If they're Asian, they might work in a nail salon, and you'd never know it."

Lele stared at her fingernails.

Mina smiled. "Yeah. It makes you wonder about all those mani-cures you got in a mall salon."

Lele bounced her eyebrows with her eyes. "Yeah... all five times." She held up her hands, exposing the tightly trimmed nails. "Nurse. You can't risk a nail catching or poking through a glove. Not these days."

As they sat back at the table, Lele's finger ran along the grain of the table. "So, mass murder, Indian reservation, and white slavery?" She looked up at Nash. "So where's the sausage?"

Nash winced. "See. And there it is. Cut it to three tiny words, and it doesn't even ring the phone at the local bureau office help desk. But paint it up with several tattoos with international associa-tions. Cut up the exsanguinated and flash frozen bodies with zero tool marks. Then, stuff them together as a single body on the largest reservations in the southwest. You're going to get some-one's attention. And that someone's desk is twenty feet from mine."

Lele hung out her finger in the air. "Yeah... What's his name? Tall with dark hair. The guy with the rifle down below the cliff. I had seen him around the hospital. Quiet guy, but nice."

Mina smirked. "Tony. He's the deputy director. And he also likes Nash's two-hundred-year-old scotch."

Lele's eyes got wide as her mouth fell open. She gawped at Nash. "Shut the front door. There's no such thing."

Mina stood. Her eyes were drooping. "You know, don't you? If you give her a taste of even the nasty stuff, you'll never get rid of her."

Nash shrugged one shoulder. "She was down in Barbados, the same as us..."

Lele's forehead stacked deep furls. "Wait. The cop. The first week. She walked into the apartment holding a bottle. But there was no label."

Nash stood. "It didn't need a label. Technically, it doesn't exist." She pointed at Mina. "Let me get her to bed before she falls."

Lele stood. "I'll clean up the kitchen and start the dishes."

The bottle stood between them. The small cordial glasses stood half-filled. "Don't sip. Just sniff."

"Why was it in the freezer?"

Nash snorted softly. "That's another case story for another time. But it concentrates the goodness and makes it flow slower."

"But it doesn't freeze."

Nash shook her head softly as she lifted her glass. "To Barbados and good times."

Lele held up her glass. "To good health and long happy lives."

7
WE'RE HERE NOW WITH

HER MORNING rarely started with a phone call before the crack of dawn. Muna rolled over and stared at the digital clock. She worked the numbers backward. It was quarter to four, and San Francisco wasn't awake yet. It didn't make any more sense than seven in the morning in Washington. But she also knew the deputy director enjoyed watching the sunrise from his office window on the third floor. Drinking coffee and watching the street cleaners in front of the capital offices was his version of a Zen wake-up.

Muna had tried it. She preferred bunny slippers, Hello Kitty pajamas, her tactical vest, and a hundred rounds of shells through each of her pistols.

Muna pulled the phone to her ear without looking at the screen. "Jambo Bawana."

The cough on the other end cleared her mind.

His voice was slightly raspy, but there also was the hint of him enjoying the joke. "Please tell me you were up last night watching old black and white Tarzan movies."

She rolled onto her back. "Who went big game hunting with an AR-15 in Colorado?"

"It wasn't like I bagged any of the game…"

She sighed. "It was the sentiment that counted. We knew you had our back... er... front, as it were. What can I do for you before the sun decides to come this way, sir?"

The silence roared through the phone. She knew he was checking the clock and doing the backward math. "Oh. Sorry."

"It's okay, sir. You only beat my alarm clock by fifteen minutes. We have a new shooting range master, and he likes the early hours. And I now have a key for any late-night shenanigans I might need to indulge in."

"But you're still on your own time..."

She sat up and rubbed her face. "Sir, do you know where I live? Where I've lived for almost three years?"

She could hear his coffee cup tick against the phone. "In the neighborhood?"

She snorted. "You could say so. I'm up in the fourth-floor dormitory. So you might say I never go home. But I like to think of it as working from home. What can I get for you?"

The muffled grunting and the movement of furniture crept through her phone. She recognized the squeaking desk chair. "I was watching ReCap this morning..."

She thought about the morning news shows popular in the nation's capital. ReCap was only fifteen minutes recapping the top stories of the day or week before. She tried to think of what day it was. Pulling the phone from her ear, she swiped up and looked at the time and date block. Saturday. It would be the week's recap.

Shit. He went to work on a Saturday. I wonder if his tie is straight and tight to the collar? "What caught your eye, sir?"

"This mass suicide thing—out in the desert."

She yawned as her right foot searched for her fuzzy pink slipper. "What about it, sir?"

The silence became quieter. She realized he had called but hadn't planned his questions or thoughts yet.

"I thought you were... I mean, the lab was doing something on the case."

She softly grunted as she bent forward to look under the metal cot. She reached out and grabbed the slipper. Sighing as she sat up, she dropped the slipper at her foot. "Yes. Bloodwork. But it's not straightforward. Yesterday, I was considering our alternative to outsource the tests to another lab for a second or more definitive opinion."

"What lab?"

"We used them a few years ago. It's the biological laboratory out at the University of California in Davis. They usually work in agriculture, but they are also set up and knowledgeable about biologicals and flora."

He snapped his fingers. "Yes. I remember. It was the case of bones in the creek. They tested the water or something."

"The mud, sir. They tested the mud."

By the slurred speech, she could tell he was rubbing his face. She guessed at a hard night. *Maybe it's a no-go on the tie thing.*

"Say again?"

He cleared his throat. "Sorry. I was asking... you mentioned flora...?"

"Yes, sir. San Diego's medical examiner got a hit on a couple of poisons and a digitalis. We've confirmed Oz's guess of it being probably Foxglove. The cardiac glycosides or digoxin are digitalis—which can kill you in a large enough dose."

He groaned softly. "But my father takes a digitalis..."

Muna nodded in the dark. "He probably is suffering from congestive heart failure."

"How did you...?"

"It's one of the oldest drugs for the heart. Don't worry. He's nowhere near a toxic level. But digitalis makes the heart pump the blood better or harder. The congestion slows the heart by smothering it. So they give him digitalis to help the heart Hulk out... a bit. When they first prescribed it, he probably made a comment about feeling many years younger. Or, at least, my father did."

Tony groaned and then chuckled. "Mom told him if he felt so

much younger, then he could go mow the lawn. She settled for them going for walks every day."

Muna nodded. "The walks are why you can still call him. The digitalis only helps. But they will watch his kidney functions."

"More knowledge from experience with your father?"

She snorted as she pulled her braid around and smelled it. "Hardly. I might have taken my hijab off, but we still don't discuss such personal things between the sexes. I'm sure my mother is aware, but she wouldn't share such information with me. No, just a few biology courses and a lot of two uncles, Oz and Mike. The bodies in the freezer case were a few college courses just in themselves."

"So, if the digitalis strengthens the heart function...?"

Muna grabbed the darker shadow on the gray of the night wall. Pulling the tactical vest over her Hello Kitty pajamas, she smoothed out the Velcro straps. "Why use it as a poison? Easy. A stronger blood flow guarantees the other poisons get full delivery. Mike is looking at a couple of plants that would lend themselves to being a paralyzing agent." She bent and grabbed the handles on her black Gladstone bag. "Look, I'm out the door. Let me go destroy some targets and get cleaned up. I'll rummage around in the lab and see if the boys made any more headway. But I know I can't call Oz. His wife won't let him answer the phone when he's serving her breakfast on the boat. I'll call you back in a few hours."

"Not needed. I just remembered why they aren't cleaning the street today. I think I'm supposed to take the dog to the vet. We'll talk on Monday."

He finally figured out it was Saturday. "Muna-day it is, sir. Have a great weekend."

She pushed the freight elevator button for the first floor. Stepping into the car, which always seemed to be where she was or nobody else used, she poked the button for the first-floor loading dock. If she was going to undo her braid and wash it, she wanted to make sure she could get it braided back tightly. Maybe even bang-tailed short. The same way Andy braided his father's dray horse tails.

———

"WELCOME BACK. WE'RE AT THE TOP OF THE HOUR. I'M Kristy Pyle, and we're talking with Bill Winston from the California State College here in San Diego." The blond hostess in the beach blanket pink dress turned to the man in the blue blazer. "Welcome to Great Morning San Diego, Mr. Winston."

The man nods slightly. "Thanks for having me."

"Now, what do you do at the university?"

He shifted nervously. "College. We're a college, not a university."

She frowned at the camera and the viewers at home as best as the Botox would let her. "What's the difference?"

"It's small these days, but a university is primarily a research institute, whereas a college is a teaching school that might do some practical research. Usually, the division of disciplines at a university is in colleges."

She waffled her hand in the air as she smirked at what she thought would be a witty joke. "So one does research whereas the other one teaches research." She smiles at the cameras.

"Exactly. We do a little research to teach our students about the experiments and theories. As where the universities do theoretical research and teach about that research."

Obviously lost in her joking and the explanation, she rolled her hand in the air. "So what is it you do at the… school?"

The man adjusted his tie and raised his hand to slick down his comb-over but stopped as the makeup artist offstage was chopping her hand at her throat. His hand floated back to the table. "I teach atmospheric physics. The dynamics of energy in the surrounding air."

She shifts at the explanation in confusion. "And how did you know Doctor Peter Lambert?"

"He was a professor in the department with me. We both studied similar dynamics of western hemisphere air quality. And with it, the potential for energy transference through temperature conferring and offsets."

She glanced down at her notes. "Making windmills work better…"

He recognized the statement. He experienced the same in grade climbing mediocre students grasping to sound better than they were. But he knew he always wanted to be asked back, so he played along. "That's part of it. Windmills were more of my field than Peter's."

"What was Peter, er… Doctor Lambert, working on?" She turned directly to the camera for a close-up of her. "Before he moved out to the commune in the Mojave Desert."

He smirked at the play. "He was passionate about harvesting potable water from the night air. Getting electricity is easy. Anybody can go down to the local home store and buy some solar panels and even just lay them on the desert sands and charge their batteries. But it's getting drinking water or water to do anything else. That's the hard part."

"Couldn't he just drill a well?"

The man shifted. "Maybe. In certain parts of San Diego County, we have wells as shallow as five hundred feet deep. But out near Pow Way, we have dry holes in the ground, which are over a thousand feet. They used to produce water, but now, even if you had a pump powerful enough to pump the depth, there's nothing down there. So, we need to get water from somewhere else."

The blonde chuckles and glances at the camera. "Well, good thing we have good wells here in San Diego."

He tilted his head. "But that's the point. We don't."

Her face almost created a crease or two through the Botox.

"Then where do we get our water? Obviously not from the Rio Grande."

He leaned forward. "You're right. You nailed it. We don't have enough water here for everyone. That's why Peter was so passionate about finding new ways to get water from the sky. San Diego County isn't densely populated... even though the traffic makes us feel like it is. But we still need more water than our wells and rain can supply. We get eighty to ninety percent of what we use from the Colorado River and the Sacramento River, which are both extremely low right now because of the drought. So Peter was trying out some unique ideas to help us bring in a couple of extra points."

"So he was a Greenie."

"If you mean he was into conserving water and finding alternatives to fossil fuels and sustaining the planet, then, yes, he was a Greenie."

She glanced at the clock offstage. It was time for the last point, and she was going to make it. "Which is why he created his cult out in the desert."

The man realized they had set him up. "It wasn't—"

She turned into the close-up camera as they cut power to the man's microphone. "And that's all we have time for today. We'll see you next Saturday morning as we make it a Great Day in San Diego. I'm Kristy Pyle, and this has been the important news you need to know."

The video clip ended as Muna kicked the leg of her desk. She spun to the dark web computer as she remembered why she didn't watch the news media or much of anything on TV.

8

IN OTHER NEWS

MINA LOOKED over at Nash sitting by the window. The soft light from behind her left her face passively in the non-committal parking lot she had seen her wife use for listening to government briefs. Or when forced to watch the news somewhere. "Are you going to be alright with this?"

Nash's head turned a fraction of an inch. "Why wouldn't I be?"

"Because you get all fainting, Nellie, with squeamish medical things—like blood and guts."

The two snickered at the old joke between them. Their third date hadn't gone as planned.

Nash had picked up some sort of infection or eaten spoiled food while working on a case. Exhausted after forty-seven hours without rest, but still determined to show up for their date.

By the time she arrived to see Mina, her plan to peck her on the lips got lost in the mental fog of exhaustion and the poisoning. In the heat of the moment, their passionate kiss shifted them back against the granite countertop.

Mina's hand flailed back and knocked over the champagne flute. Her hand snapped forward and smashed down onto the shattered, delicate glass, leaving several shards embedded in her skin. Her head snapped back silently as she brought up her bloody hand—as Nash passed out.

Both ended up in the hospital, but the doctor only admitted Nash for further observation. Mina referred to the multiple pink scars on her hand as her "battle wounds" from dating. But she wouldn't see what real battle wounds truly looked like until a month later.

They both turned at the light tap on the door before it opened.

The tiny doctor smiled as she closed the door. She pointed at the one-inch-long hair with only the tips bent. "I like your cropped hair. It gives you the look of a woman who is kicking backsides and taking names for later."

Mina passed her hand over her hair. "Thank you for not shaving it this time."

The woman looked at the scar hiding on the back of her head. "I didn't shave it the last time, either. That was the nurses in recovery. They couldn't see if the blush around the sutures was an infection or just inflammation. This is healing nicely. How are you feeling?" She sat on the wheeled stool with her hands palmed together between her knees.

"Good. We hired a personal nurse who likes to cook healthy food." She glanced at Nash. "We're sure it helped."

Nash snorted soft air. "The weeks in Barbados didn't hurt, either."

"Yum. Lamb. I loved raising the Barbados Black Belly lambs almost as much as we enjoyed eating them. Mom made a mean curry called biryani."

Mina nodded. "Lamb, goat, but mostly seafood. Our room was on the edge of the cliff. The surf pounding the rocks below was our lullaby every night. When we retire, we're going to buy the hotel and live in that room."

The doctor's freckled face crinkled. "I'll need the information on the hotel. How are the headaches?"

"Light. A couple of aspirin and a massage help a lot."

"Good." She looked over at her pad. "Cindy will be in in a minute. She'll set you up for the radiation. Tomorrow, they will want to cast a new skull cap, and then we'll start treatment on Monday." She held up her palm. "But... there have been some new studies, so I want to offer you a choice. There is a little hotter treatment, but it's only for five days. The study has shown it is just as effective as the sixteen-day procedure you did before. So there is that. It's up to you. We don't need to know until Friday if you two want to think about it."

Mina looked at Nash. Nash pushed out her lower lip and pointed her right palm at Mina's head. "It's your head. You choose. You already know my choice. Rub some dirt on it, and it'll stop bleeding, eventually."

The surgeon chuckled. "That was my father's idea of first aid."

Nash looked over with a crooked grin. "He was a leatherneck?"

She smiled and raised her hand. "Born in Guam, learned Japanese alongside English. Then street trash Tagala, Italian, and then was lucky enough to do my whole high school and college from Camp Pendleton in California."

Nash smiled. "What did he teach?"

She crunched her face. "Joint assault. Landing craft, tanks, and helicopters."

"What did he drive?"

"Helicopters mostly, but he was one of the first to get in a Harrier. He loved hiding in the coastal scrub and popping up to surprise the tanks. Dad loved the war games. I knew his wingman, and he for splashing entire companies of tanks before they could figure out where it was coming from."

Mina looked over with a fawning look at her wife. "Sounds like your kind of guy."

Nash snorted softly and rocked. "I would have bought him a few beers."

"He only drinks scotch in the backyard."

Nash nodded. "The air is cleaner there. How long was he in the sandbox?"

The surgeon cocked her head at the mystery. She held up two fingers.

Nash nodded. "You got lucky."

"Mom did. I was already up the highway at medical school."

Nash pointed at the diploma. "UC Irvine. I know some computer crunchers from there."

The surgeon sensed the conversation drifting too far afield into personal stuff. "Fine schools for both… and back to your cancer. I got clean margins, so there shouldn't be another time. This isn't a cancer that metastasizes into other areas. So, I think we're good going forward, but we're going to see a bit of each other over the next few years just to watch everything else. What with your breast cancer and the lymphoma, I feel it would be the prudent course to take." She put the tablet back on the stand. "Thoughts or questions?"

Mina looked at Nash, shaking her head with pursed lips. She turned back. "If any come up over the next weeks, I'll leave a note on the health portal."

The surgeon stood. "Okay then. I'll send Cindy in and get things lined up."

"Thanks." The two women nodded.

Driving later, Nash glanced at the orange dial of her watch. "Ouch. We missed lunch." She glanced over. "How are you feeling?"

"I could use some tapas from Guapo's."

Nash ticked her head in a cocked slant as she fingered the turn signal for a left. "Food at the bar, it is." The Hellcat purred through the turn and growled as she goosed it up the boulevard.

THE MAN BEHIND THE BAR THREW UP HIS HANDS. "BLESS saints, they're smiling down on me today. My Padres are playing strong, and I get my two favorite guapas walking into my empty bar. I get you all to myself." He raised the bridge at the end of the bar and waddled out for his group hug. "How are my favorite girls?"

Mina chuckled. "Happy… now. But we won't tell your wife."

He kissed her on the neck and whispered. "Which wife?"

He pushed them back and looked at their faces. "How was the island?"

Nash smiled. "Just what the doctor would order if she had known the secret."

He rubbed both of their outer arms. "You both look good." He looked behind them.

Mina shook her head. "I had to go see the surgeon today, so Powder got a spa day. The nanny took her."

The man looked with wide eyes at Nash. "You have a nanny now?"

Nash pointed at Mina. "A registered nurse, to be exact. One who cooks, so she's living in. We're thinking of adopting."

He turned and waved his large arm at the bar. "Please. Tell me wonderful stories." He waddled back to the gap in the bar. Closing the bridge, he turned, making his way to the middle of the dark wood bar. "What are we having?"

Mina and Nash turned their respective stool chairs. Both ran their hands along the dark walnut bar. They had marveled one day as he told them of getting lost in Spain and wound up at a large auction warehouse. The entire contents of a salvaged two-hundred-year-old bar were up for auction. The bidding was up to four thousand euros when he walked in and seemed stalled. He had asked the man he was standing next to what part of the bar they were auctioning off. The man waved his hand and told him in Spanish: todo. Guapo cried out. "For the complete bar? I'd pay ten thousand!"

The auctioneer had banged his gavel and pointed at Guapo. *Sold for ten thousand euros!*

Shipping and reconstruction cost a lot more. But the bar had come with cases and cases of expensive liquor, and Guapo never set foot in the halls of Congress again. Once a very successful lobbyist, he was now a jovial bar owner in the nearby suburbs.

"What's the best tapas today, Guapo?"

He spread his hands over his enormous belly. "Always the one in my belly."

Mina leaned forward and rubbed the belly. "Well, Happy Budda Hoti, what tasted the best?"

He held his thick hand up to his right ear. "Keep rubbing. I hear your luck changing."

The soft sound of a screen door slamming rattled from the backroom. He smiled. "I sent Lito out for more shrimp. All the market had was golden prawns from the gulf. It's the smartest thing I have ever convinced an oil company to do. Shrimp is the bane of a drill rig's existence. They clog up giant intakes they use for cooling water. So they put big screen traps in front of them. Every day, they empty the traps with hundreds of pounds of shrimp. But it's back into the gulf. Now, this little drill company sorts out the other stuff, packs down the good shrimp in ice, and ships them up here. If you need great-tasting shrimp, let me know. How you want yours now?"

Nash raised her eyebrows as she leaned in. "Tempura or beer batter?"

He smiled as he wagged his large index finger in her face. "Saki tempura. Fluffier like Guapo, and tastier. What are you drinking?" He peeked over at Mina. "What will the doctors allow?"

Mina smiled softly. "She's driving, so we're both having pineapple spritzers."

He pushed back from the bar. "Sweet or tart?"

Nash glanced up at the television snuggled into the back bar.

"Quinine on both. We got addicted to it down in Barbados." She pointed at the television. "Can you turn that up?"

"Sure…" He reached back for the remote.

Mina frowned at the television. "What's…"

The sound came up on the reporter talking over the aerial shot from a drone. The small group of houses were in the middle of an empty desert. To one side, there was a large array of photovoltaic panels. Nearby stood upright, spinning barrels on stands painted in stripes like barber poles. Farther out were tall posts that looked like square telephone poles with some sort of webbing between them.

"Energy-wise, the compound was more than self-sustaining to a point where they were selling power back to the grid. The local power company told us they produced seven times what they used. This last year, their net payback was in the six figures. Many of our viewers will recognize the large array of solar electric panels. But it is the spinning barrels, an alternative to the traditional windmills they were perfecting out here. The barrels spin with very little breeze but produce a goodly amount of power." The display returned to the woman standing in the desert.

"Murial, what are the pole things farther out?"

She looked over her shoulder at the desert as the display played the old video of the fly-over. "Those are interesting, Stu. Those posts are close to one hundred feet tall. The area between each pair is half the size of a football field. What looks like thread is a stainless-steel cable about the size of your little finger. The night air passes through the thousands of strands, and the moisture condenses on the metal. I don't know if you can see it, but the strands angle slightly, just enough to have the collected water run down to the one pole. The moving water also cools the metal more, which makes it collect more water. But at the pole, they absorb the water into a sponge-like medium, trapping the water and carrying it down into a gigantic holding tank. Each set of webs collects about a hundred gallons a night, maybe more." She turned and pointed another way. "See if you can get over there for some footage of the greenhouses, Ray." She looked at her cell phone to follow the feed. "They need the water for all the food they are growing in sheltering greenhouses."

Mina glanced back at Nash and then turned to study her. The woman's eyes were blank. She didn't see the television or hear the reporter. Mina waited.

Nash's voice was little more than her breath. "It wasn't religion."

9

UP NORTH

MUNA AND MIKE stood at the large windows facing west to the ocean. Moving their hands, arms, and mugs were as if connected. An overcast sky, to Muna's Pittsburg upbringing, meant a storm coming in. Usually from the northern coast. Gutter-flusher in the late summer or deep snow in the winter or early spring.

To Mike, it just felt like a heavy weight on his chest. When he had lost his legs, sister, and he had thought—his life. The day had been overcast. The sky had stayed gray the entire time he lay in the hospital next to the window. His view never changed. It was a battle he fought every morning after. It would start as he slowly maneuvered his way to the bathroom with a pair of shortened crutches. Showered, he would then use the mirror set close to the floor for shaving. Memories of his sister always came flooding back, usually of her teasing him about shaving almost nothing on his boyish face. Her laughter would follow him as he made his journey back to his bedroom as he dressed for work.

The tie of authority eventually gave way to an open dress shirt, especially in the days when the lab was his and his alone. Then, his palace of solitude had shattered. First by Nash, then the invasion of Muna, and finally Oz. His old teacher and fellow instructor at

Quantico. The long pants and dress shirt had shortened and eventually turned into casual levity. How he dressed coming to work had nothing to do with the job he did. When a lab coat was needed, it was there. Biohazard suits or Hello Kitty shorts were available and used as needed. He had noticed his gray days were less than his happier days.

He snuck a peek over at Muna. His sister would have been the same five feet even. He wondered if she would have ever worn Hello Kitty pajamas.

"I call drizzle by two o'clock."

He snorted in his coffee mug. "I won't steal your money. The barometer has been rock-steady for the last seven hours. This is just Bay Blues. Soft and fuzzy like gray flannel, but will never turn into a Brooks Brothers undertaker suit. If we're lucky, Marin County will get a light wash-down by next Wednesday. But the bay... nada. It's why Oz is out there now. He gets his entire week cruising from Alameda to Tiburon and way up the Sacramento River."

She sipped on her mug. "Anything new coming in?"

He stopped the mug next to his mouth. "Keep making jokes like that, and we might have to mop up the floor over here." He thought and turned his head. "Why?"

She slurped the last drop from her mug. Peeked in at the bottom of the porcelain and scowled. "I think I have a hole in the bottom of this mug."

He didn't even chuckle. It was a common problem in the laboratory or office. "Plug it with pork rinds."

She turned and looked back at her desk. "Did you split those blood samples for me?"

He nodded. "All done. Labeled, packed, and ready to ship."

She looked in her empty mug and shook her head. "I think I'll drive them up to Davis myself. I need the driving practice." She glanced over as she strode across the room toward the breakroom.

Mike turned and looked back out the window. Raising the mug

to his mouth, he sipped on the air. Looking into the empty mug, his shoulders sagged. *Damn.* The lab felt empty again—already.

———

"I THINK I'M SUPPOSED TO TURN LEFT HERE..." MUNA swung her head both ways. The GPS was proving less than helpless.

Mandy's giggle tinkled through the speakers. "If you go straight, is there a barn on the right or trucks parked along the left?"

Muna sputtered her lips. "Barbed wire and a large cow with some nasty-looking sawed-off horns."

Mandy laughed. "That's Brewster the Sperm Bank. Turn right. Left is after his pasture. Then you'll see the building down the way."

Muna nosed the car to the right. "Okay. See you in a minute." The phone clinked off. She looked out her open window. "Bye-bye, Brewster. Go make yummy babies."

The small man in a white lab coat stood in the doorway. The smile would have fit anyone twice his size. "Welcome back, stranger. I hope you have something exciting and interesting for us. Mandy needs a good, hard challenge. All we've done this summer is soil, soil, and oh yes... did I mention the dirt?"

Muna laughed as she rolled out of the car. "Good afternoon, Pi. Mandy mentioned you were being dirtier than usual. Let me grab the boxes, and you two can fill me in on all the dirt."

Mandy stepped out around the small man. Her blond hair was pulled back in a ponytail. "Don't encourage him. His mind is dirty enough. He'll just drag you down into the sediment, soil your mind with his schist, and then take you for granted."

Muna laughed as she leaned into the trunk. "It's the way he rocks."

Mandy smiled at the white foam boxes with the red drop stickers sealing the lids. She grabbed the second box and bent over in a mangled hunch as she dragged her foot. Her speech became slurred as her tongue hung from one side. "Blood. We have blood, master. Live blood."

Pi held up his fists in the air. "It's alive. It's alive."

Muna deadpanned as she looked at Mandy. "Slow season?"

Mandy groaned. "You have no idea. It's the drought. Dairy is off. Rice is down. The melon farmers went fallow or just planted cover crops because they couldn't get pickers. So everything we might have been doing... is idling in neutral. We're not kidding about testing soil. We've been begging for anything from the eleven western states." She elbowed through the door. "Can you imagine what it's like to go through volcanic dirt to tell a farmer what he can add organically and locally to improve the growth of his pineapples?"

Muna put down the box and stared at Mandy. Waiting.

The blonde grimaced. "What?"

Muna's face snapped in surprise. "Oh. That wasn't part of the soil's joke. You really worked over dirt from Hawaii."

Mandy groaned as she turned. "Hawaii, permafrost from Alaska, superfund strata from Los Angeles, we even had a farmer send us sand from Death Valley asking if it would be good for grapes. What's he going to make? Hot wine?" She frowned as she studied Muna. "New shirt...?"

Muna smiled with a smirk as she realized how long it had been since they had last seen her. "Nope, same old white cotton from Target's men's and boy's department. Wears like a French whore in Paris and washes like the face of Mount Rushmore. Federal Government approved white, end-on-end cotton from Pakistan."

Pi walked past with his nose in a tablet. "Nice lace slacks. They go nice with your hijab." He glanced up with a megawatt smile and kept on walking.

Mandy looked at the black leather pants. The furls on her forehead rolled from side to side. "I don't..." Then she looked up, and her face exploded. "Where's your hijab? Did you...?"

Muna settled into a warm smile as she leaned against the stainless-steel table. "What was that about coffee?"

Mandy jerked. "Oh. Certainly. Of course. Coffee."

Muna smiled. "Chill, girlfriend. I'll dish it all. I just need some caffeine after the drive. My stash of pork rinds ran out somewhere around Vacaville."

Pi scurried out of the back laboratory. "Stories? We get a story time? I'll have some coffee, too, Mandy. Please… mistress. Are there any story time cookies to go with the crackers?"

As the square of afternoon sunshine had moved across the floor of what Pi and Mandy called the sunporch, the story about Muna's lack of hijab wound down. The coffee pot stood empty. And the three sat relaxed.

Pi shifted in his chair. "So it was not so much a crisis of faith but a crisis of being dictated to with no basis other than because I told you so?"

Muna nodded. "Pretty much. And now, as my mother predicted, Iran is trying to stuff the genie back in the bottle."

"But here…?" Mandy shifted her empty mug. "And the rest of the world? I watch the news a lot, and it wasn't a sharp change, but I have noticed a lot fewer hijabs and maybe more of just the scarf."

Muna nodded. "My mother said even the older women in their mosque have replaced their hijabs with nice scarves and styled hair." She held out her hand and finger. "And I was watching the news of a riot in Palestine and wondering where the Palestinian women were. Even the scarves were gone. They were down to short bobs and tactical braids."

Mandy pursed her lips tightly, but the smile snuck into her twinkling eyes. "And the pork rinds?"

Muna fell back against the chair with a struck look on her face. "Always. Even with the jaw wired shut, the chef whipped up a special protein shack for me at Disneyland. Even he liked the high content of cayenne pepper with the pineapple."

Pi mused. "Oh yes. The sharp bite to offset the sweet. I can see that."

Mandy grimaced. "Wired shut?"

Muna waved her hand. "Eh... broken jaw. Another FBI story. The short run is we got blown up and shot. But only I got pistol-whipped. I'm one up on the badass queen." She beamed the row of pearls.

Mandy's mouth dropped open as Pi rested his hand on her arm. "She's staying local for a few days while we do her work. You have plenty of time for more stories. But for now, the ice is melting." He nodded toward the boxes in the other room.

Muna nodded. "Technically, evaporating or turning to a gas. We packed it down in two-stage dry ice boxes. I didn't think you needed any more contaminated water out here."

"Thank you."

Muna pushed her mug forward and folded her arms on the table. "There were nineteen dead down in Fort Mojave near the Nevada border. Once they got out to San Diego and a real medical examiner, the blood work started. They had some heads-up from the forensic photos. About half had defecated and urinated at one point." She held up her hand to Mandy's open mouth. "No, it's not something that happens all the time with death. Well, not like this."

The young woman tilted her head to one side. "What usually happens?"

Muna spread her hands as if she was grabbing a lectern. "If we take all deaths, many happen in circumstances where the bowels and bladder were under muscle control but full. Like trying to get home before you have an accident. So when death occurs, the muscles relax, and what was being controlled..."

Pi narrowed his eyes. "But if you're going to bed..."

Muna pointed at him. "Exactly. You do your ablutions before bed to prepare for being unable or not wanting to get up in the middle of the night. So there is no pressure. Hence, most who pass during the night don't. Patterns. We look at patterns."

"What were in the photos?"

Muna hooked her elbow over the back of the chair. "Along with the defecation, there was vomiting or foaming at the mouth on at least half of the bodies. So, the ME suspected poisoning, and sure enough, some of the usual botanicals showed up. But not in enough concentrations to warrant death in otherwise healthy adults."

Mandy glanced at Pi. "Even arsenic shows up in mild concentrations that we consume without thinking of it. Apples for one. Eat fifty apples a day, and by the end of the week, you'll have a problem."

Muna snickered. "I don't think I could even eat three or four a day. Even if that was all I ate."

Pi bumped his eyebrows. "No, but cows can consume upwards of a hundred pounds a day. And depending on the apple, it's either a killer or at least a detriment to their well-being."

Muna knocked her fist against her forehead. "Argh. Of course. Cow country."

Mandy shrugged her lower lip and face. "And old orchards or farms with an occasional fruit tree planted in the homestead. What was once planted a hundred or a hundred and fifty years ago as a food source can now disrupt the current food supply. Even a dozen rotten apples can cause spoiling in a cow's milk. And it's costly to quarantine her until her milk is back to normal."

Muna hummed. "Poison in the food doesn't always mean suicide."

10

TIME TO WORK

"Nash?"

"Nash?" The deputy director pulled the phone back out of his chest. "Let me get back to you. What's your number there, sir?" He flipped the roster for the Senate hearing over and mumbled while he wrote the number on the back. "Seven, eight, three, eight. Is there an extension there? Thank you. It shouldn't be longer than a few minutes... Yes, sir. If I don't call you back, I'll have my agent call you."

He carefully set the phone back in the cradle as if it was radioactive. He rolled his eyes large and stood. "Kathy?" He gazed at the open door where his secretary should be standing. The empty doorway beckoned.

Distracted, he strolled to the doorway. "Kathy?"

Four agents and a dog stood in the middle of the open center of the bullpen office space.

The woman cleared her throat to the right of him. He twitched. In her hands, she held a cake. A KABAR knife stood stuck in the center, surrounded by twenty burning candles. Nobody yelled. She stepped closer.

He read the cake and smirked. *Happy Anniversary, Commander*

KABAR. He blew out the candles and turned. The four agents were making silent explosion signs with their hands. "Thanks, guys. It means a lot to me."

Nash smirked. "Well, you took the tests and stood firm. You stuck the ground, and you've bagged and tagged. You've proved yourself field-worthy, sir. And I, for one, will have you as my wingman any day."

The deputy director blushed at the powerful speech. "I don't know how to fly."

Nash laughed. "It's not so hard. I'll teach you. Let's start with a Blackhawk and work our way down to a seven-fifty-seven."

He held up his palms. "I'd rather sit back in the back and let the professionals do it instead."

The tall brunette with the thin mustache grumbled. "Are you going to cut the cake or what?"

Kathy put the cake on her desk as the deputy director pulled out the knife.

Nash turned as her back pocket vibrated. She glanced at the phone's screen. "Yeah, Muna."

Static and electronic gravel rattled a moment, and then there were three voices of laughter in her ear. "We're on FaceTime Nash."

Nash pulled the phone around and turned it sideways to see all three clearly. "Wow. It's an old home week down on the farm. How's my favorite Pi? And it's good to see you stayed, Mandy."

Mandy laughed. "Who else was going to keep him in line? How've you been? Excluding getting blown up and shot... Yeah, Muna filled us in a couple of days ago."

Muna rolled her eyes dramatically. "They didn't believe anyone would want to damage this beautiful face. So I had to show them all the photos."

Pi rolled his finger in the air. "Coma isn't a nice thing. Any residual effects?"

Nash walked out into the hall by the elevator. "Some, but in a good way. It's a long story."

He glanced over at Muna. "Well, fly into Sacramento. We can listen to more story time over a dinner or something."

Nash leaned against the marble wainscotting and planted her one boot under her butt. Old habits die hard. She watched through the door at the others eating cake. She wasn't missing the sweet calories, like she was missing the field. "I don't think the DD would let me take the time off. Even if it's his anniversary."

Muna scowled. "And he's at work? What an ass."

Nash snorted. "Twenty years with the bureau, ass-ette." They both snorted at the sisterly jabbing.

Muna held up a slim stack of papers. "I'm sending this over. Tell him you caught a case in California."

Nash closed her eyes and almost whispered. "Mojave."

Muna growled in agreement. "Mojave."

Nash rolled her eyes open but narrowed. "It wasn't a religious commune."

Mandy and Pi both nodded. "It's beginning to look that way. It was poison, though. Just not suicide."

Pi held up a sheet of paper Nash recognized as the printout from a spectrometer. "Or, at least, not the suicide poisoning any normal person would choose."

Nash dropped her foot as she caught sight of the deputy director leaving the group and began walking her way. "Which begs the question of whether a sane person would choose suicide?"

The man put down the paper. "And I would have to point out the most famous case of all. Socrates versus the Senate."

Nash noticed the deputy director standing in the office doorway. "Case closed. And I think I need to go make my case here. We'll talk later. Send the file, Muna. I might need it." She closed the connection and holstered her phone in her pocket.

Tony sighed. "California?"

"It wasn't suicide. Muna is sending the definitive results of the floral poisoning experts. And I don't think we better make any jokes about bullshit. They're experts on that too."

He nodded. "She was taking the blood samples out to the university you guys used for the bones and the water contamination."

Nash bounced her back off the wall. "Davis. They're good. And seriously, congratulations on the twenty years."

He turned as they walked into the office space. "The knife was a little over-the-top... But yours is coming up soon enough. And I'll remember the knife." He pointed at her workstation. "Go over what Muna sent you, and then see me in my office before you leave."

She smirked. "Travel or just home?"

His eyes closed as he stopped with a heavy sigh. He gazed back. "Either. And the way things are in the dog days of bureaucracy doldrums, I might try to come with you. Anything not to go into another meeting of uselessness." He snapped his fingers at his door. "Oh, and I have a phone number for you."

"Send it in the chatterbox."

He thought about the new messaging system and how it opened a small yellow square on your desktop screen. The first week, his screen became buried in yellow squares that he didn't know how to make disappear. His head lowered with the growl. "I'll bring it out."

<hr>

"DO YOU THINK SHE'LL COME?" MANDY STOOD POURING coffee from the carafe.

Muna leaned back in the tilting desk chair. "I know late summer in Washington is called the dog days. It comes from the nineteenth century when a couple of stray dogs wandered into the hallowed halls of Congress."

Pi chuckled and bent over, looking into the small refrigerator. "Do you know the rest...?"

"Something about defecating somewhere important?"

Pi put the protein bar on the table and climbed back into the chair. As he unwrapped the protein bar, he thought back to the professor telling the story. "Evidently, the security at the time thought the dogs belonged to a representative. So, they didn't shoo them out. Nor did they pay close attention to how many dogs were in the building. Or what they looked like." He glanced up with a wry smirk.

Mandy laughed. "Because it was a pack of dogs…"

He nodded as he chewed. "The shit was everywhere. And there were reports of some bitches being in heat. So, the halls of power were awash with something other than the usual screwing."

Muna lowered her eyelids. This was beginning to sound like a story Oz or Mike would tell. "If this turns out to be a shaggy dog story…"

Pi held up his palm. "You can look it up. When Congress reconvened, there was a litter of pups under the desk of the President Pro Tempore."

Muna tossed her braid over her shoulder and leaned toward Pi. "Okay. What's the joke?"

Pi and Mandy both shook their heads. "No joke." Pi pointed at Muna. "True story. And why they call it the dog days." He turned in the swivel chair. "But now, when they break for the summer, they lock it all up tight as a drum." He hopped down and walked off. "They have litter laws now." He scurried the rest of the way into the anaerobic chamber and closed the air-tight door.

Mandy hung her head and peeked at Muna. "Sorry about that. But the dogs…? True story."

Muna glared at the closed door with the large red light next to it. "If I thought I could get away with it, I'd turn him over my knee and spank him."

"You'd get accused of elder abuse or worse."

Muna sighed. "It's just… I get non-stop dad jokes from the guys at work. And then…" She held her splayed hands out at the door.

Mandy swiveled her chair to look at the door. She wondered if there was a fresh bio-suit in the chamber. Shrugging, she swiveled back. "Have you ever thought about what you might represent to Oz and Mark?"

"Mike. His name is Mike. And, no... what do you mean?"

Mandy smoothed her index finger along the seam of the table's welded corner. "Do they have kids?"

"I think Oz has a daughter back east. She's in Jersey or somewhere. He doesn't talk much about her, so I'm not sure."

Mandy bounced her head once. "How old?"

Muna hooked her arm over the back of the chair. "I think he mentioned she had retired. So maybe in her sixties?"

Mandy's eyes grew large for a moment. "And Mike?"

Muna shook her head. "I think it has something to do with losing his legs... but no. Not that I ever heard of."

Mandy bobbed her head as she stood and grabbed her mug, the short ponytail brushing the back of her neck. "Yup." Her smile was warm but smug.

Muna grabbed her mug and followed. "Yup what?"

Mandy stopped at the coffeemaker. "You're the daughter or little sister they never had. The tormenting is what you do to the little brat following you around and pestering you. But secretly, they wouldn't have it any other way."

Muna rested her weight on her left hip. "And you would know this... how?"

Mandy snorted long and hard. "Four older brothers."

"And you talk to them...?"

Mandy poured the coffee into the two mugs. "I talk to at least one of them every week. Some weeks, it's all of them."

Muna pulled up her mug and smelled the steam. "How much older?"

Mandy tossed her head. "Kelly was fifteen and the last one still at home when I was a surprise."

"Must be nice."

Mandy nodded as she turned and leaned back against the counter.

THE WINDOWS WERE THE LIGHT GRAY OF NIGHT IN D.C. Tony yawned and reached his arms back over his head as he stretched. The tie had landed on the end of his desk an hour before. "Do we need to get a chemist in here to understand all this?"

Nash shook her head. "Muna laid this all out cleanly... well, probably more like Pi, and Mandy laid it out." She pointed at the chart. "And I remember some of my chemistry and biology."

He floated his splayed hand over the stack of papers. "But none of the drugs... er... excuse me. Herbs or plants... were enough to kill them?"

"Right." She pulled out one sheet. "Let's take the digitalis. Which we are certain is the Foxglove flower." She ran her pen down the columns. "Here are each of the nineteen names. Here are the content levels in their systems. And here is the level to cause probable death. As you can see, no one was even close. But..." Her pen moved to the last column. "This is the level needed to have effect or incapacitate them."

He scanned down the column. "They're all in the range, but it's in the bottom." He looked up with a frown.

Nash smiled. "Whoever did this was a female."

"How do you know?"

She smiled. "Because a guy would have used too much. When they poison someone, they might as well just take out a cannon and shoot them. There is nothing subtle about a male poisoner."

"But women are subtle?"

Nash shrugged a small twitch. "It's our murder weapon of choice. You guys like it more violent and personal. Black widows are just happy it works."

Tony frowned. "But you said it wasn't enough to kill them."

Nash smirked softly. "Not alone. Foxglove is only the digitalis. It makes the heartbeat stronger and pushes the blood around the system better. But we want people to be sleepy and lethargic. Too sleepy to get out of bed. So for that…" She found another sheet and turned it for him to see. "I give you Belladonna. In the hippy days, a little Belladonna would make people think they had bought really strong weed even though it could have just been oregano. But sprinkle a little Donna in there, and people calmed right down."

He smiled. "Mellow yellow."

She shook her head. "Nope. That was banana peels. Dry them and grind them up. The poison the growers sprayed on the bananas to kill the enormous spiders can cause mild hallucinations from the toxicity." She shrugged. "Or… it's just drug-addled street lore. But smoking the poison can mess you up."

He taped the paper. "But this Belladonna is the real thing."

Nash pointed down the column. "Everyone would have felt like they had taken a quaalude." She pulled up another sheet of paper.

Tony smiled. "So we have them dopey, but their heart is pumping like an eighteen-year-old going to the prom."

"So we slip them the Mickey?"

Nash dropped another page. "Nope. Caster the friendly bean." She pointed to the one word. "Source of ricin."

Tony leaned back in his chair. "I'm guessing this is an important part?"

"To screw up the racing heart. Ricin does it by making the beats shallow or weak. Enough ricin, and the heart just flutters, which is how the gas showers worked in Auschwitz."

He frowned, leaned forward, and found the other sheet. "But you have"—he glanced at the sheet—"foxglove making the heart pump like a racehorse made of iron."

Nash nodded with floating eyelids. "Have you ever heard of a drug called speedball?"

He pinched one eye closed as he cocked his head. "Yes… but I don't remember what it is."

"The old school is to crush up a couple of quaaludes and an equal part of speed or cocaine. It keeps you mellow while the heart turns laps at Indianapolis. Your hallucinations and altered perception may vary depending on your physical health. At my age and condition, I'd survive. At yours... it would tear your heart apart."

"And the Belladonna?"

She tapped her finger on the desk. "Keeps you asleep while your heart beats itself out of your chest." She scanned deeper down one sheet and grimaced. "And while our bowls and bladder let go. And there could be the vomiting, with the potential of aspirating."

He pushed the pages back at Nash. "Okay. I'm good now. I've heard enough. Call your magic man and go play with Muna. But make it right with your wife first."

Nash snorted. "I think she was getting close to kicking me out the door. It's the daughter I must convince. It's time to get back to work, and she just wants to be with mommy."

11

WHO IS THIS

The large table was a dark, empty field. Dozens of cartoon and action figures stood at attention along the small wall between the tabletop and the windowsill. Five cars in partial stages of transformation drove along the width of the dark wood sill as if it were a road or highway.

Nash looked over at Muna. "Do you think it's going to be big enough this time?"

Muna studied the table made from two desks, end to end, and covered with a large sheet of plywood. Andy had ordered the board custom cut and brought in. The table was twelve feet long and almost three feet deep. Every inch was reachable, even by Muna. She pointed at several more unused desks in the vast room.

In its heyday, the room was the office space for over fifty agents working in the domestic war effort of World War Two. Everyone had their own desk, no matter which shift they worked in the around-the-clock nature of war. Many of the desks had been removed, but the space remained and only seemed to grow. "We can always make a second or fourth desk as we need it." She fluttered one eye at Nash. "It's only plywood." She rolled her eyes. "It's not like the larger 3-D printer I want."

Nash glanced to the far end of the room. The former semiprivate office was now occupied by the current printer the small woman had gained. She had gone to a local technical trade show. In the last hour of the last day, she sweet-talked the sales team into hand-delivering and setting it up before figuring out payment.

Three of the engineers, playing at sales, kept dropping by for the next month or two—to train the young woman. After Muna employed the device to replicate essential evidence, the firm exchanged any remuneration for a write-up. The article highlighted the critical role their printer played in the federal investigation. Muna never mentioned the photos and smaller articles appearing on gamer and makers' websites. Mike had rolled his eyes and turned a blind eye to no paperwork. He later printed a sign for the glass door. *Muna's Private Printer Palace—Keep Out.*

Oz had once joked about the printer with all the attachments, reminding him of the giant laser in one of the original James Bond movies. Neither of the men entered the room again.

Nash smirked about the current printer. "The one you have will save us a trip to San Jose for more cartoon statues."

The smaller woman growled as she surveyed the army of figurines. "They're called action figures."

Nash leaned over to the fur weighing heavily against her knee. She knew the hint. "Yeah, well, these two action figures need some bedtime. Shooting at six?"

Muna turned. She knew the other agent couldn't see her blood-shot eyes in the dim light from the city. "Sure. I can sleep in."

The three turned for the elevator. Nash wasn't going to bust the junior agent who had saved her life twice. She had noticed the exhaustion at the airport. "Well, then, let's make it a sleep-in day and shoot at seven."

Muna leaned against the wood-paneled wall of the elevator as she pressed the fourth button without looking. "You're the senior agent. So no argument here."

STILL IN HER HELLO KITTY PAJAMAS AND TACTICAL VEST, Muna pointed out the five figurines. "The little monk is the Air Bender. So anything having to do with the wind turbans will go on that pile."

Nash glanced down at Powder sniffing at the pink, fuzzy bunny slippers. "Are you hiding drugs in those slippers?" In the shooting range, she had shot barefooted. Nash wondered when and where she had slipped into the slippers.

Muna looked at her with rolling eyes and the haughty look of a bored young teenager. "No duh. But they are new from China, so they probably came in with at least heroin." She picked up the tall, dark figure with the extended arm and splayed hand. "This is Magneto."

Nash frowned. "Solar doesn't work on magnets. It works on sunlight."

Muna nodded as her right hand flopped out in the air—pointing at the statue of a man's body with a falcon head. The top of the ceremonial ancient Egyptian headdress was an orange ball. "Correct. And then we go old school and have Ra look after the sun stuff."

Powder rose and put her front paws on the tabletop. She sniffed at the bulging, muscled statue with tattoos flowing into scales.

Nash snorted and then chuckled as she ruffled one of Powder's ears. "Yeah. Me too, girl. I'm sensing a godforsaken trend is happening, and it's about to get fishy." She picked up the figure. The detail was missing, but the intent was there. "Um...? Is this supposed to be Jason Momoa?"

Muna winced. "Maybe we should daytrip to San Jose after breakfast. The STL file was cheap. I got it off a fanboy site. I should have done a little more research on the programmer." She rolled her eyes. "His handle was *Crush it like a tin can*. It should have been *Crush it like a fourth grader*."

Nash frowned. "How much did you give him?"

Muna turned as she pulled her pursed lips to one side. "A Grant... but I'm not finished with him." She smirked. "Turns out he lives in Orange County."

Nash started chuckling. "How close to the play school?"

Muna held her face up as she removed her tactical vest. "About ten minutes on his bicycle. Breakfast?"

Nash stopped her with her hand on Muna's shoulder. Nash's eyes narrowed as she growled. "How old is he, and who's in charge?"

Muna smiled innocently. "Boy, you have a nasty mind. You think all geeks and nerds want to do is corrupt innocent children or something. Sheesh."

The growl deepened. "Who, and how old?"

"The Slug Six took him over as a mascot. But Momma and Jazz are going to get him a straight-up set of tutors for all the other school stuff he needs."

Nash softened and straightened. "Why?"

Muna chewed at the side of her thumb. "Because his computer is a breadboard, he cobbled together from parts he found in dump-sters... and he's bullied at school for being homeless."

They turned in the elevator as Muna pushed the button for the fourth floor and a change of clothes.

Nash looked at her bare feet. "You know... they had some exten-sive greenhouses..." She peeked over.

Muna bounced on the balls of her feet as the door slid open. "That's why they are holding a Baby Groot for me down at the Fanboy Shop."

COLBY DREW HER RIGHT LEG UP AND TUCKED THE FOOT under her left leg. Her eyes sparkled as she watched the birds flying in the morning light. The little paper tags and strings hung over the edge of her mug as she sipped. "I never tire of this view." She turned her head toward her brother. "It seems you're having a good day today."

He sipped on his tea. "Wait until the breeze picks up. I'll be hiding in the office, sucking on the oxygen. I get the mornings. The dust and pollen are grounded by the morning dew. So this is when this vampire gets some sunshine."

She nodded. "You've got to take life where you can find it."

He paused with his lips near the mug's edge. "And where is Colby Chiller finding life these days?" He frowned. "Didn't you find heaven out in the desert somewhere? Some fort sandcastles or something."

"Fort Mojave. It's an Indian reservation. A lot of agriculture, but the water in the Colorado River is drying up."

He coughed lightly and then folded forward in a severe jag. As he calmed, his throat was strained. "How deep are the wells?"

She resisted telling him her concerns. He had heard it all for too many years. "Most are past the thousand foot. The seven city wells are past fifteen hundred, and they'll start on two new ones they think will hit two and then run laterally for a mile or more."

He nodded as he peeked at his handkerchief and then stuck the folded cloth back in his shirt pocket. "Same as fracking. Chasing the water." He looked over at his younger sister. "What were you doing about water?"

She sipped on her tea as her eyes followed the two birds dancing in and around the trees in courtship. "We were pulling it out of the night air. The conversion rates for the investment in the standing arrays to the liters of water gained would have sucked. Except, we ran closed hydroponics in the greenhouses. It used a third the water as the drip in the other houses."

He rasped softly. "To open field?"

She shook her head. "For an acre of greenhouse, we out-produced five of what would come off a field. We were experimenting with eight-foot verticals, and it would have quadrupled our yield. There are some twenty-foot vertical indoor farms in New York City turning in some eye-popping numbers."

"I saw an article in an agricultural magazines a few years ago. Do you think it could be commercially workable?"

She rocked as she sipped. "Already is. There's a farm producing most of the cherry tomatoes, miniature carrots, and Brussels sprouts for the restaurants in the city. Last I heard, they were optioning land to quadruple their production. They want to expand into other markets. Even at the more expensive mark, they are organic and direct delivery instead of trucking for days."

Turning, he studied her. He could tell from her constant eye movements that she was distracted or nervous. Her body said relaxed, but all their lives, he knew her eyes told the actual story. "Ready to talk about why you're not down there farming?"

She focused on where the birds had gone. The tip of her tongue danced along the dry edge of her lips as she exhaled deeply. Closing her eyes, she turned toward her older brother. Her rock. Her champion. "They're all dead."

He frowned as he fished the handkerchief back out of his pocket. "The plants? The greenhouses?"

She rolled over on the wooden chaise lounge. Her eyes locked on his as she frowned. "You really don't watch the news, do you? Not at all…"

He winced. "When we moved up here… and the VA told me to just go home and die…" His head movement was soft and tired. "No. Not in the last year or two. I get the farm report on my computer. It gives me the weather and spot prices on fertilizer and my apples. Otherwise, just the talk when they deliver."

She wiggled around to pull her phone out of her back pocket. She glanced at the bars. It was iffy but worth a try. Poking at the search, she pulled up the first news clip. She passed it over for him to watch.

Colby resumed watching for the birds in the dimming light. The news wasn't talking any differently than it had the last week.

Nothing had changed. If they had gotten any new information, it wasn't changing the narrative. She smirked a soft snort when the anchor mentioned the Heaven's Gate cult and even got the meteor wrong. Hali Bop, in her mind, wasn't even close to Hally's Comet. But as someone once said, you only need to be right for a day. Then you can bury a retraction or change notice on page twenty-eight, right under the ad for pantyhose at half-price.

He passed the phone back. She turned it off and dropped it in her lap.

She sighed and thought. "I only had a few bites of vegetables and a biscuit that night. Everything else had ingredients I was allergic to. Later in the night, I got up feeling feverish and nauseous, so I drove to the clinic in town—but it was closed when I arrived. Still not feeling right, I drove to San Diego to stay with a friend for the weekend and be near a hospital, just in case. When I tried calling the compound in the morning, there was no answer. A few days later, I heard on the news about what had happened."

He leaned his head back and blew out a soft breath. "So out of you twenty… you're the only one who survived."

"Twenty-one. We laughed about being a winning hand. Laughlin, Nevada is right across the river."

He furled his forehead and rolled his head over to face her. "But they said nineteen."

She sat up and looked at her hands. "They either miscounted or just got it wrong. There were twenty-one of us."

12
SORTING PEOPLE

THE AIR BLOWING through the vent was tepid. And then it stopped.

The deputy director froze. His eyes narrowed as they shifted to the dark, screened rectangle high on the wall. The quick intake of breath puffed his cheeks as he blew the air out of his pursed mouth. He glanced at the time block on the computer screen. Six-oh-one. To save energy, the government buildings were turning off the air-conditioning after the official workday was over.

He fell back into his last comfort—his seven-year-old fake-leather, fake-executive desk chair. The hydraulic piston had stopped working the month after any kind of warranty would apply. Maintenance had applied layers of duct tape to extend the life until the ten-year cycle might replace it if the right administration was in the White House. Tony had his doubts if there was such a magical entity.

As he thought about leaving, a yellow square showed on his screen. He leaned forward, moved the cursor to the square, and clicked.

He recognized two of the five figurines lined up. In the distance was the San Francisco forensic lab. A smile tugged at the right side of his mouth. The youngest figurine was one of his favorites—and this statue was of its time in the small flowerpot. Like millions around the world, he had instantly memorized the characters' single spoken line for any situation. He growled his best. "I am Groot?"

"Oh shoot. We weren't ready yet."

The laughing face slid past the computer as she reached out, trying to stop herself. A boot at the edge of the screen kicked at the arm of the chair, stopping the slide.

Tony snickered. "I'm booking a flight to come work out there. Muna, I need you to set me up a remote desk. It's six o'clock, and they just turned off the air-conditioning for the building."

Nash rolled a chair into view and plopped down into it. "I don't think they can legally do that. There are over two stories, and the entire air exchange relies on air-conditioning. They even deliver the heat in the winter through the air-conditioning."

He fluttered one eyelid. "Care to come argue the case for three thousand workers?"

Nash barked a short laugh. "Hell no. It's sixty-seven degrees here. We're freezing in our shorts and T-shirts."

He held up his palm and waved it back and forth at the computer screen. "Oh yes. I can see how exhausting the working conditions are."

Nash reached out her left arm and put Muna in a headlock as she covered her mouth. "It's Muna's new file sorting system. If she was here right now, I'd let her explain it."

Muna's eyes were wild as she waved her arms and legs around in the air.

Tony rolled his eyes as his face slowly lowered into his one palm. "Maybe you can explain it to me. Or should I ask Powder?"

At her name, the dog's paws and head appeared above the desktop. The bark was more of a soft fluff of air out of the sides of her mouth.

Tony laughed. "Yes. We're talking about you, Powder. I see

you're in charge out there." He frowned. "Um... not to be conventional or anything. But... where are Oz and Mike?"

Nash turned solemn. "Um... it's *that* day. So Oz took Mike down to his boat to sit and talk near the water."

He looked to one side at nothing but his memory. "I thought his accident was...?"

Muna moaned and then growled. "Not THAT day. It's his annual review day."

Tony's face lightened, and then scowled at Nash.

She waved her two splayed hands. "No problem. You did the review the night you two stopped in for some scotch. I filed the paperwork for you. You were busy." She jerked her thumb at the beaming mini version. "Same time as I filed Muna's review. I think her ammo allotment needs to be increased. The extra range time might bring her up to standards."

His right eye narrowed as he looked back and forth at the two known for more than a little high jinks. "I'll sign-off on the increase... but which standards are we talking about here?"

Muna shrugged. "We already got your sign-off. And the shooting competitions start next month."

"Competitions?"

Nash rolled her eyes. "Nationals, internationals, or Olympics... take your pick. The ophthalmologist signed off on her having seventeen twenty with both eyes. So even trick shooting isn't out of the consideration."

He pointed at the five statues. "Shooting and this...? Is the workload out there hitting the doldrums?"

Nash rolled her eyes. "On the contrary. In fact, if you transfer your desk out here for a few weeks, we could use the help."

"And my partner would be...?"

Muna pointed at each of the statues in turn. "Take your pick. Ra manages solar steam, Thor controls wind power, Mystique morphs photovoltaics, and Aquaman steals water from the air. And, of course, there is your little friend and the greenhouses."

"Okay... um... I see the compartmentalization... but why the statues?"

Muna beamed as she leaned forward to the keyboard, and Nash stood up. "And he finally asks the important question." She grabbed two of the figurines as Nash's hand came into view from the top and grabbed the other three. Muna poked the keyboard.

The deputy director's screen changed to a view from probably the ceiling. The scene was of a large table next to the windows. More figurines lined the deep windowsill. On the table sat five stacks of paper. Muna and Nash came into view.

Muna waved her arm over the large table. "This is probably going to become too small, but it's a start. We have nineteen bodies. Each has a name, a story, and an expertise. Those educated skills were why they were out there in the desert and what they were working on." She placed Thor on the first stack. "These people had education and experience in thermal dynamics and airflow engineering. So we are assuming they were working on the unique wind generation units."

She kissed the top of Aquaman's head and placed the figurine on top of the next stack. "This is a unique group and will require a lot of digging into their past to figure out exactly what and how the water gets stolen from the air."

Nash placed Mystique on the smaller stack at her end. "Photovoltaics is kind of mainstream now, but I'm sure there was something unique going on out there at the compound."

Ra walked like an Egyptian to the next stack. "We think this is where the physicists were playing. But also, there is a plumber in the group."

The thinnest stack became the foundation for the Groot sprout. "And there was the food. They were growing it in some interesting greenhouses. And if you know anything about greenhouses, intense sunlight and heat are not your friends. So, again, there will be some interviews to conduct. Also, the poisons were all botanical..."

Muna turned with her hands clasped behind her back like most professors wrapping up their lectures. "So you see… It's not exactly the doldrums here. But we could use someone to oversee the table while we're chasing down all the interviews. Sir."

Tony lowered his eyelids to what he hoped looked like narrow slits. "Who are you hiring?"

Nash sat on the edge of the large table. "He already works for the bureau. Tell me your wife wouldn't like to get out of the heat of Washington for a couple of weeks. And what better place to vacation than in beautiful San Francisco?"

Muna pouted her mouth and held out her one palm. "The room price on the fourth floor… you can't beat."

He laughed. "I'm not so sure my wife would want to stay in a testosterone townhouse…"

Nash tilted her head forward as Muna exploded. "Excuse *me*…"

He held up his palms. "I misspoke. I'm sorry."

Muna dropped her weight onto one hip. "Well, it's not as if I've hung any frilly curtains or anything."

Nash growled. "She tried. I threatened to burn them in situ."

Tony cocked his head with a narrowed eye.

Nash growled as she waved her hands. "Oh, hell no. They were saffron tie-dyed with potato-stamp-printed blue bunnies. Powder gave them one sniff and immediately shit on them."

Muna hung out her one hand with a pointed finger as she rolled her eyes and nodded. "Preach it, sister."

Tony cleared his throat. "Is the report done?"

Nash and Muna snapped into the definition of stunned deadpan. "Are you coming out?"

"No."

"Then, obviously, the report didn't hit its mark." Nash pointed at Muna. "I'll need her as a document herder in Southern California. But we seriously need someone to run herd over the table and keep track of what is going on."

He leaned in on his desk. "Today was the seventeenth day over ninety-six degrees. People are killing friends and family. I have at least a dozen meetings to attend this week alone. I would love to come out and sing kumbaya with the children, but I have forty-seven in this office alone to handhold. Forty-nine, counting the two who are never here." His head twisted. "So who are you going to hire, steal, borrow, or kidnap to do your bidding? Because I'm guessing Mike and Oz aren't going to work."

Muna smiled broadly. "Can I hire someone outside the bureau?"

He sighed. "How far outside the bureau?"

Muna's eyes looked at the ceiling, away from the camera. "A consultant from an NGO."

"Do they do work for the US Government?"

She nodded. "Critical infrastructure."

He shrugged his face and held out his palms. He didn't want to get any closer to the answer. "It's your computer."

Her head vibrated. "Oh no. I'd compartmentalize her. Otherwise, I'll have her bring her own system."

He nodded. "Yeah, have them bring their own laptop."

Muna glanced back at Nash and smirked. "Oh no. I don't think Chips would bring a laptop. If she's coming for a few weeks, she'll bring a tower."

Nash snorted. "Or build one here."

Muna pushed her index finger back over her shoulder at Nash. "And there is that. So I'm good?" She pulled her cell phone out of her pocket and held her thumb over the screen.

Tony had a sense they had set him up. "Clear it through, Mike and Oz. It's their lab."

"Roger Wilco." Muna waved her hand in the air and snapped the thumb and fingers together. It cut the connection off.

Muna turned toward Nash as her thumb pushed the screen. "See, given the right provocation, it's easy peasy."

Nash shook her head slowly as she reached over and fondled the fuzzy head and ears. "How about a walk, girl? Your sister is going to be on the phone for at least an hour."

Nash smiled as they turned in the hall.

"Hey, Ming. I have a deal for one of your crew."

The elevator pinged.

"No. I want to borrow Chips for a few weeks or a month."

"Just some light drudge labor, but the rest of the day, she can work remotely for you."

Nash looked down at the brown and green eyes as the elevator door slid shut. "Your sister is up to questionable shenanigans. I didn't say she was a bad influence, but she will corrupt you."

13

SUNSHINE AND SAND

Chips peeked back over her shoulder. "Do they have script books with all those jokes hiding somewhere?"

Muna laughed. "If you find one, burn it. Please. But you can also tell them to stop."

Nash laughed from the driver's seat. "It won't do any good. But you can tell them."

Chips pulled at her short blond ponytail. "Nah. I just write them down and send them to Slug and the boys. I guess it's a guy thing. The thumbs-up responses are piling up. So, where are you today?"

"Cal State San Diego. Doctor Peter Lambert should be under Mystique. He was the spearhead of the project out there. So we thought we would get some background on the man himself. We caught a snip on the news, and they're still pushing the religious cult thing here."

Chips rolled her pale blue eyes. "Not just there. I wrote an algorithm to troll for news on the top twenty-five. Anytime the group, project, cult, or religious group comes up, I get a hit. Yesterday, it was forty-nine to seven for cult over project. Almost nobody is using the terms doctor or education. It's as if some Bubba gathered a bunch of people and walked off into the desert."

Muna moaned. "I think there was a story like it in the bible."

Nash turned left. "Every religion has its stories about messengers leading people out into a desert to die. It's a requirement for it to be a religion." She glanced over at Muna's fluttering eyes and bored face. "Look it up. It's in the rule book."

Muna busted her deadpan face into laughter. "Rule book…" She rolled her eyes at Chips on her phone on FaceTime. "She's as bad as the boys sometimes. Anything else on the sorting?"

The young blonde shook her head. "I've looked everywhere I could: DMV, power company, tickets, and even called the local mini-mart at the gas station. I still only come up with the nineteen we have."

Muna nodded as Nash nosed the car into a large parking lot. "Okay. It might be all there is… but Nash has a gut feeling it isn't. And when it comes to out of the ordinary—I'll take her gut over anything else staring us in the face."

Chips watched Muna and Powder looking around and could hear the car being turned off. "Alright, you're there, I'm here, and we both have work to do. Hug Powder for me. Caio."

The connection snicked off in Muna's hand. Her lips furled as Nash looked over. "You have a bad feeling, too?"

Muna's eyes narrowed as her head bobbed. She sighed through her nose. "As I told Chips, when you have a feeling in your gut, I get a tingle, and then my hair stands up…"

Nash leaned against the door and studied Muna.

The smaller one grabbed her door handle and looked back at the silence. "What?"

Nash rolled her hand in the air. "Go ahead. I want to see your braid stand up."

Muna growled softly as she unbuttoned her shirt sleeve. Pulling it up past her elbow, she stuck her arm out.

Powder sniffed and then licked a short touch. Nash leaned over close and looked at the arm but didn't touch it. "Oh yeah. Your arm. But where are the hairs?"

Muna pulled her sleeve down and re-buttoned the cuff. "Ass."

Nash pulled her door open. "Hairless, but good to know you can back up my gut." She looked at the large buildings with people walking everywhere. "Where are we going?"

"Engineering building." Muna waved her hand in the general direction of the air as her voice took on a cowboy twang. "Over that away."

Nash snorted softly and wagged her head. "Y'all sure it ain't over thar?"

Muna rolled her eyes. "Ask the locals. And make sure you tell them we're pilgrims."

The young woman walking past looked at Muna and laughed. "Pilgrims? From where? Orange County?"

"Oh shit. You can hear us?" She snapped her head in horror at Nash. "You said the cone of silence would work here. You guaranteed it."

The young student stopped. Now, with a bored look on her face, she shifted her weight onto one hip. "Okay... what's the social experiment, and where's the camera?" Her index finger circled a lazy circle in the air.

Nash pointed at her ears. "She cheated. She doesn't have those plug things in her ears."

The redhead's eyes fluttered in boredom. "Now you sound like my dad. I'm gone."

Muna laughed and held out her splayed hand. "Wait. We can share our hatred for dad jokes while you show us where the engineering building is."

The woman turned back and frowned. "Which engineering?"

Nash smiled. They hadn't thought there would be more than one. "He worked with solar electricity... but..."

The woman gave a soft snort of boredom. "Doctor Lambert?" Her eyes rolled. "I should have known."

Nash squeezed one eye shut. "Um… yeah. But how?"

The redhead's almost transparent eyebrows arched. "Know?" Her snort was sharp. "On this campus? It's all everyone hears from you…" She rolled her eyes. "Pilgrims."

She looked Nash up and down. "But you're obviously not news crew. And you aren't a student. What with your matching white shirts, leather pants, granny boots, guns, and badges…" She knelt to look closer at the badge on Powder's tactical vest. Her head jerked. "Seriously? FBI?" She straightened. "You need to call wardrobe. Those idiots wear crappy gray suits. They dressed you two more like a Los Angeles lesbian mafia hit squad."

Muna tilted her deadpan head in a shrug. "Some do… in the beginning. But… Doctor Lambert?"

"Physics. But he doesn't wear a suit either. He's more of a T-shirt and board shorts kind of professor." She pointed down the large walkway. "Follow along until you see the wagons circling the single Indian."

Nash shied her head and narrowed her one eye. "Wagons? Indian?"

"News vans. Wagons. The school threw the lowest of the teacher's assistants to the wolves about a week ago. So she answers the questions. But it also answers the question about how we embrace foreign students who pay four times as much in tuition as we do."

Muna got closer. "Indian?"

The coed nodded. "I mean, she doesn't sound as bad as the tech support for my laptop, but you can tell she's from there."

Muna nodded her head slowly up and then down—once. "There. India."

"One of those tech support countries, but she doesn't have the red dot on her forehead. Just look for the news vans. You can't miss them. They all have those big radar dish things on top of them." She turned left and walked off.

Muna watched Nash watch the retreating young woman. "What? The Indian thing?"

Nash tilted her head toward her left shoulder. "I don't know. It's kind of…" She turned, but her eyes were closed. "She had the reference about circling the wagons, but… then it became about people from India, or Pakistan, or even Bangladesh. And I'm wondering if she thinks the Indians who the settlers circled the wagons against… were from those tech support countries?"

She turned with a confused look on her face. "But her whole… I'm not sure what. It had tones of prejudice, but her comfort with it all suggested it was just the nature of the world around her."

Muna leaned and scratched Powder's head and neck. "And a really off-hand sympathy for the cost of education for foreign students."

As they strolled down the wide sidewalk, they watched the students and other adults. Age and status didn't seem to provide a demarcation for clothing. Beach and sunny California seemed to prevail across all boundaries. Nash looked Muna up and down as they walked.

Muna caught the action out of the side of her eye. "What?"

Nash snorted. "Lesbian Mafia hit squad?"

As they cleared the one building, the parking lot came into view. Five white vans stood clustered as near to the sidewalk as allowed. Women in office dress stood clustered—comparing notes. Their camera crews grouped in other clusters, either admiring each other's cameras or scrolling through their phones.

Nash stopped Muna. She nodded at the reporters. "This explains why no matter which channel you flip to, the words and ideas always seem the same. The video is only slightly different because they're standing next to each other."

Muna coughed in her fist. "And we're the mafia hit squad?"

Nash rolled her eyes. "Come on, Sundance. Let's go find an office to rob." She looked down. "No drug sniffing. We don't want to scare the kids."

Powder looked around like she was ignoring anything Nash was saying.

The building was cooler. Not chilled, but cool. Nash waved her hand toward the one open door.

"Excuse me."

The three turned at the sharp female voice. The woman, who could have been their third sister, strolled across the lobby from the hall. Her dress wasn't Southern California as much as it was young New Delhi casual. But in San Diego, it passed for office chic.

"No pets allowed in here."

They waited for the woman to get close enough to recognize the three badges and two pistols. They knew they had found the school's mouthpiece.

The young woman stopped a few steps away. "Oh."

Nash and Muna opened their ID wallets. "Special Agent Muna al-Faragi, and agents Nash Running Bear and Powder. Please don't pet. Her tongue will remove half of your makeup in a heartbeat." They slipped their wallets back into their back pockets. "I'm assuming you're the contact person about Doctor Lambert?"

The diminutive woman eyed Powder. "Siri Desai. How may I help you?" Her voice had the tilt of the British influence but not the usual sound of customer service.

Two students walked out of the elevator and passed them without looking up from their phones. Nash watched the two ghosts toward the exit. She turned back around. "We're doing background as to the people who were in the compound at Fort Mojave. Did you collaborate with him?"

The woman's arms flexed slightly tighter to her body. "No. I only started last spring."

Muna glanced back at several people entering the building. "Can you direct us to someone who did collaborate with Doctor Lambert?"

The man with the large, weathered bag over his shoulder stopped and turned. "Pete? Maybe I can help you."

The young woman relaxed and smiled at the help. "Ah, Doctor Byrd. Thank you. That would be most appreciated." She turned. "Doctor Byrd, these two are from your Federal Bureau of Investigation."

He held his hand out. "Nester. Nester Byrd."

"Nash. Nash Running Bear. And this is my partner, Muna al-Faragi."

He adjusted his heavy bag. "Please, come on up to my office. I need to drop this bag before it kills me."

The small, windowless room held a minuscule desk. Three walls of floor-to-ceiling bookshelves oozed folders, papers, and nonsensical trinkets of academia. The desk, appearing to be half consumed by the wall of books, became filled with the man's bag.

The fourth wall barely held the long leather sofa, showing decades of use. A testament to the teacher's popularity with his students. The wall above was a free-form posting of years of event flyers, notices, and a single sign reading: Office Hours are when I'm Here.

The man chuckled at Powder sniffing the leather. "Go ahead. It's safe for humans or beasts. My Scotty spent most of her life curled on the west arm. Students brought her treats. I never knew if they came for discourse with me or her affections. But it's safe to sit. With an earthquake, only this seat is in the kill zone."

With a whoosh of air from the cushion, Muna sat. "What was your Scotty's name?"

He smiled in warm memory. "Scotty. She was a Siamese blend of ally cats. Her purr jittered like the time Spock and Kirk got trapped in the transporter, and their communicator jittered." He laughed at Muna's blank stare. He fanned his hand as he sat. "Never mind. You kind of had to have been there."

Nash tapped a flyer on the wall. She turned with a question on her face. Her fingertip was still touching the flyer.

He squinted at the flyer. "Oh. Yes. Hali-Bopp. The vigil was small but memorable. It wasn't about the comet. On the night of the comet, we had a marine layer, so we never saw it. But this was for the Heaven's Gate members. Several had gone to school here. We shared memories until well past midnight." He pointed at the other end of the wall. "Buried in the deeper end of the wall is a flyer about welcoming back the Vietnam Veterans on the tenth anniversary of the end of the war. But as students forgot about the war, it was history to them, so they papered over it." He ran his fingers through his graying hair. "But I remember them and the flyer."

She turned and sat as Powder took her place and curled up between her and Muna. "Did you serve?"

"My older brother did. By the time I turned eighteen, I had a couple of pounds of metal keeping my spine straight. Scoliosis."

Nash nodded. "Doctor Lambert…"

He sucked in his lower lip as he pulled a thermos out of his bag. "Yeah. Pete."

14

PETE

NESTER BYRD RAN his liver-spotted hand over his thinning hair. The chair squealed quietly as he leaned back. "Pete Lambert..." He blew a sigh out of his pursed lips. "Where to start?" His head leaned back as he looked at the single poster thumb-tacked to the ceiling of the small office. The poster touted a band named Cheap Trick as the opening act for the Grateful Dead. "We were so young..."

Nash glanced up and then squinted at the date. "Nineteen seventy-nine."

He rocked his head. "Joe Mathias's old hippy van ran—but no money for gas. Seven of us kicked in for gas and cheap food and piled into the old Volkswagen. It was a long eleven-hour drive to the Bay Area. It's worse coming home. We knew the old Volkswagen would never survive the Grapevine coming back. So the thirteen-hour drive down the one-oh-one became a long day and a half when we shredded the fan belt a half hour south of San Luis Obispo. But the concert was epic."

Muna slumped down and wrapped herself around Powder. She was getting used to listening to Dad's stories, as well as the jokes. "Is that how you met Doctor Lambert?"

He squinted his left eye. "No... Well, kind of. But mostly no." He rolled his head forward. "We were in a survey class a year before." He pointed at her. "You know what a survey class is?"

Her soft bark was half snort and half chortle as she rolled her eyes. "Stacked tiers with seven hundred students looking for an easy four-point-oh. The professor reveals a long list of required readings with a thirty-page term paper. Then, he points out the midterm test is at the beginning of week three and is half of your grade. All the while, he rests his hand on the deep stack of drop cards. Yeah. Been there, done that, got the A."

He smiled. "What was the class?"

She shrugged. "My favorite? Social Anthropology of Astronomy."

His eyes lit up. "I'd take that class. Do you remember any of the books?"

"Sure. Still have them. One was a brief survey of astronomy in the sixteenth century. It was the heavy book at a hundred pages or more." She held her finger and thumb about a half-inch apart. "The other seven are basically pamphlets on different astronomers like Tycho Bagh, Galileo, Copernicus, and a few others. One was the Thomas Williams treaty on the megalithic yard."

His lower lip pushed up his top lip. "Wow. It must have been an exceptional class to have inspired you to remember it all."

"It was the hardest grade I ever enjoyed working for."

"Do you remember what percent of the class survived the midterm?"

She nodded as her eyes fluttered in a slow blink. This wasn't idle chitchat. This was an academic's admiration for a master class. "The class was down to about two dozen by the time we took the midterm. Half flunked. There were only two of us, with over ninety percent."

He smirked with a soft snort. "The other was a Curve Beater."

Muna's laugh was a quick snap. "Mildred was no beater. She drove a concrete truck through bell curves. She was a grandmother of nine, and she barely had time to take one class a quarter. I only beat her because our final exam was we had to teach our term paper as the lecturer of the day. English wasn't her first or even second language."

"What were your papers on?"

"She grew up in the same village as Tyco Bragh, so she chose Copernicus's theory of dual galaxies. She should have stuck to Bragh."

He winced. "Ouch. And yours?"

"Roman use of the stones of Salisbury Plain."

He leaned his head back with his eyes closed. "Yeah. I'd love to take that class."

Nash cleared her throat.

He sat up. "Oh. Right. Pete." He blinked a few times. "We hung out a bunch of our senior year. But when I left for Washington for my doctoral, he headed out to Arizona." He noted Nash's one eye squinted and pointed up. "Our Washington. Not D.C."

"But you stayed in touch?"

He pushed his lower lip out as he nodded with a wink. "Absolutely. We both had access to academic phones, so we talked all the time. I took a couple of winter breaks down in Arizona, and he came up to Seattle for a couple of summers. We were both doing work in the photovoltaic field, so it was a natural."

Muna frowned and shied her head to one side. "Seattle is a natural for photovoltaics?"

He bounced his head. "It sounds counterintuitive, but even with all the rain and overcast, Seattle is barely under the national average in annual solar hours. His work in Arizona was about overcoming the heat. Back in those days, we were experimenting with Arco panels. The panels were a foot by four feet and barely pushed out fifty-watts at peak. The heat of Arizona could easily suck out half of that. Same as a rainy day in Seattle. So, we were working on the same thing, but from the two ends of the damage."

Nash hung her hands in supplication between her knees. "Was he religious then?"

Nester burped a soft chuckle. "Religious? You've been watching the news too much. A couple of those idiots interviewed me. Those interviews never made it to the six o'clock news or even to get buried in the late-night cycle. Someone took one look at a bunch of people out in the desert and stopped thinking the moment someone thought of Jim Jones or Heaven's Gate. Nobody ever wanted to hear the good news about a bunch of people getting together in the environment to solve the greatest problems the world is facing. And with time and the rise in temperature, the problems will get worse."

Muna nodded. "Water and power."

He pointed at her. "And food."

Nash stretched her arms in place. "So he wasn't religious...?"

He rolled his head. "His folks were Methodists or Presbyterians or something like that. But they were only CEOs. So his religion was what he liked—the three Bees."

Muna's face crinkles with a frown and narrowed eyes. "CEOs and three Bees?"

Nash snorted softly. She'd heard the term before. It explained a lot about the reservation she had grown up on. "Santa and bunnies. But I can only guess at the bees."

He pointed at Nash but explained to the confused ad hock student. "Their going to church and religious fervor was limited to Christmas and Easter. Pete and I went to a midnight mass here in San Diego one time. It was all in Latin. He commented how much better it was to exercise his Latin instead of playing on his supposed guilt. The music was delightful as well. Probably would have been great if we hadn't done the pinner of junk weed and gone for the fatty. But it was what it was."

Muna chuckled at the casual dismissal of religion. "And the bees?"

He held out his hand toward Nash. "And your guess...?"

She sighed and turned her head to one side. "Girls or women would be a G or W… so I'm guessing booze?"

He snapped his hand back. "Nope, you were on target. Yes, to the booze. Or, in his case, beer. But yes, the females, in those days, always got categorized as broads or book bunnies. But the other was his studies."

"Books." Nash smirked and rolled her eyes closed. "Did he ever marry?"

He shook his head. "No relationship was long enough. He never even lived with anyone more than a long school break or to go tramp through Europe. Pete, for all his goodness, was a lothario to the end. True to his nature, he was one hundred percent a Peter Pan. And in some ways, the compound out in Mojave was his ultimate Neverland."

Muna rubbed her left thumb along her right index finger. "Anyone else from here?"

"Out there? Sure." He leaned back and closed his eyes with his head tilted back. "Um… Norman Brotman. He was probably running those greenhouses. He ran the ones here. Horticulture was his jam. I think one intern went with him as well. She worked in the gardens here." He rolled forward and opened his eyes. "If you have a list, I can see if I recognize anyone."

Muna pulled out her phone and stopped. She scrunched her face on one side. "Which is the Wi-Fi here?"

He turned and started digging through his bag. Pulling out a small pad in a case, he opened it. He looked up. "Is a fruit plate okay?"

Muna snorted softly at the old term for an iPad. "Sure, I've suffered under worse conditions."

He turned it around and held it out. "It's pretty barebones, but I don't know enough to load things on it." He rolled his eyes. "And my granddaughter is away at a sleepover camp in Joshua Tree with her scout troop or something."

Muna looked at the icons. "What word processor do you usually use?"

He blushed slightly. "That's my first fruit plate. It was a gift from a former student. But normally, I'm a Seattle brat."

Muna's fingers were already moving. "I'm loading an academic version of the whole desktop so you can do spreadsheets and power points as well. Any games while I'm shopping in the toy section?" She looked up at his red neck, threatening his ears. She held her finger over the screen. "Just say the word. There's no judging here. We have close friends who game internationally."

He shook his head slightly. "Old school. It's not stuff you would know about."

Her snort jumped her shoulder. "Pong, Treasure Quest, Ms. Pacman, and the Sims it is. Your icon is the dragon from the quest. The boys loaded about twenty of the all-time greats into the package. Somewhere, there is a golden ticket to go download their top one hundred greats." Her fingers flew over the screen, and then she turned it around and handed it back to him. "Here's the list of the nineteen people."

His eyes sparkled as his eyebrows rose. He glanced back up at her as he shrunk the program to peek at the five new icons on the desktop. "Wow. Thanks. Um…"

She shook her head. "Nope. All legal downloads and programs. They automatically registered to that pad. You just can't share or transfer them. But Deep Six fully donated them, and if you need any more help—use the golden ticket. They're up in the Irvine area, but they travel."

"Thanks." His voice was soft as he turned it around and leaned back to study the list. His finger held a place as he continued reading the rest of the list. His forehead furled. "Brotman is here… but not his intern." He crushed one eye closed as he turned his head. "Janice, Janet, Jan… something like that. But she's not on here."

"Anyone else?"

His finger slid down. "Lawrence Toliver. He was here for years but then moved up to a better position in solar studies at UC Irvine. Speaking of Irvine. I think he was on their solar race car project. But yeah. He's big into the photovoltaics."

Nash stood and pulled out her wallet. Sliding out a card, she handed it to him. "We appreciate you giving us your time."

He held up and wiggled the pad. "Trust me. I got a lot more out of this brief visit." He turned to Muna and stuck out his hand. "Thank you very much."

"No problem. I do the same for the two uncles I work with."

He rocked his head softly. "Lucky guys."

Nash leaned, scratching Powder along the side of her neck. "You have no idea. But they're learning."

He pointed at Powder. "Your dog is off leash…"

Nash narrowed her eyes. "Yes."

"Drugs?"

Muna curled up her lip. "Nah. We don't let her do them anymore. But she does great at finding treats, dead bodies, and bombs."

He turned his head as he chuckled. "I'm guessing you give the uncles as good as you get."

Muna smiled as Powder eased off the couch. "Every day and every chance I get."

15

SIFTING SAND

CHIPS LEANED into the computer screen and, therefore, the camera and microphone. Muna pushed back hard into her seat as the face grew on her screen. Chips whispered in a breathy hush. "Who are all the suits?"

Muna's forehead became a deeply plowed field of furrows. "In San Francisco? Where are you? I warned you to stay away from the Embarcadero."

The blonde leaned back as she pointed down. Muna got a clear view of the woman's sweatshirt. The Deep Six logo was their computer battle uniform. A cross-hatch was spray-painted next to the large hand and middle finger. Deep Six's backhoe and name logo were graphically tattooed on the back of the hand. "No. Downstairs."

Nash walked past and stumbled at the statement. "Oh, no. No, no, no... Girl, tell us you did not go into the front office."

Chips' exaggerated grimace pulled her few freckles flat. Her voice was soft. "I was in a hurry. And didn't want to walk all the way around the building to the loading dock. So, I figured I could cut through the front... office..."

Muna's face was animated. "Shut the front door..."

Nash snorted and blew out her breath. "What did they do?"

"I was Facetiming Bunny and walked straight toward the back." She rolled her eyes. "I guess, right past security or something. But one suit blocked the guard guy who was going to tackle me." Her eyes expanded. "Those guys are serious."

Nash rocked as she slowly blinked. "You know how serious Jazz gets when someone is messing with you girls?" Her hand rested protectively on Muna's shoulder.

The little girl's voice was pure fourth-grade and drawn out. "Yeah...?"

Nash blinked and rocked her upper body in the best Auntie Nash she could muster. "Those guys are eight times more serious and were born triggered. It's the main reason we only use the loading dock and the elevators. And you don't even want to know about the second floor."

The blonde bit her lower lip and drew it out slowly. "Got it. But Mikey and the Oz Man are cool. Aren't they FBI?"

Muna unclipped her badge from her belt and held it up. "Go ahead. Ask the boys where their badges are?"

Nash laughed. "A hardass who had just graduated from Quantico was taking a course at the Body Farm. I don't remember what the shit shooting was about, but he held out his badge at Oz and accused him of not even being a real FBI agent. Oz leaned in and examined the man's badge. His comment was how amazed he was the ID numbers were now six digits long. And then he pulled his out of his back pocket. It was only four digits. He had gotten his badge before the agent was born, grew up, served in the military, and then served his required five years as a cop. It was the only time I ever saw his badge. But... he's still the Wizard."

Muna rocked. "Ask Mike for his badge. I've never seen it... But he makes a mean pickle and chili shake."

The blonde lowered her head and looked through the tops of her eyes. Her cheeks bumped as she faked throwing up a bit in her mouth.

"I'll pass." She leaned out of the camera for a second and then sat up with some papers in her hand. "I'm sending you a copy of the authorizations you need to enter the crime scene out in Fort Mojave. You'll need to stop in at the local sheriff's office to check in. Jazz says they get really triggered when Feds come snooping around their territory."

Nash rocked. "Especially tribal. They don't give a damn about WIFLE."

Her hand stopped halfway through combing back her blond hair. She frowned. "Tribal? Wiffle? As in wiffle ball?"

Muna nodded. "Indian Territory. The tribe is Fort Mojave." She shook her head with one eye closed. "Don't ask. It's more confusing than trying to figure out the conversion from assembly language to compile. It dates to the mid-nineteenth century and a bucket-load of old dead white guys."

"Okay, well, it's in your buckets. And I'll send the short chop to your phones. But... wiffle?"

Muna nodded. "Women In Federal Law Enforcement. We've been around since the seventies. Ask Oz. I think he was around when they formed."

Chips rolled her eyes but with a smile. "Oh great. Another dad story over lunch." She glanced over her shoulder. "Oops. Gotta bounce."

The connection faded from Muna's laptop as the two started laughing. Muna choked slightly into her fist. "I ran into the suits at the shooting range a few times. That's why I go early now. I can just picture her with that shirt..."

Nash twitched her head. "I can't imagine wearing that shirt..."

Muna stood and stretched. "I think the gaming guys call it their jersey..."

"Still."

Muna looked her up and down with a smirk. "I think you could pull it off. It's no more threatening than the USMC, or the FBI sweats you run in. I've run behind you. I've watched people's reactions. You scare the hell out of most of the guys running in Golden Gate Park. Women as well."

Nash gave her a hard eye. "If they're not breaking the law, they have nothing to fear."

Muna closed her laptop and slid it into the case and her suitcase. "Let's make some tracks. It's a long drive."

EVEN IN THE DARK, FORT MOJAVE DIDN'T LOOK ANY LESS under-impressive. After they crossed over onto the Arizona side of the Colorado River, the single main road drove straight up the middle of the shallow valley. Farmers planted some kind of agriculture or another on both sides of the highway. The water source was a hard football kick away.

Muna yawned as she scrolled her pad in the passenger seat. Powder had long given up on anything interesting and snored softly from the backseat. "I would have thought we were in Nevada."

Nash pointed ahead. "The tip of Nevada will be at the north end of the valley. Most everything is here in Arizona."

Muna waved the back of her hand at Nash's side of the valley. "But the media keeps saying it's Fort Mojave in California."

Nash slid her eyes into a bored side-eye as she rocked. "Most of the Mojave Desert is in California. Technically, the parts of Death Valley we were in, with the freezers full of bodies, are part of the Mojave Desert. And it stretches down to butt up to the backs of Los Angeles, San Bernardino, and San Diego counties."

Muna blew out her breath through pursed lips. "That's a lot of cactus and tumbleweeds."

Nash snorted softly as she eased into the parking lot of the motel. "Very little of both. Mostly sand, yucca, Joshua trees. Home to lizards, snakes, and the elusive and endangered California desert tortoise." She glanced into the backseat. "Potty, girl?"

They stood waiting for Powder to find her spot. Muna sniffed.

"It doesn't feel dry. I mean, it doesn't feel like I would think a desert would feel."

Nash glanced up at the stars. "Did you notice all the agriculture?"

"Kind of hard to miss."

Nash rocked her head. "Back in the middle of the last century…"

Muna snickered. "When Oz was a little boy…"

Nash paused with her eyes focused on Orion's belt. "More like when he was born. But yeah." She glanced over. "Ass."

Muna licked and smacked her lips wetly as she rolled her index finger in the air.

"Back in the forties and fifties, doctors suggested people move to Phoenix for the dry air because of their asthma and other lung problems. But the people pined for their original home, so they planted their favorite flowers and trees. By the sixties, they were bored, so they took up golf. By the eighties, people in California had found out it was cheaper to retire there instead of in Florida. So more flowers and trees from everywhere else. And a bazillion acres of water to flood the hundreds of golf courses and million yards. Soon, the humidity was worse than Southern California, and everyone was allergic to everything now growing there."

Muna rolled her eyes. "You realize you just said that in Oz's voice? But I get it. Water the desert, and you get steamy agriculture." She frowned. "So, what do they grow here?"

Nash pulled out the small plastic bag and started to where Powder had done her business. "I don't know… Green stuff. What were you looking up while we drove here?"

Muna turned her head as she smacked her lips in embarrassment. "Um… STL files for the 3-D printer… maybe…"

Nash looked back with a twisted face. "For five hours?"

Muna leaned back against the car. "Well, when I had connections, I had to consult with Ming and Chips."

Nash chuffed as she dropped the small bag into the garbage can outside the motel's office. "Yeah, consulting about how to pirate a toy."

Muna raised one eyebrow as she pulled open the door. "You know… the word pirate is a very pejorative word." She checked to see if her humor had gotten across. It hadn't. The hard eye of Nash stalled. "It was more personal…"

THE GREENHOUSE STRETCHED WELL PAST A LONG CITY block. A powered pallet jack whined between the rows of hydroponic tomatoes. It carried a large wooden box behind the driver. The box held many of the tools needed to tend to the hydroponics, as well as the pruning shears and clippers for the plants. Five days a week, the box was the same. The other two days, they swapped the toolbox for the cardboard lug boxes and helped harvest tomatoes.

"Juan?"

The older man stood at the end of the long row of plants. In his hand was a crescent wrench. His eyes crinkled with his smile. "Si, Debra?"

She slowed and stopped the power jack. "Something is plugging the fresh line between four-nineteen and four-twenty. I noticed it's down to a dribble. I don't know if you can ream it or just replace it. But I'm only getting about a third of what I need for that end of number four."

The older man warmly smiled as he removed his hat and wiped his arm along his brow. "It's good to have you back, *mijita*. The others don't see the feeder lines or even the system. They only look at the tomatoes and dream of salsa cruda." He flipped his hat back on his head. "I'll go take care of it next. I'm almost finished with this mixer."

"Thank you, Juan." Her head and face jerked her short blond hair in a violent twitch as her tongue stuck out in a fat sausage to lick her lips. "It's good to be back. Hydroponics was my focus study in college. So the system is like the blood system in our bodies." She twisted the handle, and the power jack whisked her away.

She slowed as she pushed the power jack and the large crate of a toolbox through the doorway of hanging plastic panels. They controlled the airflow through the greenhouses, as well as supplied a barrier to flies or other flying pests. In the greenhouses, there were no natural enemies of the pests, nor were there any chemical deterrents. She turned right and entered the third greenhouse in the block of five. They all started with the letter H.

She liked these four greenhouses. Everything was edible but were all herbs. The smell was intoxicating. She smiled at the large rainbow graffitied hat. The brim spread out to cover the woman's shoulders. The colorful hat brought the woman joy but also made her easy to spot. Debra wasn't sure how much longer since her mother had mid-stage Alzheimer's.

She let the power jack coast to a stop. Debra let go of the trigger as she stepped off. Stepping over beside the older woman, she reached out for a gentle side hug. "Hello, Dorothy. How's my favorite gardener?"

She could see the woman was pruning plants that weren't to be harvested for weeks. It was minor damage for the joy of having her close and busy. When Debra convinced the company to let her mother putter, she promised she would pay for any damage. Within weeks, management had received overwhelmingly positive feedback from the other workers. So they even put her on their medical insurance, along with a small wage.

The woman stayed in the small dormitory with others to look after her while Debra needed to be away on a research project. But now Dorothy would move back out to live with Debra in their small house in the desert.

16

DOUBLE GLOVE

THE AIR ACHIEVED a full stop before the door swung open. Muna gasped at the already stagnant heat of the early morning. She pulled her dark glasses on before stepping anywhere near the desert sun. "Well, that cuts it. I just went from naturally curly to hard-baked, crispy hair."

Nash stepped out around her as she pulled on her gold-tinted aviators. "Suck it up, cream puff. That's why you used up all three bottles of cream rinse in the shower. Your hair is bulletproof."

Muna shouldered the strap of her workbag. "How do you know I used their cream rinse? I might have brought my own."

Nash opened the trunk of the car and dropped her workbag in. "Nope. Powder hasn't come near you all morning."

Muna looked at the dog, walking shyly ten feet behind her. "Traitorous snitch."

Nash opened the driver's door. "Don't blame her for you not packing the right supplies." She flicked the turn signal and turned the key to the auxiliary position. She walked around the car, checking for anything that might have changed during the brief night. "It's why I have Tracy ship us her soap, shampoo, and cream rinse from up Harkin Way. It comforts Powder with the smell of her childhood." She smirked as she passed the smaller woman, checking the car by walking counterclockwise. "It's also why I packed two extra bottles of each in my go bag. I never know how long we're going to be out on a case anymore."

"Right turn." Muna walked around, dropped her workbag in the trunk, and closed it.

Nash turned the lever up and started counterclockwise around the car. "My cases used to be cleaner and more straightforward. Now, it seems more like they only give me the case if it has a whiff of strange and might take a month or more."

Muna slid into the passenger seat. "Are you bellyaching about the per diem?"

Nash closed the door and turned the key. "Money was never the problem. I'm more comfortable in the cheap shacks than the nice places. If the little soaps smell like a French whorehouse, they creep me out."

Muna held her hand up toward Powder's head. The dog leaned closer to Nash. Muna growled and pointed at the street. "Coffee."

The low stucco building squatted in its own small field of asphalt. The entrance looked more like a converted motel or restaurant than an office building. Only the small herd of SUVs and the flag at half-mast marked it as a Tribal Police office.

Muna frowned. "I think we're in the wrong state." She glanced around. "The crime scene is in California."

Nash smirked as she pulled the key out of the car. "The crime scene is in the nation, not a state, Kemosabe. Only a lazy white man let the river draw boundaries. Tribes know it is better to be on both sides of a river so you don't have to cross to gather fish." She looked at Powder. "Potty?"

Nash and Muna held up their identification wallets for the woman behind the desk. "Special Agents Running Bear and al-Faragi to see whoever is running the case across the river."

The woman rolled her eyes. "Across the river is California."

Nash recognized the traditional nation-to-nation challenge. How much do you know about me? She snapped her wallet shut in midair. "And about sixteen hundred acres of Mojave tribal land. Give or take."

The woman smirked. "Which tribe?"

Nash leaned her knuckles on the low desk. "Paiute. Northern California."

The woman pointed at Muna. "Her."

Muna leaned in and mirrored Nash's knuckle stance on the desk. Powder rose and took her place between them. "My father is Shahsevan." She glanced down at the dog. "Agent Powder is full-blood Paiute and FBI."

The woman's mouth tugged west. "I saw the badge. Never heard of any tribe called Shah Seven before."

Nash growled. "It's where the term for a leader comes from. Shah. As in the Shah of Iran. In some circles, they considered Muna a princess. In other words, she's the undisputed champion." Her eyes locked on the woman, and she didn't flinch.

The woman's eyes finally closed in a slow blink as she rocked back in her chair and let her head fall back in a zombie drop toward the door behind her. "Moose. The FBI is finally here. You must have filed the report by a tortoise."

The man filled the doorway. The squeak of the voice didn't match the size of the man. "About time. What took you?"

Nash stood as she examined the man's shorter braids and a distinctive scar spreading like a tree from his left jaw. "I can't believe the corps let go of you."

He warmly smiled as he turned. Waving his hand, he stepped out of the door. "Coffee is on. And a damn sight better than we had in Fallujah."

Nash smirked at Muna. "His company lined up every morning next to ours. His Hummer or MRAP was parked next to mine. At the whistle, they went uptown, and we went down."

Nash leaned against the high counter where the coffee service was. "You guys lost your LT. But we never heard if you got a new one or they just field-jumped you."

He looked over as he passed her a mug. "They wanted to. It was my second tour. But I wasn't a Marine—I was Guard. I was supposed to be there for eight months. But by the fourth year, they tried to weasel me into the corps. Heck, even your old team was asking for me."

Nash squinted. "If I remember right, they called you Lucky Charms."

He blushed. "Probably because I like the cereal."

She pointed at his cheek. "More like lightning only strikes once."

He lifted his left leg. "It's a bull-pucky saying. The joints are all metal now. Those MRAPs weren't as armored as they liked to tell the public back home. We have one here. It looks good in the Christmas parade with Santa throwing candy."

They moved to the table as he looked at Muna. "Shahsevan, huh? We had an interpreter who was Shahsevan. Do you speak?"

She shook her head. "More Polish and gutter Irish. I grew up in Pitts. South of the river. But I'm learning restaurant Cantonese and Spanish. I'm based in San Francisco." She sipped on the coffee and smiled.

He laughed at her appreciation of his coffee. "Yeah. One of the few benefits of having a casino." He glanced at Nash. "So you drew the wackiest of whack-jobs."

She nodded. "What do you know about it?"

He grimaced. "We saw a lot of shit in the box. But this..." He shook his head. "What's your paperwork say?"

Nash pointed at Muna. "Full access. Including any background anyone has done."

He nodded in a rocking motion. "They were over there for the last five years. But only the last two or three were they always there. They had a lot to set up the first three. A fella named Roc

Reese or Reed was the first guy. He was setting up the solar stuff, so they had power."

Muna scrolled through her pad. "They had windmills as well."

He sat forward. "Finish your coffee, and I'll give you the guided tour."

MOOSE POINTED OUT ALONG THE SOLAR ARRAY. "THERE are more of the barrel-shaped windmills along the ridge. Their power line ties in with these solar arrays." He turned as his finger drew a line in the air toward the buildings. "Which goes into this building, which acts like their power distribution."

He turned and pointed at a small forest of telephone poles covered with what looked like spider webs and nests. "Over there, the standing array somehow catches water out of the air. In my humble opinion, it doesn't catch enough. But it gives them all the water they need for those large greenhouses. I guess it was some of the experimenting they were doing out here. All the people were eggheads from universities and colleges."

Muna nodded. "We've been doing deep dives on all nineteen. Some were even physicists. But most were doing research and authoring papers in their fields."

Moose turned. His shoulder and head bobbed. "We've got masks and gloves in the main building."

Nash snapped the second set of gloves at her wrist. "Let's start out in the outlying rooms and work back here."

Moose flicked on the lights as they entered. "Or did you want to use your flashlights?"

Nash juddered her head. "Nah. We're good. You've probably had several teams through here already." She looked down. "We're just walking Powder."

The dog looked up as if she were rolling her eyes. Her walk was careful and measured. The large man watched.

"What kind is she?"

Muna snickered. "Paiute puppy."

Nash rolled her eyes. "Have you ever had a reservation dog?"

He chuckled. "Didn't you mean to ask if a rez dog had ever adopted me?"

Nash rocked with the common knowledge. "Ever known or had a white man dog?"

"We had them in the box. Some were good. Others were only good for the IEDs. If they retired the K-9, they had to retire the handler. The dogs were no good for anyone else. Most, they ended up putting down."

Nash's chuff barely moved her chest. She knew the dogs. "Think about what you'd like Powder to find in these buildings."

His head twitched in a shake as he frowned softly. "As in what? Drugs, bodies, bombs, weapons? What?"

Nash smirked. "Yes. Just yes. She's a rez dog."

He looked back out the front door of the cabin. "Okay... dead bodies."

Muna frowned as she looked up from her pad. "Why? Didn't you find all of them asleep in their beds?"

His head twitched. "We didn't release it to the media. One was in the bathroom throwing up when they died. A little late to have second thoughts."

"Anyone else?"

He looked at Nash. "Most of them had thrown up in their beds. Some were sleeping on their backs..."

Muna nodded. "Aspirated."

He nodded and looked hard at her. "Aspirated. They drowned in their own vomit."

Muna twitched her head. "More often than not, the vomiting is a death convulsion response. So, technically, it was the poisons killing them—not the vomit. But I'm sure we found some vomit in their lungs. Just not enough to kill them."

Nash touched the man's shoulder. "Muna is the head mother

hen for the San Francisco forensics lab. She's had her hands in more cadavers than you've seen dead bodies. With or without the Sand Box."

He rocked. "Big surprises in little packages. Okay then." He turned and pointed toward the two doors. "This is Hoover and Livingston. They were..." He squinted to remember.

"Physicists." Muna looked up. "Hoover was from Cal Tech, and Livingston was UCLA. From their backgrounds, I'm guessing they were responsible for or attached to the water collection." She looked down at the pad. "Hoover had worked on a similar experiment in Angola." She shook her head. "Too dry."

Nash peeked in the rooms. A large stain spread across one pillow of the rumpled beds. Glancing around the spare common room, she looked at Moose. "Next."

The smaller cabin had a single bedroom but also a bed in the front room. Both with the sheets rumpled and thrown back. It lacked the cloyed smell of dried vomit.

Muna looked at her pad. "Kristine Anne Cline, electrical engineering at Fullerton College."

Nash looked at the suitcase with the gold initials KC and pointed at the second bed in the front room. Muna grimaced as she cocked her head. "Nobody."

Nash looked at Moose. He shrugged. "She was the only body." He pointed at the bedroom.

Nash looked at Powder sitting by the front door. "Powder. Find the other body. It could be anywhere. When you find it, come get me."

The dog blinked and turned out of the door and was gone.

Moose blinked; his eyes wide open as he turned to Nash. "Just like that?"

Nash nodded. "Just like that. But don't ask her to fetch you a cold beer. She'll bring you a dead skunk. She hates beer."

17

BAD MATH

SURVEYING all the living accommodations took hours. As the buildings got more complex, the living arrangements became more interesting. According to the records, only one couple was married, and they were living in separate buildings.

Some tags on suitcases didn't match with the body found in the location. One room had two suitcases tagged to two people, and they found only one in the building.

Muna shrugged. "Sometimes I like room nine, and sometimes I like the smaller room five. In the summer, five faces to the east and gets light earlier. And it's closer to the bathroom."

Nash smirked. "Exactly." She pointed from the shade of the main lodge at the outlying buildings. "All totaled. There are twenty-four beds. Twenty-one, according to evidence, were slept in."

Moose bobbed his head and then sucked the bottle of water dry. "The main dining table has places for twenty-two without crowding."

Nash looked at Muna. "We're missing something." She turned her attention to the dog looking out from the shade of the large lanai. "Powder?"

The dog looked back.

"There were no dead bodies? Not even old ones?"

Powder sat and then walked her front paws out to lie down on the cooler concrete.

Muna snickered. "And there is your definitive answer. No. Nope. Nada. Zip. KaBoom. Mic drop. End scene, curtain down."

Moose harrumphed. "Who runs who?"

Nash rolled her eyes. "Oh, trust me. We're her team." She rolled her head to Muna. "What was Oz's list?"

Muna pulled up the file. "Belladonna, castor bean, foxglove, hollyhock, phlox, rhubarb greens... all botanicals."

Nash sat back, thinking.

Moose rumbled. "Yuk. How do you get people to eat that stuff?"

Nash's head snapped to look at him. "Exactly. You don't. You make the food too good to resist." She stood with her hands resting on her hips. The distant hump in the low hills reminded her of something in a desert long ago. She glanced back at the large man. The large tattoo on his left arm was the one she remembered hanging out of the Humvee. "Which road did you take to get to Bangtown?"

He smoothed his hand across his face and scratched his jaw. "I don't think it had a name. We just called it I-5 because it was the smoothest and with the least choke points—it was like a freeway."

Nash nodded. "Which route did the locals lavish the most tender loving care on?"

"The five."

"Which route did they plant the most IEDs on?"

His voice was soft and small. "Five."

Nash nodded. "When I got there, the outgoing commander showed me the snowplows on the MRAPs. He told me to never let the weenies talk me into taking them off. We also never drove the five. The plows could clear a car or minitruck at thirty miles per hour. A vendor cart, fully loaded, was easy at fifty. A woman in a burka walking slowly down the middle of a street sided by buildings was an enemy combatant unless they stepped to the side."

Muna's face was sheer horror. "You would run over a woman?"

Nash glanced back. "A dog would get out of the way. But it wasn't a woman… it was a burka. And probably a young man trying on his jihad wings. If he could slow down the column, they could pick us off from the rooftops. So you never slow down. And never go back. If you even think about it, you're done."

The voice was deep. "So what has the five got to do with poisoning people?"

Nash's smile was sardonic and cold. "They made the five the most seductive they could. What food do you pick up and not even think about?"

"Fry bread or jerky."

Nash dipped her head. "Yup. And when did you stop asking what the jerky was made from?"

"Why ask? Meat is meat."

"And if they season your frybread with hollyhock instead of sage?"

He hummed as he rubbed his face.

"Exactly." Nash turned on her heel. "I need to look at the kitchen."

The large island only had a few pots and pans on it. The large drainboard and rack were full of dishes. Nash did a quick count and turned on Muna, holding the pad. "I get twenty-one."

Muna looked at the inventory list. "Check."

Nash turned to the smaller rack of glasses. "Twenty-two glasses."

"Check."

Moose frowned. "One extra."

Nash pulled out the silverware from the drying rack and laid it on the island. She counted out the forks, then the knives, and finally the spoons. "Twenty-two main forks, twenty-three spoons, and twenty-one dessert forks." She looked up at Moose. "Twenty-one at the table. The cook was sampling here in the kitchen. It's hot, hard work." She pointed at the rack of glasses standing upside down. "They used the extra in here to keep hydrated."

Nash rested both hands on the stone square leading into the large island. Her hands spread out as she looked at Muna.

Muna paused at the silence and looked up. As she recognized the dead flat of the eyes, she lowered the pad onto the counter and waited.

Moose's face wrinkled. "Wha...?"

Muna held up her hand. She could feel the time ticking in her watch. In Nash's watch. Anywhere there was a clock or watch ticking—it counted heartbeats. Small noises of the desert drifted in the back door. She didn't move.

Nash twitched.

"Nash...?"

Nash looked at Muna. The tiny spark of light in her eyes relit. "She cooked dinner. She was the cook. They never questioned... They didn't know."

"Who was the cook?"

Nash looked at the large man. "The killer. She was the only person who knew how to cook for so many. It's why she was here."

"Because she could cook."

Nash's head ping-ponged gently. "No. She was here to kill them. Or at least one of them."

Muna grabbed the pad and tapped it to wake it back up. "What else?"

Nash winced and peeked at the large man.

Muna waved her hand in dismissal at the giant as if he was a gnat. "Forget him. What else did you see? You were gone a long time."

Nash leaned back and rested her butt against the drainboard counter. "It was confusing. My mother and father were arguing about whether to tell me. I don't know why I was there. It was when I was six. My little moccasins had the sign of a shaman I had drawn, but I think my mother had beaded some of the pattern. The last thing was my father telling me families aren't always what they appear to be. Many things and people hide in the shadows of the family tree." She looked at Muna. "I don't know what it had to do with the cook. Or why they would come to me now…"

The man stood at his full height with his arms crossed. His face was clouded.

"What?"

He swallowed. "You… you're a shaman."

Muna turned, rolling her hip along the island's edge. "Does that make a difference?"

He frowned down at her. "If she sees things, yeah. It does."

"Why?"

"Because she didn't see the IED and got her Humvee blown to shit."

Muna closed the gap between them. "She and I both got blown up a while back. She didn't see it either. It doesn't work like that."

"Stand down, Muna. He's not the enemy."

He looked at the stern face of the senior agent. "Well?"

Nash shook her head softly. "She's right. It doesn't work like that. There's no control over it. I don't have a crystal ball or something. I just touch something and see what it needs to show me. Sometimes, it makes sense. Other times, not so much. My parents were both shamans. I never knew about my father. Looking back, he was probably more powerful than my mother. But she was the one who had the reputation of seeing things. I hated it. I never wanted to be my mother… but here we are."

Muna frowned. "Wait a minute. When we showed up, you didn't even know we were coming or who was coming."

He nodded gently.

"Then how did you know we got blown up in Colorado?"

Nash's head dropped to her chest as she slumped.

His head snapped toward the former Marine. "You got blown up again?"

Muna put up her hand. "Wait. What do you mean, again?"

Nash's face was bashful as she looked up at Muna. "We were in the Humvee in the sandbox. At least nobody lost body parts then."

His head was still playing a tennis match from Nash to Muna and back. "Didn't they fly you up to K-town or something?"

"Landstuhl. Ramstein at first. But when they cracked my skull, they moved me into K-town."

He pointed at Muna. "Then what's this about Colorado?"

Nash deadpanned the question. "Need to know."

He knew he was beaten. His breath sounded like "Jarheads." He pointed at Muna again.

Nash burped a sharp laugh. "Oh, trust me when I tell you you do not want to go there. If I knew she existed back in the day, I would have wanted her as my wingman for Bat shit crazy days on San Clemente Island. Open her packet of C-4 at your own risk." She turned her head. "Powder?"

The dog wiggled her way around the other end of the island.

Nash smiled. The dog had been waiting her turn. Pointing her fingers at the drawer pulls, she explained what she wanted. "The person we're looking for is the cook. She probably touched all these knobs. I want you to get a good smell and then show me where she slept."

Powder walked them out to the third building and waited at the door. Nash looked over at Muna.

Muna scrolled through her notes. "I'm getting there. I'm getting there. Just hold your horses." She looked up. "Nobody."

Nash opened the door and waved her hand at the rumpled bed in the corner of the tiny cabin. "And yet, we have a used bed and a confirming nose."

Muna tapped a few times and swiped the folder. "Got it. Killer in cabin three."

As the pad swung to the bottom of its arch, an alarm blared. Moose jumped, and Nash twitched.

Muna swung the pad up and tapped the screen in the corner.

The screen lit with two hands, pulling on blond hair. "Go for Muna. What's up Chips?"

The woman didn't move.

"Chips? Is everything alright?"

Her head rose as she slowly ground it from left to right. "I was going to tell you a joke about popcorn. But I decided not to."

Muna smirked. She knew her boys. "Why?"

"Because it was too corny." She leaned in and held up an old battered three-by-five card. The handwriting was distinctively Muna's. The lettering read, *SAVE ME*.

Nash licked her lower lip as she drew it into her teeth. She had seen the card a few times in the early years of Muna's getting used to the men. "Anything else, Chips?"

She held up her hand. "First, and I didn't know this when I came up here, but Deep Six knows many people up here."

Nash tossed her head. "It makes sense. They've been dredging the bay for over a hundred years."

The blond pointed at the screen. "Yeah, that too. Anyway, there are a couple of Navy guys who started a little radio station called vlog during the pandemic. It's called KGoat. They're based out on Yerba Buena Island, also known as Goat Island. And the big television station here is KGO, so they ride off both of those." She waved her hand to erase all the previous. "So they do a call-in format about anything getting a lot of airtime in the news or something."

Muna nodded. "Yeah. I've caught it a few times when things were slow..."

Chips tossed her rolled eyes over her shoulder. "Well, I haven't. But I might now. I thought these guys were just talking heads in their parent's basement..."

Nash wanted to chop things off. "What have you got, Chips?"

"I don't know what Jazz's connection is with the Navy... but they reached out to her. She said they knew she would know the right place to reach out and find someone interested."

Muna growled before Nash could get there. "Chips..."

18

YOU HAVE IT ALL WRONG

"I JUST DUMPED it in your box. It's not short. These guys vetted her."

Muna looked at the pulsing orange blob in the upper left corner of her screen. "Okay. Thanks, Chips. We'll call it up on a better machine for sound. Say hi to the guys for me. Have Oz take you down to dinner on his yacht."

The small tip of her pink tongue poked out of her lips as she slowly quaked her head. Her one eyelid fluttered closed.

Muna and Nash chuckled as the connection broke. They both looked up at Moose.

Muna softly elbowed Nash. "I have the laptop in the trunk. And I'm starved." She eyed the man with her head cocked. "Where are you taking us to lunch?"

Nash held up her watch. "Linner."

Moose laughed. "I haven't heard that term since the sandbox. If it's going to be a lunch dinner, then we'll have to go to my sister's place."

Nash pointed at Powder.

He waved. "Nah, she's good too. She can play or ignore the other mutts in the joint."

NASH LAUGHED AS SHE NOSED THE CAR INTO THE parking lot behind the truck. "You won't find My Sister's Place in San Francisco. I can smell the grease from the fry bread already. And don't make any smart remarks about wanting a roadkill sandwich. This kind of place can provide it."

They followed the big man through the tall gate into a shaded garden. Nash only guessed at the eucalyptus trees until she stepped on a nut. Stooping, she picked it up and smelled it. Smiling, she handed it to Muna. "Here. Rub this through your hair."

Muna sniffed. "It smells kind of like the vapor stuff Mom used to rub on my chest when I was sick."

Nash held her fingers a couple of inches apart. "A small bottle will last you almost a lifetime. It's eucalyptus. It originally came from Australia. But when the hippies found out the acorns were great for making necklaces for their dogs, they planted them everywhere."

"Why necklaces?"

"Fleas hate the smell right until it kills them. But we use it to open our sinuses. It's kind of like the Foxgloves and Hollyhocks. They're pretty in the garden until they kill you."

Moose had stopped to talk to the receptionist. The young woman nodded, and Moose waved them to follow. "It's nice out here, but I figure we'll need privacy. We're in the banquet room."

The larger screen on the powerful laptop reminded Nash of watching the old TV at college. It wasn't as large as sitting in front of a large monitor in San Francisco, outfitted by Muna. But it was easier to watch than the government standard on her desk in Washington.

They split the screen to watch both vloggers at the same time. The format was based on the old call-in radio broadcasts of the past, or still hanging on at the few AM radio stations left in rural

America. An advantage of a vlog was they could play a video clip of newscasts to set up the discussion.

The three brief clips were basic examples of the news reports over the last few weeks. It is low on facts, has less knowledge, and is fattened with conjecture and popular theory.

Mike: "And across the nation, which is the reporting they have subjected us to for weeks. We're not even sure if what they played today wasn't the same video clip we watched two weeks ago. The one reporter seems to wear the same top... But that isn't what we're talking about this evening. Welcome to The Goat Review. I'm Mike, and this is my partner in crime, Chase. Tonight, we're discussing the nineteen people found dead in the Mojave Desert near the Arizona border. Chase?"

Chase: "Thanks, Mike. Right. And we're going to assume you have not been hiding under a rock all this time. But we have some breaking updates you may or may not be hearing in the news over the next few days. But let me explain." He picks up a paper. "First, we only have a few of the names of the victims..." He holds up his hand. "Because they haven't notified all the families. With so many, it's a long process. Sometimes, it's not as easy as calling your parents. So, hang with us on this, and we doubt any of you out there tonight would know any of the victims, anyway. So, if you're thinking of calling in to harangue about the government not releasing information, you're listening to the wrong channel. Go dial-up Conspiracy dot com."

Mike: "We knew from the start, the leader's name..."

Chase: "Right. Peter Lambert had been a teacher at San Diego State College until he retired a few years ago and bought the land in Fort Mojave."

Mike: "Not a small lot of land either."

Chase: "Exactly. The property total is a hundred acres. For those of you who are trying to get your head around that number, that is eight blocks by eight blocks. Or a tenth of Golden Gate Park."

Mike: "Gives whole new meaning of walking around the block

or a walk in the park when it's out there in the scorching desert. But what is the new information?"

Chase: "What we now know is a lot and very little. Before I give you the two unknown names..." He holds his hand up to the camera. "Yes, only two. But you'll see why." He holds up the typed paper to read. "They have identified all nineteen people. Just have not released the name. But! Sixteen of them were teachers or professors at colleges. Two were physicists working, or they believe, in think tanks. And the last one was a spouse of one professor but was also a medical physician."

Mike: "So not your run-of-the-mill nut jobs running off into the desert to grab a ride on a late-night asteroid to the promised land."

Chase: "Quite the opposite. It looks like they had set up their own research center to plan for days ahead. According to the records we could get from the local electricity provider, they were producing and selling back into the grid with more energy than they consumed. For water, there was a nearly defunct wellhead. But their impressive six-acre greenhouse always had something to offer, like tomatoes and lettuce at the farmer's market. Obviously, Dr. Lambert and his colleagues knew how to make it work."

Mike: "Which brings us to our question of the night. Religious cult or a research project gone terribly wrong? Let's hear your thoughts."

Chase: "Caller from San Leandro. You're on the air."

Caller: "Hi. Yeah. Um... what time is the Spurs game supposed to start tonight?"

Mike: Rolling his eyes. "Dude. You missed it by four days. They played last Friday. Time to go sleep it off. Thanks for calling."

Chase: He looks at the ceiling for a moment. "Can I just block San Leandro?" He reaches out to his computer. "No, just joking. San Jose, illuminate us with your scintillating knowledge."

San Jose: "Even with all the stuff about solar and growing food, I still think they were out there for religious stuff. Didn't Moses haul a bunch of people out into the desert?"

Mike: "I think Moses was more of a road trip than let's go live in the wasteland. So, what makes you think religion?"

San Jose: "I don't know, man. It just seems like every time it's a bunch of people out in a desert... like it's a cult. Manson was out in the desert, too, man."

Mike: "I thought he shacked up at the Spahn Ranch in Chatsworth?"

Chase: "Yes. But they arrested him and his bunch when they camped out in Death Valley." His face pulled to one side, playing for a laugh or levity.

Mike: "Okay. Thanks for calling. We now have one vote for cult. Caller in Bodega Bay. Good to hear from the Northlands. Cult or think tank?"

The voice was hesitant but female. "He...hello?"

Chase: "You'll need to speak up, Miss. You're on the air with Mike and Chase. We're discussing the group of people found dead in the desert down south..."

Woman: "Is this better?"

Mike: "Perfect. Any ideas on tonight's subject?"

Woman: "There wasn't anything religious out there. Most of us didn't even think about religion. Bradley was the only person who had a bible. But he hollowed it out to hold a small pistol. He kept it on the nightstand next to his bed."

Chase frowned as he leaned in. "You said *us*. You used the term *us*. Are you implying you had lived out there?"

Her sigh was audible over the phone connection. "Yes. I lived out there for over a year. I worked in the greenhouses."

Both men shifted in their chairs—agitated.

Mike: "If that's true. Why did you wait until now to say something?"

Woman: "Because I was scared. I still don't know what happened that night. I didn't feel well, so I left to go to the clinic. It wasn't open. So, I drove to my friends in San Diego. I still don't know what happened that night."

Chase: "Bear with us here. But you're just a voice on the phone that is saying you were there. How do we know you're telling us the truth?"

Woman: "You said they haven't released the names yet, but you have a few more. Are the married couple two of those names? You haven't told anyone yet, right?"

Chase looked down at his paper. "I believe so." He looked up.

Woman: "That would be William or Will and June Robinson. We just called her Doc. She was an endocrinologist, but her specialty was epidemiology. They had lived in La Jolla but moved out to Fort Mojave shortly before I did. What about Norman Brotman? The greenhouses were his baby. And then there was his assistant, Jana Bright."

Chase glanced at the paper. "I don't have those names."

Mike scribbled furiously on his own paper.

Woman: "What about the solar guru himself, Doctor Lawrence Toliver?"

Mike: "Listen, can we call you back, or you hang on? You're releasing names we don't have clearance to name. Nor do we have the resources to check them out..."

Chase: "You said it was *not* a cult. What was going on out there?"

Woman: "Research. During the summer, the temperature in the desert can hit the low teens. That's a hundred and the teens. It's a brutal place to survive. People are out there because the river is there. But the river is drying up. Soon, with this long-term drought, agriculture will be unsustainable out there and in a lot of other places as well. They do crop circles with overhead sprayers. It's one of the most wasteful forms of watering in hot, arid countries. But they weren't growing food like we were. Half of the greenhouses weren't even being used, and we had more than what we took to the Saturday market that we just gave away. We took hundreds of pounds of vegetables over to Bullhead City every week for the homeless, or almost homeless. But we were still experimenting with the system to draw the moisture out of the night air. It was good, but it needed to be better."

Mike: "Moisture out of the night air?"

Woman: "If you look at pictures, there are like large spiderwebs between telephone poles. Those collected hundreds of gallons of water each night. Pure, clean, fresh water. It's what we drank and cooked with. Our showers came from the old well. Trust me, nobody would want to drink that water."

Chase: "And the sky gave you enough water to water all the plants?"

Woman: "More than enough. As I said, we also used it for our potable water as well. But Norman was working on a more sealed aquaculture loop so we could produce more with less water. He also wanted to set up some fishponds and raise our own protein... um... fish. But once the fish had... um done what fish do in their water, it's already fertilized with good nutrients for the plants. And then, what little was left, he planned to divert to the toilets. Which ends up going back into the ground."

Mike: "It sounds like they were all thinking about the long game. Many years."

Woman: "It was Peter's retirement. All he wanted to do for the rest of his life."

Chase: Looking up at the schoolroom clock on his wall. "That's all the time we have tonight for The Goat Review. Check in next week, and we'll dig into more of the breaking news. I'm Chase, and my friend Mike is still talking on the phone to the pretty girl, saying goodnight for now."

The screen flickered but didn't go dark.

Mike nodded and quietly hung up his phone.

Chase leaned in. "Well?"

Mike leaned his chair back. His fingers steepled with a small piece of paper between them. "Interesting turn of the show tonight."

Chase wadded up a piece of paper and tossed it at him. "Ass. What did she say?"

"Dude. She really is frightened. I'm amazed she even called. And if you think about it, I'd be scared as well. She said there were twenty-one people out there on the compound. But in every news cycle, they only talk about the nineteen. That means—She's not the only one alive. And she says she grew up Quaker. So, she wasn't the person doing the poisoning."

"So what now?"

"Now... we try to help her. We need to find out who is doing the investigation and somehow safely put them in touch."

19

MORE SIFTING SAND

NASH BLINKED AT MUNA. "I did not see that coming."

Moose rumbled. "In the lodge, you said you saw the woman cooking. But she was poisoned as well?" He pointed at the frozen image on the laptop. "Is she the one you saw?"

Nash chewed on the side of her lower lip. Her head shifted back and forth gently. "I don't think so." She cringed and looked at the now-darkened window. "No. It wasn't her. But she said there was someone else. Another woman."

Muna nodded and pushed the cursor and play block back. The video rewound. She stopped and clicked on the play arrow, and the video resumed.

"... haven't told anyone yet, right?"

Chase looked down at his paper. "I believe so." He looked up.

Woman: "That would be William or Will and June Robinson. We just called her Doc. She was a retired endocrinologist, but her specialty was epidemiology. They lived in La Jolla but moved out to Fort Mojave shortly before I did. What about Norman Brotman? The greenhouses were his babies. And then there was his assistant, Jana Bright."

Chase glanced at the paper. "I don't have those names."

Mike scribbled furiously on his own paper.

Woman: "What about the solar guru himself, Doctor Lawrence Toliver?"

Mike: "Listen, can we call you back, or you hang on? You're releasing names…"

Muna stopped the video and snapped her fingers. "Jana Bright. Got it."

She pulled up another app and input the name. As the little wheel turned, she clicked on an icon on the lower bar. The dog turned into a small information block. She groaned. "Ugh. I can get better speed out of a ten-speed bicycle with two broken wheels and no chain."

Nash growled. "Easy tiger. You're on someone else's home turf. Not everyone has high-end gaming needs."

Moose pointed at the laptop. "How much speed do you need?"

She looked up at the big man. "A heck of a lot more than this dial-up stuff."

He snorted wetly. "Whose Wi-Fi did you sneak into?"

She pulled up the information block again. "Cactus King. It's barely hitting a Megabit in the upload. But the download looks more like some people are already streaming it to death."

He wagged his head. "Not videos. He's running an illegal online gaming parlor. There's nothing we can do about it because he's here in California, and his uncle is the sheriff. But I'll talk to his home-room teacher tonight. I'm sure she can make him see the error of his ways during detention."

Muna smirked. "How old is the kid?"

The man rolled his eyes into the top of his head. "My wife teaches advanced placement English for the combined seventh and eighth grades. But I think the kid is still in the sixth grade." He pointed at the computer. "Find Lil Sis fry bread."

Muna ran a search as her mind whirred. "What does the kid want to do?" She glanced over.

Moose closed his eyes. "He better be focusing on staying alive long enough to grow some hair between his legs instead of trying to skin folks out of the little money they have."

"Found it. What's the password?"

He leaned in. "It's *unclem00sesaysletmein*. All one word and lower-case. Oh, and the ohs in Moose are zeros."

She typed, and a few seconds later, the spinning wheel became solid. She leaned over and squinted.

Nash frowned. "What's wrong now?"

Muna sat back. "Nothing. I just wanted to make sure it was turning instead of going to stone."

He chuckled. "You should have about sixty downloads. The Mighty Mouse doesn't get off work until eight. Then she'll start dragging the speed, but you can still download a movie or two in an hour. Even when she has both battle bots overheating the bathtub."

Nash mashed one eye shut and looked with the other at Muna.

Muna waved her down. "She's a gamer who probably knows Slug and the boys. Or at least know about them."

"Speaking of which…" Nash pulled out her phone and found the number. She typed in a text and turned the phone face down. The phone immediately sounded like a large motorcycle revving its motor.

Muna laughed and pointed. "Oh, you didn't."

"I certainly did." She swept the phone off the table as she looked at Powder. "Time for potty?"

They walked out the back door. "Hey Jazz." She glanced back at the door. "Yeah, we just watched it. That gives us one more name we didn't have. Now, if she will just talk to us, we'll have all twenty-one beds accounted for. How well do you know the two guys in the video?"

"One is the little brother of a Coastie I've been dating. It's a straight-up deal. We can come up and do the introductions."

Nash rubbed the back of her neck. "Let's stick a pin in that for a moment. Muna and I are out here in Fort Mojave. We flew into San

Diego to interview some people who might have known the ones on our list. Then we drove out."

"You have the list of all the names? Jeez, girl. Don't let it get out. The fucking media would kill to know those names."

Nash snickered. "No trouble. I have Miss Goofball to protect me." She snapped her finger at Powder. "Get out of that garden. Those plants are legal here."

Jazz grunted a laugh. "How tall are the plants?"

Nash rocked with a knowing snort. "Stubby. The dry heat isn't the best for them." She bent in to look. "But it looks like they'll get some decent buds off their effort. If the customers don't come back here first."

"When are you coming back?"

"I'm beat. I drove all day yesterday. So, we'll leave tomorrow. I can drop the rental in Orange County if you want to fly up with us."

"Just a minute." Nash could hear the phone being covered, but the conversation was enough to hear. "Hey, Tree? Do we have any extra room for a couple of federal escorts for the team?"

Jazz was chuckling as she pulled the phone back to her head. "That got the girls worked up. Come on in. We'll drop your rental, but we can show you around for an extra day. We're flying the teams up to a big gaming conference and such in the Silicon Super Bowl. So, I guess it penciled out for Tree to charter one of Alaska's team specials. You can look official and be their FBI escort when they walk into the conference. And then, while the kids play, we can go up north and meet the boys."

Nash chuckled. "It's not like we have any RoboCop armor or anything that stands out..."

"Trust me. With these things, black suit jackets and ear-wires stand out more than neon signs."

Nash pulled on the back door. "I'll call tomorrow evening when we hit town."

"Come hungry. I'll make reservations for the restaurant down in

Crystal Cove. I'll put Frank and Tink on notice that he is to be on his best behavior."

"I'm not sure we're up for anything fancy."

Jazz snorted. "My guess is if Tink isn't working, she'll be in a T-shirt or scrubs. Frank will be in some rude T-shirt, board shorts, and his huaraches. And if Ming comes with us, he damn sure better have painted his toenails."

Nash chuckled. "Manana, chicha."

"Later Gator."

Nash found another number and sent a text of three purple hearts. As she slipped the phone into her back pocket, she felt the twitch of a vibration from the return. She glanced at her watch. It would be shortly after midnight in Washington. She'd talk with Lele in the morning and find out how Mina was doing.

Muna glanced over her shoulder as Moose looked up. "How did it go?"

Nash sat down as Powder jumped back into her seat. "We're heading for Orange County tomorrow. We have a layover. And then we're working shore patrol for both teams." She pointed at the laptop. "How about yours?"

Muna frowned. "I turned it over to Chips and her sisters. Jana Bright turned up over seven thousand hits. So, it's probably an alias. When you say both teams, are we talking Slug and Herra? The whole Deep Six? Where? I didn't bring my passport, just my ID."

Nash hung her head to one side. "No trips to Paris. Sorry. Probably San Jose. It's something called the Silicon Super Bowl?"

Muna's eyes grew enormous. "Only the hugest event, like, ever. It's the most badass gaming conference this side of the Bifrost. Are they going to play?"

Nash shrugged. "Who knows? But Tree rented a seven-thirty-seven just for us. I would think they are going up there to inflict major damage points. Or whatever they do."

Muna looked at Moose.

He chuckled. "Yeah. I know what you're talking about. If the

Mouse was a few years older, she'd be pounding on her uncle to take her. So, who are these people?"

Muna rolled her eyes. "The people your niece would want an autographed poster of to tape up on her bedroom wall. Major international contenders." She smirked. "Don't say anything to her, but we'll work on the poster angle and any other swag we can funnel out this way."

THE EVENING WAS PERFECTLY PLEASANT AS THE OCEAN tickled the edge of the sand. A couple of dolphins played just outside the flattening. But the trained shooter's eyes caught the dorsal fins dancing among the small swells.

"There's a pod of five who make the cove their home. We surfers don't molest, and they have fun hanging out with us. On flat surf days, it's just lying in the sun. I've had the older female sleeping next to my board. It reinforces my belief in living with nature." Frank reached over, ran his fingers over Powder's head, and played with her ears.

Nash jutted her chin out at Powder. "Your coyote? Does it let you pet like that?"

He turned to the blonde in powder blue scrubs next to him. "Does she let you pet her?"

Tink shrugged. "Peewee? Not like her mother used to." She turned to Nash and Muna. "Dog was more like a domestic dog in bed. She'd sleep between us. Groan when you moved wrong. Roll over and offer her belly—all the usual stuff you would expect from a family dog. But the year Frank was in the hospital, we cuddled a lot. We both missed him."

The man snorted. "Except when she went out and got knocked up."

Muna cocked her head. "But she was feral?"

Frank chuckled. "Not hardly. Feral infers they once were domestic. But my coyotes are all wild. We just get to share the bed with them. The first one, Dog, was still a pup when she dragged into my shack. One night, it was storming like crazy, and without thinking about it, I closed the door. A while later, I woke up, and there was a little hot water bottle snuggled up under my blankets, snoring softly. So, I went back to sleep." He shrugged. "What the heck. I was already feeding her, and I'd rigged up a continuous water pan on the porch. So, sharing the bed wasn't a stretch as long as she didn't smell."

Tink gently backhanded his shoulder. "Dog never smelled."

He laughed. "Duke did."

She cringed. "Oh god… I'm still trying to figure out where he found a skunk. They don't roam around the headlands. Do they?"

Muna snickered. "What an eccentric life. Living with wild dogs."

He smiled. They had shared their bomb stories, and Frank had let them run their hands over the mechanical spine in his back. "Not so eccentric, really, and no wilder than getting blown up." He put his fist out. Muna and Nash both bumped into it.

Nash raised her glass. "Here's to no more bombs."

Jazz, Ming, and Tink joined the three.

Frank leaned in with his elbows on the table. His Ramones T-shirt was cut off halfway, and it looked like the boys were bellying up to the bar. "So, Jazz told me you caught the poison case out in the desert…?"

Nash laid her head over to one side. "And it looks like a break in the case just fell in our lap. Thanks once again to a certain crew."

Ming held up her hands. "Oh no. It wasn't us." She pointed at Jazz. "This one is all on her."

Frank chuckled. "Like my old partner always said, it's good to know all the right people in all the low places. A mayor is only as good as a mayor can get. But the street sweeper, they can get you the dirt."

A beeper sounded, and Tink closed her eyes as her head dropped. "No restaurant for the weary."

Frank gave her a hard eye. "At least the assholes waited for you to finish dessert."

She pulled up the old-fashioned tech and looked at the readout. "Seven cars on the five. They are warming up three operating rooms for our share. Kids, it's been fun. Come stay longer sometime. Maybe you can meet our kids." She slid out from the table.

The night manager stepped over. "I heard the beeper, Tink. If you want, I can run you up the hill in the cart."

"Thanks, Greg. I'd appreciate that." She waved as they scurried out the back way.

Frank's sigh was soft as he played with the small spoon on his dessert plate smeared with chocolate syrup.

Nash twitched her head to one side. "Nurse's life?"

His lips furled as the other four women were quiet. "She's one of the top trauma surgical nurses in Southern California. So, the big shit gets shoveled their way—a lot." He looked up. "What do you know about blood and surgeries?"

Muna and Nash both vibrated their heads. Nash smirked. "Rub some dirt on it. Everything stops bleeding eventually."

Frank rocked back with a smile at the old SEAL, saying. "Everyone knows a surgery has a good chance of using some blood. But they don't know how much. The cap is thirty-six units."

Muna's eyes swelled large. "Four gallons?"

He pointed. "That's whole blood. There's no cap on plasma. But the problem with plasma is it's the stuff that makes blood runny. So, you also need platelets to hold it all together. But all in all, about five gallons before they must step back and let nature take its toll." He pointed his finger at Muna. "Call the time of death."

"But surely those cases are rare…"

Frank drew in a deep breath and looked at Ming. She closed her eyes and nodded her head to one side. She was young, but she had gotten used to the story. "The first time, when I was blown up and I lost my detective partner, I went thirty-two. But they were done with the extenders. So, they were scrambling to find three more units of type-O." He tossed his head slightly. "A few years ago, I got lucky and only went twenty-seven. But that's when they had to open the whole back all over again to replace the caterpillar."

He reached over and scratched at Powder. "Her unit gets those at least once a week. It wears on her, but sitting on the sidelines would kill her. She has an apartment near UCI Medical Center, but she stays at my shack most of the time." He looked over with sad eyes. "I'd like to think it was my boyish charms, but I know it's the same reason I live there. The quiet on the edge of the cliff and the dogs calm the soul. It won't heal it, but the calming helps you work on the rest of it. I think her blood pressure is better than it was a few years ago. Or… at least I'd like to think so." He looked at Jazz. The woman softly nodded as she looked at the tablecloth.

Nash rocked with understanding. "Duty is more than just a calling. It's breathing."

He rocked.

Nash looked at him. "So how do you manage retirement at what… fifty?"

He smirked. "Don't let the childish good looks fool you. I'm fifty-three. But it's the kids that keep me young."

The smile tugged at Nash's mouth. "And chaperoning up to the Bay Area…"

He smiled toothily. "Who knows? Maybe you need to pick my brain."

FLY WITH THE EAGLES

POWDER SNIFFED every seat while the large young man held everyone back. He watched as the dog took her job, the length of the aircraft built to only hold a football or basketball team and their staff. Every seat was First-Class. Several were in pods of four—facing each other. Several near the back could lie almost flat—for sleeping.

She worked her way to the end and then came and sat next to one in the middle. Slug smiled at those behind him. He had asked Powder to find him the winning seat.

As he approached the seat, he searched for any clues. It differed from the rest in only one way. He noted a small plaque just under the right armrest. The mark on the plaque read 8B. He thought through all the gaming knowledge he had amassed. Smiling, he presented her with the jerky. "You found it. Number eight black."

Bunny stopped right behind him. "You're colorblind, Slug. It's blue. Just like all the rest."

He snorted and pointed at the tiny plaque. "What's your seat?"

She scanned the other seats. "Why does your seat have a plaque and the others don't?"

He shrugged as he slumped down into the seat. "I don't know. I just asked her to find me the uniquely winning seat."

The flight attendant stood to one side. "The dog is right. And we don't know why. I've flown this unit for four years. Every time, the most valuable player or highest-scoring player has sat in that seat. And as she pointed out, they all look alike. Except for the plaque that nobody notices."

Slug reached into his shirt pocket and drew out another stick of jerky. Tearing a bite from the stick, he patted the seat next to him. Powder eased herself up into the seat and accepted the rest of the jerky. Both seemed to smile as they chewed.

Frank stepped onto the plane and took the first seat. It faced backward and the rest of the plane.

Nash waved Muna to the window seat as she sat across from Frank.

Jazz wandered past. "I need to keep the kids settled down back here. I don't want any of them hacking into the plane's systems with their cell phones."

Ming and Tree were last on. Tree went over some details with the pilot and the senior flight attendant as Ming came and dropped her computer bag on the small, low table.

Curling her legs into the roomy seat, the diminutive Asian wiggled and smiled. "I always love these seats." She looked at Muna as if they were the same height.

Muna snorted. She knew her Asian twin was questioning her both feet on the floor. "One, we grew up much different. And two, I was never that flexible. These pants hide a lot of heavy-duty walking meat. And San Francisco seems to just add more."

Nash snorted softly.

Muna slapped the other agent's arm back. "Can it, Marine."

Nash nodded at Frank in the backward aisle seat. "In the Hawks, did you always take the pilot's wall and hang your leg out?"

Frank's face pulled back on one side. The question was one only a team lieutenant or captain would understand. "First in the water or sand." He pushed his jaw forward. "And your favorite seat?"

She showed her full smile of large teeth. "One C. Right next to the bucket of scotch, no ice."

The steward leaned over. "I've got twelve or eighteen… Your travel agent was only vaguely specific, ma'am."

She smiled and hummed. "Yes. Magic Rick is still in training. Whichever has the word Glen in it."

He nodded and looked at Muna.

Muna held her hand to her chest and then pointed at Ming. "I think we are the high-test coffee twins, please. Frank?"

"Just water for now."

The steward straightened. "Very good. We'll be taxiing in about five minutes. The pilot expects clear air, but we still enforce the seat belt rules, please."

Frank focused on Nash. "I know the girls have been trolling the dark and light for the alias. But do you have any feelings about where she may have been from or may go now?"

Nash snapped her seat belt. "My gut is she's from the Orange or San Diego region. I think she knew some people before the research collective. Hopefully, this gal up north can shed some light on that." She flopped her head toward Muna, opening her electronic pad. "I don't remember seeing any dusting powder in any of the buildings…"

Frank winced. "They probably didn't. Sometimes it's resources. And other times, when they don't think murder, they don't think fingerprints. It's screwy, but it's a human nature thing."

Nash squinted one eye as she cocked her head to one side. "Or it comes with the territory. For most people, suicide is a squishy area. It doesn't make you think straight. I've seen it with mass murders as well."

Muna held out her pad in landscape—showing the enlarged report page. "No box ticked."

Nash rolled up and pulled out her phone as the steward arrived with the drinks. "Do I have a couple of minutes for a phone call?"

He snorted softly. "As long as we get pictures with the Deep Six team for bragging rights, you can chat all the way to San Jose. But it's better if you use our Wi-Fi. The access is Alaska seventeen, and the code is *we are* and hashtag and the number one."

She punched in the code and then found the phone number.

"I'm just sitting down to lunch. This better be good."

Nash laughed. "Are you home or at Sister's?"

He chuckled. "Hey, Federales. You just can't stay away?"

"Just some follow-up. We noticed nobody dusted for prints."

The growl was low and harmonized with the jet's engines. "At the time, we all thought it was suicide. But, in all fairness, I think you ought to pull one of your teams out of San Diego or Los Angeles and get it done right the first time. Those boys will cover everywhere, and even the plants in the greenhouses will be black."

Nash nodded. "I'll have them reach out before they come. Enjoy your lunch."

"Nope. Just peeked inside the burrito. She's getting funny. It's bean and kale. I need to cross the river."

Nash breathed a chuckle. "Yeah, those diets can be brutal. I'll check with you in a few days, Moose." She thumbed her phone closed as she caught Jazz's look. She smirked. "His daughter wanted to come with us. But she's only fourteen. So, she made him a bean and kale burrito."

Ming's head twisted into a curious cock.

Nash chuckled. "He makes Jazz and me look like you and Muna."

Muna nodded with a raised eyebrow. "He has to duck to get through the door sideways."

Nash rolled her eyes as she found the next number. "Hey Mike?"

She could tell they had her on a speakerphone in the autopsy room. The echoes had a distinct stainless-steel ping to them. "Hey. It's the wandering waifs. Or is that waves? Whiffs?"

Nash growled. "How about stop while you're ahead?"

She recognized the muffled characteristic of Oz wearing a full bio-suit. "What can we do for you, agent?"

"Hey Oz. We need to have the whole compound dusted. It was murder, and we need to identify the female who did the cooking and was in the cabin designated as number three."

"Kitchen and three. Got it. I'll reach out to a friend in Los Angeles. I like her work. Anything else?"

Nash's mouth hung open a moment as she thought. "Maybe ease up on Chips with the dad jokes. Save them for your niece. She'll be back soon enough."

Muna glared at her.

Mike laughed. "She built a computer wall in the corner and disappeared from sight. We haven't seen her for three days. But we're good."

"Behave. We'll see you tomorrow or the next day sometime." She thumbed the screen and pocketed the phone.

Muna growled. "If they terrorized the girl…"

Ming laughed. "Chips? Hah! The girl is stainless steel wrapped around a cast-iron core. She grew up fighting with older brothers on a ranch or something. If she's hiding behind a computer, she's on the dark side. I'll reach out tonight. She usually surfaces around ten o'clock."

Nash sipped on her scotch as she eyed the quiet Frank. Her chin notched up.

"So, this is how investigations go these days…"

"Not always this lucky. They will never replace the boots on the ground. But with federal stuff, I do a lot of flying around these days. More than my fellow agents in Washington."

He sipped his water. "And that's another thing. When I was with the Orange County Sheriff's, we interfaced with the Orange County

FBI office and only occasionally Los Angeles. But here you are... all over the west coast."

Muna started pulling on her fingers. "And New Mexico, Arizona, Northern Bum Fuck Egypt, as well as getting blown up in Colorado —twice..."

Nash rested her hand on the smaller hands. "Easy tiger. And I only got blown up the second time. Felix blew them up the first time. I was just in the line of sight."

Ming giggled. "Was that when you destroyed the hot car?"

Nash glanced at Muna and tried to mimic the squeakier voice. "May... be...?"

The two smaller women laughed at the bad impersonation.

Nash growled as she turned back toward Frank. "When you worked for the sheriff, you had a beat or jurisdiction."

He nodded.

"About the time I thought I was working the jurisdiction dictated by the area around the District of Columbia, I would get sent to Florida, Ohio, or Louisiana. So, I started thinking my jurisdiction was just screwball cases. Or the cases the locals didn't want to touch. It's hard to explain to a white guy, but the officers of color get the crap jobs. The First Nations get the jobs they wouldn't assign to another minority because it might look like what it is. But the Indian won't speak up."

Ming snorted loudly as she hid her face.

Nash's eyebrows rose as she looked at the young woman. "You have input here?"

She pointed at Frank as she rattled off something in Cantonese.

Muna laughed. "I almost got that."

Nash looked at Muna.

Muna looked at Ming. "Something about that you have the wrong man, or this is not the droid you seek."

Ming laughed at the Star Wars reference. "No. You're talking about the wrong white guy. If anyone understands being at the bottom of the shit pile, it's Frank. If anybody is the odd person out in our group, it's Tree. She's cis chick and likes a cis dude with certain curly hair." She flashed a smile at Muna. "But your Cantonese is coming along great. It appalled my mother that I'm learning Cantonese instead of Mandarin."

Muna rolled her eyes. "But it's more Californio."

"True dat." They fist-bumped.

Nash turned her wide eyes back to Frank. "I owe you an apology."

He shrugged it off. "You couldn't know. I'm white. I surf. And I'm a dude. The pink toenails are something... well, it takes some time to understand. But I fully get the shit pile command structure. So, what's the reality about how you're out here so much?"

"When you were in the corps or in the sheriffs, how many First Nation did you work with?"

He squinted one eye. "My partner, Kalani, was First Nation Hawaiian. I think there were a few guys with Mexican heritage, but if they went back to Inca or Aztec... I doubt it."

Nash nodded as she set down her drink. "So, there's a noise disturbance of a large party having a luau. Dug up the yard and roasted a big and all. But it's gotten out of hand. So, who got the call?"

"Well, if it was a real luau... Kalani might have already been there. But I see your point. We got calls like that. They're called affinity calls. Send the Hawaiian to the luau, the black to the black neighborhood, and the gay cops to the gay bar. So, you're on suicide watch?"

Nash pushed up one eyebrow. "You had gay cops?"

He wobbled his head. "There were teams that were better with certain calls."

"Humf." Nash blinked one eye. "No, I'm not on suicide watch. But the case is on Fort Mojave tribal land. And I'm the token as well as the wiffle with the most waffle. So, I got the job."

Ming twisted her head. "Wiffle?"

Muna glowed. "Women In Federal Law Enforcement. We're a thing."

Frank leaned his head back and looked over his cheeks at Nash. "And that's it? You're the token Indian?"

Muna scoffed. "Hardly. Mass of dead bodies in the middle of nowhere." She glanced at Ming. "Sound familiar? No signs of gunshot wounds, no stab wounds, no signs of a struggle. Ringing any bells? Let's try the trifecta. This is just strange enough to turn left and get weird, like the twisties in a jet pilot. So, when it turns into the wild ride from sanity, you want the most experienced and her team of misfits." She pointed at Nash.

Frank furled his lips as he looked up and to the side at Nash.

Nash opened her hands and slowly weighed them up and down. "At first, we had a group suicide on tribal land. But now, we have a mass murder, so it gets bounced to the federal level, and because the tribal land straddles the state border, it's FBI. And the token Indian is me. So now I'm out here—again. And now we're chasing a ghost who knows poisons—again. If it doesn't get any weirder, we just need to identify and find the killer. While we protect a witness, we haven't corroborated whether it is legit or even real."

Muna rolled her finger out into the air, pointing at Nash. "Which means... she gets it."

Frank frowned softly. "And the team of misfits?"

21

WALK LIKE A WINNER

AMID THE CACOPHONY of the indoor corridor, electric golf carts weaved among people, heading every which way. Some of them were wearing regular garments, others had team outfits, while a few sported inflatable unicorns or T-Rex costumes. A young girl wasn't watching where she was and got side-swiped by a large T-Rex tail. Nobody laughed. A few helped her back on her feet, but everyone had been in this circumstance before. This Super Bowl wasn't about two overpriced teams of testosterone. This was a game open to even a high school team wearing hand-painted T-shirts who arrived on the city bus. If you qualified, you played to win. The final prize money grew by each hour, but everyone knew it was well north of the base million dollars, floored by several tech companies.

Slug huddled the crew. "Okay, for you new teamers, this is the one. There are four levels of elimination. When we get past each of the sorting levels, they wipe everything out, and it all starts on reset. That includes the deaths and any levels of armor or magic you won. We all start at the beginning levels all over again. Each level of elimination is a new game. You've all been playing these games until we get to the finals. That is when they unveil this year's new

143

game. So, literally, nobody goes in with any experience. So, until that game, we played our usual strengths. In that ultimate game, everything changes. You, Herras, and Chips will be the lynchpins. You figure out the game and feed us cannon fodder the tactics. We're all earwigged into each other by squads. So, pay attention to what you're hearing." He pointed at the lanky redhead. "That means you too, Slapper. No zoning out. This is two hours or ten hours. There are no breaks, but stay hydrated. Our chairs are all set up. The roadies set them up and ran the diagnostics last night. Questions?"

He looked around at all the faces. His nod was crisp. "This is Paris all over again. But this time, we're making an entrance to blow them away. Because…?"

The team smiled and chanted together. "Intimidation is everything."

He turned. "Line up. FBI, you're in the front. Frank, I don't recognize you in the suit, but I guess for today, you're part of the shock troop. Powder can run point." He looked at the chubby blond with the braced shoe. "Petey?"

"We're hot." He held up his pad. "As soon as I give you the signal, your mic is live."

They shuffled up to the large double doors. The two sheriff's deputies stood with their hands on the pulls. The one winked at Jazz.

Petey muttered quietly. "I'm in. And three… two… one." He pointed at Slug as an enormous wave of shock noise exploded in the now pitch-black arena. As the deputies pulled open the doors, a set of spotlights lit the doorway. More lights banged out step-by-step, tracing a line across the arena to where Deep Six's chairs were set up, and they would battle for the Champions of the World title. The roadies had done the actual job they had hired them for. Half of the crew were movers but for the large, sensitive computers. The other half had installed the lights and hacked the system so Petey could take temporary command of the lighting and speaker system.

The oldest of the hackers had remembered his father's time at Cal Tech. There weren't real electronics then, but there were large cards a block of the stadium would turn to spell out the team's name or cheer. Cal Tech had broken into the storage room where they kept the cards. They switched out only some cards. When the University of Washington Huskies had performed their card routine, instead of reading Huskies, the large block of cards read Cal Tech. Great pranks only need to happen once to become a legend. It had been over sixty years since the cards, but they still held it as the greatest stunt in Bowl Game history... until today.

Nash and Muna snickered at the sound of Slug's altered voice. It sounded like they had rented an announcer from the wrestling championships.

"Ladies and gentlemen. Combatants and guests. Please stand. Help us give a warm welcome to the Women in Federal Law Enforcement and their partners as they escort this year's team, Deep Six... and your next... World... Champions."

MUNA SAT QUIETLY IN THE WINDOW SEAT, PETTING THE sleeping Powder. Her eyes reflected the dark glass and the twinkling lights atop the Golden Gate Bridge. The inner part of the table had circled back and forth many times during dinner. Most of the talk was about procedures, protocols, and past skirmishes, both military and law enforcement. None was in her realm of expertise or interests.

Nash put the glass down. "That would be more of Muna's expertise." She looked at the younger woman. "Muna?"

Her head slowly turned as she brought her attention back to the other three. "Yes?"

Nash frowned. "We were talking about the... Are you alright?"

Her voice was soft. "Yeah. Fine. Just a little tired. Talking about what?"

Frank waved the air. "It was just talk. What's going on? You were halfway to the bridge out there."

She shifted on the bench seat as Powder moaned. Her hand cupped in around the ear and jaw, holding the head to her thigh. "I was just thinking about today."

Jazz raised one eyebrow. "Which part?"

Muna pooched out her lower lip as she looked at the woman with the bright-red tipped spikes of shorter hair. "All of it... but mostly walking into a standing ovation of a hundred thousand people who didn't know I existed."

Frank snorted an avuncular chuckle. "More like a hundred and fifty thousand, but they do now. And I bet they'll be talking about it for years to come. Maybe not you personally. But I think there were some young girls out there today who were running their search engines on their phones about WIFLE and wondering about the dog. No matter how the teams do tonight, I think you three made the biggest hit."

Jazz coughed in her fist. "Of course, credit where credit is due. Petey hacking into the arena's lighting and PA system... that was just short of brilliant as well." She knew the truth lay in the groundwork by the roadies.

Nash rolled her eyes. "And I'm sure they will never repeat the stunt at any venue."

Jazz laughed. "Nobody would ever try. There is the first, and then there is the copycat or also tried. And in the computer world, we derogatorily know those people as script bunnies. And Deep Six's reputation is nothing but cutting-edge. I'm sure we will get back to the office and find the stunt has generated a lot of new contracts or interest in what we do."

"So, nobody will get in trouble over this?" Nash looked at Jazz.

"Respect? Yes. Trouble? Hardly. Check with WIFLE in the next week or two and see if there isn't an uptick in inquiries." Jazz turned toward Muna. "But I don't think that was what was worrying you."

Muna waved her hand through the air. "No. It was nothing I was worrying about. It was something I had never wondered about. But now I know."

Nash frowned at the woman she respected for her prowess at researching and knowledge of esoteric information. "What?"

Muna looked over and blinked. "What Taylor Swift must feel like when she walks out on a stage."

"DID I EVER TELL YOU I HAD A SON?"

Debra was getting used to the disjointed memory of Alzheimer's in her mother. She dipped the sponge in the bathwater and gently smoothed it over the slender shoulders. "Yes, Dorothy. You said he was nice."

The older woman nodded. "He always wanted a kitten. But we were poor. So, from scraps of cloth, I sewed a quilted kitten doll. I patched that doll a hundred times from all the loving he gave it."

Debra blinked. The doll was still on the bed the woman slept in —patches and all. "Let's wash your hair today. Shall we?" She submerged the large sea sponge in the shallow water and squeezed it to pump in a load of fresh water.

"Is it Wednesday?"

Debra hummed. "It is Wednesday."

"Well," the woman nodded. "Wednesday is hair day."

Debra pulled the dripping sponge to the top of the woman's hair and squeezed. The water cascaded over her head as the woman squealed in glee. "Wednesday is a wet day."

The daughter brought one more sponge full to the head of wet hair before she squeezed a small dollop of shampoo into her hand. With both hands, she worked the soap into the thinning gray hair as she looked out of the window at the new houses dotting the desert like fresh squatting cacti.

There had been better days. But they always seemed tempered

by the restrictions of circumstances. The young single mother had never aspired to become the electrical engineer she had dreamed of as a young girl. The rape and resulting pregnancy had forced choices. Strict religious families don't have daughters who get pregnant. And an abortion, although legal, was not a moral option to a young woman who still carried her bible to school. So now, the daughter of the daughter, who never knew her grandparents, washed her mother's hair.

She brought the sponge up to rinse the hair and head. The woman hummed. She had long forgotten the words she had sung to her child, but the melody still abided. Even if it was only in bits and pieces, it was one of the few comforting moments of Debra's growing up.

Debra pulled the plug out of the bathtub. "Let's stand you up now so I can dry you off. Then I can put you in your nightgown, and you can listen to the radio before bedtime. Does that sound good?"

The woman struggled to stand from the small stool in the tub. "I need my diaper too. I don't get up in the night."

Her daughter gave her an affirmative nod, for this was the tedium of their nighttime routine. Her head and face jerked her short blond hair in a violent twitch as her tongue stuck out in a quick, fat sausage to lick her lips. "Yes, Dorothy, double the pleasure, double the fun. We'll stuff them on your little bum." She repeated the lines her mother had sung to her each night for many years, though it felt impersonal and distant now.

The older woman giggled.

Debra gently toweled the wet head and shoulders as she watched the red car drive along the distant road to the cream house. The new roof was terra-cotta clay red, but she knew it was only aluminum sheets. The traditional curved tiles were too expensive for the younger new residents seeking savings in the desert. Or just finding privacy among the prickly cacti and the dwindling miles of sand.

2 2

FINDING TRUTH

THE DAY WAS a rare fall day, with clear blue out until it joined the darker blue on the horizon. A lone ship broke the surface of the darker. Not even an aircraft spoiled the sky. The walk through Golden Gate Park had been relaxing. The time spent gave a better understanding of how a broken-up former detective, a former deputy turned lawyer, and a bunch of genius kids got together. It was as straightforward as a man and woman cohabitating with wild coyotes.

Muna was half-turned along the bench, with her hand half draped over Powder's shoulders. Her hand absently kneaded the fur of the neck as they both watched out the window.

Jazz turned toward Frank. "Ming would love this view."

The man burped a chuckle. "Don't bring her here. Ming would buy this view." He frowned at Nash. "Is the service always this slow? Or am I missing something?"

Nash glanced at her orange-faced dive watch. Frank recognized the Doxa. It was one of the favored watches for SEALs and serious divers alike. Nash smirked. "They're a little late… but, speaking of views…" She held her hands out at the windows.

149

She smiled at the small snap of Frank's head. "Holy... Is that roof opening?"

The waitress quietly set down a full carafe as she picked up the empty. "It certainly is. And a glorious day for breakfast, alfresco it is."

Nash chuckled. "Wait for it..."

Gently, the table and two seated gentlemen came into view. As the lift reached its summit, the men looked out to sea. The one said something to the other, and they both chuckled and then turned and waved at the watchers in the restaurant a block away. Muna and Nash waved back.

Jazz's mouth fell open. "You know those guys? Why aren't we having breakfast with them in the magical house?"

Muna sat back around. "No. We don't know them. But we figured they realized they had an audience, so they started waving."

The waitress tinkled in amusement. "Their names are Jean Pierre and Claude Dumont. I met them at the market a month ago. I told them we watch their magical roof every day. They're retired engineers or something and love their view." She rested her hand on Nash's shoulder. "I think it was last year... we didn't see them for a few months. They had gone back to France. One of their mothers was dying or had already passed. Anyway, they took time to tie up all the loose ends. But now they're back."

Nash nodded at the enlightenment and nodded at Jazz. "What would you like for breakfast?"

Jazz held out her hands at the table. "Is there a menu?"

The waitress smiled and shook her head. "No."

Jazz looked around at Frank and laughed. "It's the same as your shack."

Frank chuckled and wagged his hanging finger at Jazz and himself. "Waffles drowning in strawberry compote. Two eggs over easy with a side of pig."

The waitress held her right hand on her hip. "You want the eggs on top or the side?"

Frank and Jazz both held up their fists and capped them with their other hands.

The waitress snorted, turned, and walked toward the kitchen. "Three awful bleeders. Soft chicks on top and run the pigs in the side yard."

Jazz started laughing as she looked at Frank, turning red. "Oh gawd. She's Danny's sister."

Nash cocked her head.

Jazz laughed even more. "Danny is his manager, waiter, wayward, whatever. When Frank spent the year in the hospital, Danny had to rebuild the restaurant. So he renamed it the Surf Shack, raised the prices to ridiculous, and got rid of the menus. He hired old waitresses who could remember anything and then call it out in the most arcane way." She pointed toward the kitchen. "Just like she did."

Frank snickered. "Except my girls usually like to throw in things like a heart attack on a shingle, run the roadkill, and dead chicks. The fancy youngsters come and pay stupid just to get abused and listen to what would be anywhere else, upsetting orders."

Muna smirked. "Does it work?"

Jazz rolled her eyes. "You once asked if all we did at Deep Six was play games..."

"But your work is just another form of the games."

Frank nodded. "And it pays well. More than we ever thought."

Jazz floated her finger out in Frank's direction. "Danny could stop working and never have to earn another dollar. Frank doesn't even know what he pays Danny because Danny takes a cut of the business. He hired the best waitress with a reputation in the area. He asked what they had done in the last two years and said that was their base salary. They all walked through the door with fan clientele willing to drive out to the shack. Danny is only open from the early morning to two in the afternoon. The shack makes more than most of the fine steak houses on the coast."

Nash frowned. "What kind of food?"

Jazz and Frank both snorted. "What do you want for breakfast?"

Nash's eyes narrowed. "Jerky machaca huevos rancheros burrito."

"Wet or dry?"

Nash smirked at Frank. "Wet."

Jazz snorted. "Red chili sauce or green chili?"

Muna remembered their time in Pueblo, Colorado. "Christmas." The mix of the two colors.

Frank smiled and turned to the smaller woman. "Did you want that jerky beef or venison?"

Muna smiled largely. "Lamb. And it better be Halal."

Frank shrugged and looked at Jazz.

She rolled her eyes. "I don't know. I'd have to check with Cookie."

The waitress brought a large tray and set it on the other table. She placed a large bowl in front of Powder. "One Halal lamb and rice burrito, hold the sauces." The still-rolled burrito laced with crosses of red and green was placed in front of Muna. "And one with Christmas wrappings."

The other three were duplicates. "And three heart attacks and bleeding."

She wiggled the half-empty carafe. "And a warmup on the coffee. Anything else?"

THEY HAD TRADED OUT THE CIVILIAN MODEST SUV FOR the official Explorer. The heavier vehicle nosed up to the base checkpoint. As the guard stepped out of the guard shack, Nash held up her ID, as did Muna in the passenger seat. Frank and Jazz held up their wallets the same way they used to flash their deputy sheriff badges. They knew that a full second of exposure was more than needed.

Nash rolled forward and then asked for directions. The guard snapped off all they needed without the long explanations. She glanced back at Jazz as they rolled quietly along the buildings. "I assumed you hadn't been here before."

The woman set her mouth and twitched her head. "I've never even met Mike. But Maria said she'd call and lay the groundwork for our being here."

Nash eased the Explorer to a stop in front of the two young men. "Are you coming with us?"

Mike laughed. "You are definitely not Jazz. My aunt's tastes run toward short and wild hair."

Jazz pushed the button to roll down her darkened window. She laughed at his face. "Will this do?"

Ming had dusted the tips of the red spikes with a tint of green. The five tiny gold Day of the Dead masks upholstered her left ear.

The young man laughed. "Now that looks more like the photo Tia Maria sent me." He opened the door. "No, we're not going with you, but we've set up a conference with her. You can talk to her from here, or she at least gets a look at you guys before you go invade her territory."

The camera was on a tripod, but the computer screen was smaller than Muna, Nash, and Jazz were used to. The woman looked fragile.

Nash turned her head to look at the others. "It's just an offer. There will only be the four of us and the dog. But, for some people, that's a lot."

Colby shook her head. "No. No, I'm fine. I don't know what I expected. Why did I even call the show that night... I just... well, I was just tired of hearing all the wrong things about good people." She looked up at the camera. "When are you coming up?"

Nash glanced at her watch. "The GPS says about three hours to get to you. So now is the best time for us. What about you?"

Her head was jerky as it moved back and forth. "Now is good. I'll plan on you guys for dinner."

Nash held up her hand. "Okay. See you in a few hours."

Chase cut the feed as Nash stood. "We've got bottles of cold water, a couple of toilets, and maybe something to snack on the road."

Muna snickered. "Any Beyond Scoville pork rinds hiding back there?"

Mike laughed. "We've heard stories about those. But no. The best we have are jerked cheese puffs and Slim Jims."

Jazz draped her arm over Mike's shoulders. "Maybe just the six-pack of water. You don't have to bribe me. Your aunt does enough of that. But if you see your way clear, she would really like a visit. You're the only relative who she talks to regularly."

The man winced. "Her folks... she can write off. I'm still working on her sister, but Dad will never change. He was an altar boy, and her being gay would never find a place in his smudge-blackened heart. I love my dad, but even I can't stand his religion or politics." He looked into her eyes. "I get down soon. I'll see what military hop I can catch."

Jazz vibrated her head. "Don't bother. You make the time, and then call me. I'll get you the ride down to see her."

"I'd appreciate that. Things are kind of tight for us right now. Chase has a baby on the way, and I'm... well... the car took a crap about a month ago."

Jazz nodded a knowing tick. "Who sponsors your show?"

He snorted. "Nobody. The Navy gives us some unused space, and we scrounge for the equipment."

Jazz shoved her chin out toward Frank. "Let me talk to the boss. I don't know anything about the electronics end of what you do, but I bet you could use an infusion there as well."

"But you guys are in dredging or something."

Jazz smiled. "Or something. We just chartered a big jet to bring our multi-player video game team up to compete at the Super Bowl. We don't write games or make any direct income from competing, but we do it for bragging rights, and it brings us in clients. But we have a few other interests we're developing, so keep in touch and come down. My girl is missing her pequeño."

He blushed and smiled. "I'll work with the commander."

She jostled his shoulder. "Good. I'm glad I got to meet you."

His mouth hardened. "The circumstances suck."

She clicked her cheek. "Major suckage, but still some good will come of this." She nodded toward Nash and Muna, talking to Chase by the door.

23

APPLE FARM

MUNA AND FRANK stood at the edge of the gravel driveway, looking down at the short, grassy slope. Powder rolled in the fresh-mowed smell. Frank chuckled. "Makes you want to go down and roll around with her?" He watched the thin lip curl.

"Growing up, I had a purple goldfish. Rolling around on the grass is something I would imagine a surfer might do." She looked peeked over with narrowed eyes. This man was no match for the hardened warrior who battled daily in words with the two best. She just still wasn't sure if it was flirting or just what older men did with a female who was romantically off-limits to them.

Frank's silence grew as the farrows carving his forehead deepened. "You mean a Black Molly?"

Muna turned as Powder made her way back up the slope to them. "Nope. His name was Rikki. As in Rikki Tikki Tavi, the mongoose. My mother had bought him at a street bazaar. I think the cloth was originally dark blue but had faded to purple. I just liked the stitching of the patchwork. My mother has probably enshrined it in my old bedroom."

Frank turned to follow the two. His mouth pursed at being

beaten at his own game of banter, tease, and entrapment. *I need to spend more time with the girls and less lying on the surfboard.*

Nash turned toward the young man with the cane, walking their way from the farmhouse. "I gotta go. I'll call her this evening." She thumbed the red icon and slipped the phone into her pocket. "What did she say, Steven?"

His lips firmed in tight rolls. "We weren't expecting four of you…" He looked around. "Or a dog."

"Jazz is Mike's aunt's… well, let's just leave it at family. Frank is also a former Orange County deputy and is good at hearing what people are saying and what people aren't saying. But if they need to stay out here, I can live with it. The dog can stay with them. I don't think drugs or explosives are involved with her talking to us."

He winced. "I can see how… well, let's just say I understand team dynamics. On a ship, the quarters might be tight, but everyone has a reason for being there." He glanced back at the house. "We've got a large party table in the backyard…"

Nash snorted as she gently waved her arm and hand at the sky. "In this crappy sunshine weather? In Washington, D.C., we're getting ready for arctic blasts and balmy rhetoric from politicians. I'll take seventy-two and sunny all day long."

He nodded. "How about all of you head on around back, and I'll go get her?"

Nash put her hand out to stop him. "Make sure she understands at any time she feels uncomfortable that we can take a break, ease up on the people, whatever she wants. She's in the driver's seat here. We can even turn this into a two-day or three-day event. We just need her information. She was the only survivor…"

He rocked as his eyes closed with his nod. "That's what has her scared."

Nash fished her ID wallet out of her back pocket and unclipped her badge. "She needs to be completely comfortable that we're the guys in the white hats. Here is my ID and badge. She can ask the operator on any phone to be connected to the FBI in Washington. I'm with Special Investigations under Special Operations. She can ask for any of that and give them my name. They will patch her straight through to my boss. He knows we're here. She can ask him anything. He's a good guy and will answer everything—right down to my two hundred-and-fifty-year-old scotch. If she mentions scotch, he'll know she's talking to me. If he licks his lips as he mentions the two-fifty, she knows it's him."

His eyes narrowed. "Do you really drink scotch that old ?"

Her one eye closed as her smile softened. "I have a bottle. He's tasted it once or twice. If we can figure this case out, I'll owe her more than just my gratitude."

The man snorted softly. "We don't drink. But making it safe for her to live her life would go a long way." His chest heaved as he coughed into his fist. Finally, he wiped his mouth. "Sorry. But as you can tell, she's losing enough of her life soon enough."

Nash cocked her head to one side. "Cancer?"

He nodded. "The Navy says it wasn't their fault." He pointed at the house. "I'll get her rolling."

"We'll meet you around back."

The five gathered as they wandered toward the back.

The two-story farmhouse sat perched atop a low knoll overlooking the highway and the orchard fields. Two sizable barns hunkered at the height of the apple trees. At the front of the house, there was a big parking lot and a gravel driveway. But along the back and side, gently sloping grass spread out for what seemed like an entire football field's length. Painted Adirondack chairs dotted the field.

On the swath of stone patio, an outdoor feast table stretched out, prepared for groups of celebrants numbering in the dozens. Nearby stood a kitchen area resembling a castle. A wood-fired baking stove formed one tower. The other included enough grilling space to feed an army of starving marines. Between the two was a grand sideboard for serving. Jazz and Frank snorted. "Looks like home."

Nash and Muna thought about the cafeteria at Deep Six. The tables could go from intimate seating for six to a boisterous gathering on a single long table in a matter of minutes. All at the whim of the diners.

They all turned at the squeal of the spring on the screen door. The young woman, although younger, was a twin of the man. The few freckles on her cheeks exposed the hidden redhead nature of her blond hair and seemed incongruous with the T-shirt and bib overalls. She squinted at the sunlight as she took in the people and the dog to one side. "Is she friendly?"

Nash smiled. "If she likes you, she'll wash your hand or face. But she's waiting to be invited. Her name is Powder. As in, powder your nose."

The woman patted her thigh. "Hello, Powder."

The dog strolled to the woman and sniffed. Licking the hand, she then sat, allowing the woman to pet her head and neck.

"She's gentle." The woman looked up shyly. "I noticed the badge on her harness. What does she do?"

Nash took the few steps. "Sometimes it's the important things like breaking the ice and making friends. Hi, I'm Nash. Agent Nash Running Bear. Powder's partner."

The woman held out the wallet and badge. "Colby. Colby Bachiller. These are yours. Your boss, Tony, asked me to go easy on you. I think he wants some more of that scotch."

Nash softly snorted as she clipped her badge on her belt and pocketed the wallet. "He needs to go down to Barbados and earn his own bottle."

The woman grimaced with a smile. "That's a long way to go to a liquor store."

Nash turned. "Closest I know for that drink. Let me introduce you to everyone." She pointed at Muna. "This is the Robin to my Batman. This is agent Muna al-Faragi. And if you don't mind, she'll video-record you while she takes notes. Sometimes back at the office, days later, we pick up on little things we miss originally."

The woman smiled at Muna. "In my world, it's called gleaning. Sometimes, the second harvest produces the better fruit."

Muna smiled as her head dipped. "Absolutely. And nice to meet you."

Nash continued. "You talked to Mike over the phone, and this is his aunt's… um…"

Jazz stepped forward and held out her hand. "Girlfriend. Hi, my name is Jazz. Just like the music."

Colby took the hand and shook. "I like your hair. It's really… out there." She twisted her finger in her blond.

Jazz nodded in understanding about wallflowers. "I use it to scare the bejeezus out of my boss, Frank."

He stepped forward, frowning at Jazz's comment. "Hi, Frank Pounds."

"You were a detective or something?"

He grimaced. "Was, and occasionally, I still get roped into a project or two. Mostly, I just listen. I like a good story. And I understand yours is the topper."

She held her hand out at the table. "I don't know anything about being a topper… but it's my story. And it still scares the hell out of me." She turned to her brother. "Steve, could we get a pitcher of apple cider… or lemonade, or even water? It's going to be a minute."

He looked around with raised eyebrows. "How many apple ciders? Or lemonade?"

Nash smirked as she pulled out a chair. "It is an apple farm. Show us your stuff." The others nodded.

He spun on his heel. "Two pitchers it is."

Colby glanced back to see he had closed the screen door. Her eyes were closed as she turned back. Her sigh was deep as she finally looked at Nash and then at Muna. She saw they had pointed the small camera on the top of the laptop at her.

Swallowing. "Let me first just say, when I left that night, I don't know if they were alive or…" She grimaced.

Nash put out her hand on the table. "Let's start at the beginning."

Colby rocked. "That would be about three years ago. I had gotten a job in the Imperial Valley. The farm was experimenting with growing organic tomatoes. They had many acres of natural cultivation. But the insects made the produce only good for canning. Also, the spring is great, but the heat then retards the output, and then there's another uptick in the fall. But the demand is year-round. So when the production slumps, the buyers move on to where they can fill their orders. The answer is shade and cooling, even though the plants need a lot of sunlight. The greenhouses and hoop tunnels create the difference."

"Was that where you met Lambert?"

She nodded. "In a roundabout way. Stephen Clark had deep roots in the world of agriculture. And you can't grow food commercially without developing close ties to colleges and universities. They're doing research to grow food more productively, and they need growers to let them experiment with larger scales of commodities. They also need our feedback on what we find to be working. Or with climate change, what has stopped working."

Frank frowned. "Stopped...?"

She blinked. "Growing the tomatoes in the sun. Lettuce will be next. The temperatures have increased. Instead of growing things, the summer kills them. Hot in the Central Valley used to be in the high eighties. Now they have weeks where the overnight temps never get under ninety. You can't water enough to cool the plants. We're running out of water as it is." She clenched her grimace and then sighed. "Look, you all know about the canary in the coal mine. But in climate change, there are many canaries. The coral reefs are dying from pollution and heat. But ingrown food, tomatoes, and lettuce or the foodstuff canaries. Look at the wine. Italy and Napa were the hotbeds for wine. Now Italy can only grow heated wines, and even the famous Rhine wines are moving to northern England and Scotland. Most of what they grew in northern California is now in Oregon and Washington. Even Canada is having success at growing cooler white wines. We're dying." She noticed the hardened passive faces and hung her head. "Sorry..."

Nash cleared her throat. "Doctor Lambert...?"

Colby blushed. "Sorry. Food production is a hot button... But Lambert. He had already heard I was working the greenhouses for Stephen. So he approached me about the greenhouses they had just built in Fort Mojave. They didn't have to make a lot of money, just pay for themselves. Well... to start. But by the winter of the first year, we had dialed in the cherry tomatoes and were working on the larger salsa ones, like beefy Tomas and Romas. More meat with less juice and seeds. We had all the Mexican restaurants pounding down our doors. They were really the ones who financed everything else. The solar arrays, wind water spider webs, and the barrel turbines... all of it. The tomatoes paid for it."

Nash pushed her finger along the crack on the table. "So you were there when it all started."

"In the beginning, there were only four of us. Lambert, Holstrom, and a physics teacher from UCLA by the name of Don Parsons. But I think he got a job offer somewhere back east and left. But yeah, it was just us."

"You ran the greenhouses alone?"

She snorted as she shook her head. "It takes three to five people for each of the large houses. We harvested a lot of produce. Just about a truckload every day. That's a two-ton box van. When the carrots and cucumbers were running, they would jump to two trucks a day easily. At peak, we had gypsy truckers swing in for anything they could take and sell to restaurants down in Arizona. But the usual was one truck for Fort Mojave and Bullhead City and the other for the casinos in Laughlin, Nevada. So we had another couple of guys who could legally drive the trucks."

"They were locals?"

"Yes, a couple were Mojaves, but mostly Latinos. But they didn't live at the ranch. They lived in town or across the river."

Nash looked at her notes. "You said there was a twenty-first..."

Colby nodded as she poured the apple cider into the glasses. "Yes. I've read your list. You were only missing Jana Zabriskie and me. They hired Jana to help in the heavy harvest but mostly to cook meals we could stand to eat. Some of the early attempts by most of us were a disaster. I think there's a large pot with oatmeal concrete and a wooden spoon in it parked somewhere out in the north forty. We didn't try our hands at making large breakfasts after that."

"Where did she come from?"

Colby shrugged her shoulder and face as she sipped on the cider. "I think she just randomly showed up one day. Strange, now that I think about it. One morning, we scrambled with dry cereal, and that night, we sat down to pot roast. Or whatever she cooked that night. I think the next morning, there were pancakes, bacon, and eggs. Then, it was a never-ending stream of the home cooking your mother never knew how to throw together for four... much less twenty-one."

Muna narrowed one eye. *Zabriskie, not Bright?* "Did anyone question the flowers and herbs she was putting in the food?"

The woman's eyes widened. "You live for years thinking the biscuits out of the refrigerator in those exploding rolls are the best. Then, you wake up to biscuits with fresh lavender or fresh chives on your omelet, and then there are pinion nuts in the quiche. You stop pinching yourself and don't even think about asking what all the yummy smells and tastes are."

"Until they kill you."

Nash studied the confused look on the woman's face. She nodded and pulled up the small list on her phone. "Wolfbane, foxglove, hemlock, belladonna, hollyhock, castor bean or ricin. Does anything sound familiar?"

Colby nodded. "There was some foxglove down in house three. I think the hollyhock was by the back door. It was a beautiful red bush..."

Muna nodded. "And extremely deadly."

The blond frowned. "Where did you get the list?"

Muna glanced at Nash. "Tox screen in the autopsy report. It's some of what you all ate for dinner. But you didn't die."

She shuddered with a grimace. "But I was very sick. I never throw up. But I woke up at about eleven and threw up. I knew something was wrong. I had put my stuff in the van during the afternoon because I was going to go spend a few weeks with friends camping on the beach down on Baja, so I grabbed the last few things and drove into town. Usually, the clinic was open until midnight, but they were closed. I had thrown up four times since waking up and felt a little better. So, I gassed up and headed for San Diego. I heard the news a couple of days later."

Nash looked at her list. "What did you eat that night?"

"The doc and her husband were going to go down to Columbia with another doctor to do surgery with Doctors Without Borders. They would be gone over Thanksgiving, so Jana made a no-holds-barred-everything Thanksgiving dinner. I had a little of the turkey, some of the baked sweet potatoes, and a small salad, but I wasn't as hungry as some others. And I'm sensitive to rye, and the biscuits were rye-based... so I didn't. Oh, and there was flan for dessert, but my system doesn't process the sweet or the dairy so good. So I didn't partake."

Frank cleared his throat. "Do you remember Jana eating?"

Colby's eyes narrowed as she looked at the table. Searching for the answer. "She hardly ever sat with us. She was always serving. It was kind of like a waitress in a restaurant. Nobody questioned it. It was just the way she worked—always cooking, serving, and then cleaning up. Some of us would ask if she wanted any help, but she never did. So we stopped asking." She slowly blinked as she looked up at Frank. "But to answer your question. I don't think she did. And if she did, it was out in the kitchen. But not with us."

Nash looked down at Frank. He shook his head. She looked at Muna typing on her other computer.

Muna looked up at Colby. "Are you sure about her last name?"

She squinted one eye. "Maybe a correct spelling? I had run on what you said on the radio: Jana Bright. But now I'm running Zabriskie, and I'm getting nothing."

Colby shook her head. "Some Fridays, I would see the small envelope tacked to the notice board. Lambert's handwriting was shit, so he printed it. It was Zab and then a small space before the risk and a space before the final I and E. I see patterns in things. I always saw the risk in her name and chuckled at how risky she was. We never knew how risky it was to let her cook."

Nash frowned. "What's wrong with Zabriskie?"

Muna looked up. "All I come up with is an old move. Zabriskie Point. No driver's license or person named Jana."

24

DETAILS

THE AGENT in the Tyvek suit and slippers groaned on the floor. "Why?"

The woman looked down from the ladder with a harmonic sneer of sympathy and understanding. The twirling brush paused and pulled back from the cabinet door. "Because the instructions said every surface from the floor to the ceiling. And if you don't enjoy wallowing around on the floor, you can always try to climb up here again."

She knew her partner had a fear of step stools, much less the ladders required to do a proper job of dusting on upper cabinets. She had provided prints on one case where everything else had been clean or smeared. The criminal had reached all four fingers deep and high on an upper cabinet. Ever after, she dusted to the ceiling. An agent never knew when another killer would stand seven feet in their stockings.

Another agent in a bunny suit stepped into the doorway. "We're just wrapping up in cabin three. How are you guys doing?" He looked down at the agent dusting the lower cabinets. "Other than lying down on the job?"

The agent on the floor held up his middle finger.

"Bingo!"

The investigators' eyes fixated on the woman perched atop the ladder. Her index finger was gently touching the corner of the door—holding it open. A hand's width in from the door frame, a set of black fingerprints stood out amid an otherwise dust-covered cabinet door. Her smug expression confirmed their suspicions. All the traces elsewhere in the kitchen were smudged or wiped away with a powerful cleaning solution.

They all looked at the other doors of the kitchen. Every door's surface was dust gray from the graphite-based powder, but there were no prints. Not even smudges or smears. She turned on the ladder. "How did you do in the cabin?"

Another agent shuffled up and looked in the kitchen. He took in the woman on the ladder and the man on the floor. The woman pointed at the prints. The agent groaned. "We have a little more to check out."

"Chop-chop. Time is miles to escape."

The men all groaned. They had all heard the same words drilled into them at Quantico, Langley, and now from their team leader in Los Angeles.

OZ LEANED BACK AND SMILED. "I BET THEY WISH YOU would retire."

She smiled. "The day I retire, it will become a testosterone slugfest between Miami and Chicago. The only reason we have the highest clear rate is because I keep on their asses to do the job right the first time."

He snorted with a soft exhale. "And the lessons come hard in the field. Good catch on the hand touch in the middle of the door. What made you think of dusting the middles?"

"Oh Oz. How many dinners did I have you over for in Quantico?

Unlike you, I work in my kitchen to get it dirty. Not dusty like yours."

He smiled. "It would surprise you at how much I've grown up since then. The only time Kathrine cooks is when I don't come home on time. But around here, we do a lot of eating in. It beats the heck out of sack lunches. And at least I know Mike is getting at least one warm meal a day."

"How's the new kid?"

"Boat or agent?"

She chuckled. "Both."

He rolled his eyes. "At least I don't think I have to haul the boat out this year. Last year's dry dock almost killed my bankroll. But this year, it's all about varnishing the woodwork."

She smiled. Their mutual love of sailing and boats stopped at her, listening. She'd rather fly or drive. "And the fledgling agent?"

His face was passive but not inattentive. "I don't know anymore whether you're talking about Muna or Mike. Her office space is larger than our entire forensic laboratory. She's about eighty pounds and only five feet, but she fills the space. Her computer, which she built herself, I may add, is more powerful than the one the twenty agents downstairs share. Her organizational skills are off the chart. And if we need some scut labor, she's already doing it. She's into work before either of us are, and I've called back late at night, and she's still answering the phone."

"Rumors have it she will shoot the combat Olympics this winter."

Oz washed his hand over his face. "You didn't hear it from me, but I think she will be the name to beat in marksman, combat, or sniper. And if she competes in the sniper, the team will be with Nash Running Bear. And they will probably shoot as the other team as well. We looked it up. They can do both teams. Muna shooting for one and Nash shooting for the other."

"What do they shoot?"

He rolled his eyes. "On our long range, they shoot the center out of the rolling target. Nash with her nine, and Muna has fallen in love with a Luger my father brought back from the Second World War. They may have to change the rules."

"And if they have to shoot rifles?"

"I'm not sure how Muna is with a rifle. But Nash is qualified. I think I saw her Marine best, which was better than a thousand yards. I don't know what she hit, but they marked it as a kill. And it wasn't her rifle. It was her sniper's fifty. He was getting his body stitched back together."

The woman sighed and picked up a folder. "So your junior might be our savior on these prints." She looked over at her monitor's camera. "It would be nice to know someone is backing up my hard work."

Oz nodded with a small dip of his head. "Muna is in the field right now. But I sent the file to her and into the next room. She knew we needed someone in the office to keep Mike and me on our toes... so to speak. So she arranged for a temporary replacement. The girl is at one of those computer competitions, but when she gets back, she can start on the file and doing the intensive search we're capable of."

The voice echoed out of the dark corner of the office. "I got back four hours ago, Oz. Takeout Chinese already came and went. Yours is in the refrigerator to nuke if you get hungry. And if that's Agent Margerie Atwater, there were no initial hits in the California crime database. The federal takes longer, but I have Arizona and Nevada already running."

Oz rolled his enormous eyes. "My mistake. She's back. No hits in California, so she's already running Arizona and Nevada and the federal government." He leaned in. "She has scary connections, and I know there will be others scouring the internet as well."

A bowl of orange sherbet landed on the desk. "We aren't scary. Just not understood. I'm going to bed. The computers are running."

He leaned to his left and watched the gray sweats with a large backhoe on top of the stacked words Deep Six printed on the back.

Team Slug graced the backside of the pants. Oz called out. "How did you guys do?"

She held up her right middle finger. "We're number one in the world." She disappeared into the dark of the office room and turned left.

The other agent in Los Angeles laughed. "I can see you have your hands full. Are you going to keep this one, too?"

His eyes closed as his head wobbled slightly. "We can't compete. Our pay is a stipend compared to what she started at a few months ago. And she doesn't like guns, so there's no interest."

"Have they tried to steal your junior away?"

"They offered last year. They have a dorm but no shooting range. So we're thankful for what we have and her commitment to duty and service. Or whatever keeps her here."

The woman nodded. "I always double-count my small blessings. Well, I have a dog to go home to, and the Santa Monica Freeway should be at least somewhat cleared out."

"Keep safe, Maggie. And thanks for the great work."

"I'll send you the bill, Oz. Don't sink the boat."

The screen dulled to a murky shade of gray, illuminated only by the neon FBI logo in its center. Oz slowly rose from his chair, stretching out his creaking joints. A smirk spread across his face as he flipped off the desk light, still clinging to the ancient ritual he practiced for so many years. The rest of the laboratory lights glared brightly overhead—as if in defiance. They mocked him with their LED luminescence—an impenetrable force refusing to yield control back to the office personnel. He grudgingly acknowledged the times had changed, yet still felt incensed at being unable to control the lights on his own terms.

He grabbed his jacket. As he walked out through the darkened office area, he stopped. He looked at the ceiling of darkened lights. Only the corner behind Chip's wall of computer screens had a flickering glow. He had watched Muna's computers long enough to know the flickering fireplace light was an algorithm running comparisons. From the almost static glow, he also knew it was doing so at an extremely high speed.

He glanced back at the fully lit archway to the laboratory and back up at the dark ceiling of Muna's empire. His small smile pulled at one side of his face. *I need to remember to ask her how she hacked the system.*

THE FIVE-LINED THE FRONT PORCH, WATCHING THE DARK street. Frank moaned. "I'm stuffed. But if he walked out here with another platter of those oysters…"

Jazz unsnapped the snap under her loosened belt. "You'd have to fight me for them."

Muna leaned over and scratched the offered belly. Her voice was quiet but carried. "See what we don't have to suffer with? It pays to eat logically."

Nash crossed her legs on the woven reed ottoman. "I noticed Oz sent you a file…" She rolled her head to look at the small face looking up. "Fingerprints?"

Muna nodded. "They got a clean set of fingers from their right hand. From the report, the perp had wiped the entire kitchen with a bleach cleaner. What wasn't cleaned off was at least smeared into streaks. They pulled some of those, but they had nothing to salvage."

"And the four prints?"

Muna's snort was soft as she sat up. "Better than the ones you rolled at the Q. Even at only two hundred percent, I could see the loops, whorls, and what looked like an old childhood scar. So hopefully, we can get a perfect match."

Nash frowned. "How could you know it was from childhood instead of last year or something?"

Frank chuffed. "Easy. Your hand has gotten larger since you were sixteen. As the length grows, it stretches lateral scars in width. As you get past your twenties, you put on a bit of beef, and the thickness will pull it across the pad."

Nash rolled her head as her narrowed eyes looked like they could shoot lasers. "Speak for yourself, white boy. I've been this height and weight since I played varsity volleyball and basketball as a freshman. Maybe you packed on beef."

Jazz shook her head. "Nope. He weighed a lot more when he was a detective. I think even with all the steel in his back, he's under his old uniform weight. And don't you dare look at me." She rolled forward slightly to look at Muna. "Where's the scar?"

Muna chuckled as she held up her middle finger. "Diagonal through the lower part of the center of the pad. The tearing is minimal, but there were four signs of pull from lengthening. It's been a few minutes since I was taking those courses at Quantico, but my guess is she cut herself in the kitchen when she was maybe eight or ten. It's an awkward time when fine motor skills haven't translated to tools, so it's a common age for deep wounds." As she drew back her hand, she looked at the pink line across the heel of her left palm.

The gravel of Frank's voice was the call to bedtime. "What power of enlargement?"

"I was only at five hundred. The screen on the laptop can only do so much. Back at the office, I can go ten thousand, but the file isn't good enough. So maybe six hundred. But even at five, I saw plenty of the tearing."

Nash leaned to scratch at the head now, at the arm of her chair. Powder was ready for a small walk and then bed. "Did you ask Chips to run the systems?"

Muna rolled forward. "Didn't have to. She got it the same time Oz did. Nothing came back from California's general search. It probably was the garbage dump of state and local employees. She's running the outlying states tonight, as well as starting the federal systems."

Jazz rolled back and buckled her belt. "When we get back to

your office, I'll see if I can't get you into the Orange County, San Diego County, and maybe Riverside and San Bernardino County's systems as well. A lot of stuff gets into the county systems and never makes it further. States and counties have been screaming for decades about needing a central interstate system, not only for fingerprints but for everything. But the knuckle-dragging continues. They can bust a burglar six times in California. He serves several months but still has no record that an Arizona Highway Patrol stop can call up. And the perps know this. So they drift from state to state, picking up and paying or serving petty terms because they don't have two strikes in that state."

25

HARVESTING

Oz LOOKED at the enlarged set of prints spread over the two forty-inch screens. Muna played with the contrast, but it was already clean. "Maggie said it was one of her cleanest harvests yet." He pointed at each of the four as if he were shooting targets. "Clean. Crisp. Complete. And crunchy." He smiled at Nash.

She chuckled. "Don Juan Olynyk." She rolled her head over to look at Oz. "He loved his alternate alligators of alliterations."

Oz chuckled.

Muna looked over her shoulders at the others and then went back to the computer. She called up her specialized search engines. "Frank?"

Jazz snorted. "Wait a minute. He's getting out his flip phone. But meanwhile, here." She laid a perfectly printed URL down in front of Muna. "I would have typed it in for you, but after seeing what kind of monster this is, I'm not touching it."

The disjointed voice rose from the corner. "I was thinking about tweaking a few things, but I peeked in the box and realized you were hiding a server somewhere else."

Muna laughed. "The server is in the Cayman Islands. But if you have any suggestions for the farm, I can pass them along. But anything here, short of one of Slug's old throwaway water-cooled gaming towers, I'm all in."

Chips rose in the dark. The computer screen's eerie greenish flickering firelight lit up her face in an early talky look. "What's wrong with water-cooled? And when does Slug ever throw anything away?"

Jazz groaned. "He doesn't. He enshrined his first winning diaper in a plexiglass case. It's next to his first commodore computer and his first two mice."

Muna leaned back to one side and frowned at Jazz. "He had mice for pets? What are they—stuffed?"

Jazz rolled her eyes closed. "His first wired mouse and his first wireless. Really? Slug? Near an animal? The closest he ever got to a pet was listening to Frank talk about his coyotes."

Frank growled. "Cut the kid some slack. His computers bring us in a boatload of money."

Chips walked around the end of the table. "Not boats. They are called dredges, barges, or tugs. No boats. And if it's larger than twenty-five tons, it's a ship. So what's wrong with water-cooled?"

Muna swung around and held up her hands. "Hey. To each their own. I just don't trust water in my tower."

Chips pointed over Muna's wall of screens. "Have you peeked in my tower? I'm running dual EK Matrix water block systems with a four-twenty extra thick radiator with push-pull fan fields. It's my seventh water-cooled tower, and there are zero leaks. My clock speed is twice yours, and I'm nowhere near over-clocking. Maybe you need to get off your purist high horse and try some perks the twenty-first century offers." She spun on her heel and returned to her empire in the dark.

Nash leaned into Jazz and muttered. "What just happened?"

Jazz smirked. "You just watched the dick measuring and smack-down these nerds do all the time. Watch for your nerd to be doing some serious research and then spending a butt-load of dough on new tech stuff soon." She waved her hand at the wall of six monitors. "And the girls do it better than the guys. The only guy Chips hasn't pecked off the tower is Slug. But only because she respects him for what he's built. But the betas are all fair game. And it's what we do—game." She smiled at Nash's small nod.

"Yes. Yes, you do."

Nash pointed at Muna, typing on her dark web keyboard and screen. The letters looked a lot like what Chips had just rattled off.

Jazz held out her hand. Nash quietly slapped it as they both nodded.

Jazz yawned. "It's been a long day. I'm going to go investigate room five." She smiled large and toothy. "The one getting the morning light. What time do you go shoot?"

"We're on the allies by six." Nash frowned. "Did you bring a weapon?"

Frank smiled and pulled up his sweatshirt to reveal his pistol grip. Jazz pulled up her pant leg. "I only brought the PPK."

Nash pushed out her lower lip. "You're both on the Orange County Reserves, right? We have ammo for both. Muna runs a hundred rounds through her PPK before her personal Luger and then her issue Sig and finishes with what's left in her hand with a Desert Eagle."

Jazz thought about the litany of the guns and how Nash had said them. Her head twitched back. "I've always wanted to try a Desert Eagle. But doesn't it push her around a lot?"

Muna tilted her head back. "I'm right here, you know. And not anymore. I've gotten used to it, and I also got it double magna ported. The flares take a bit of getting used to, but it's gentler than the Sig."

She spun the chair around. "Let me sleep on it. But I think I can let strange hands caress my eagle." She smiled at the sexual innuendo. She tapped the corner of the running algorithm. "San Diego has four possibilities so far, and two in San Bernardino. Orange and Riverside are still zero. So I would say our girl is a San Diego girl. We'll know more in the morning. See you at five."

Jazz frowned and pointed at Nash. "Nash said six."

Muna and Nash both nodded. "We'll still be on the range at six, but we start at five. Come down when you want. Just push the basement button and hold it until it stops. The range is in the hidden second basement."

Jazz looked over at Frank.

He fluttered his lips. "What. No dog to wake me up at the crack of dawn…? I'm sleeping in."

The range master glanced up at the clock before watching the four switch weapons. He gave a little smirk as he watched the two less experienced shooters hitting their targets in random areas compared to the agents, who had an impressive ability of precision. The master dropped his head and went back to reading his manual on how to improve his racing engine's power.

Maybe the new guys will get better by six o'clock.

DEBRA LOOKED ACROSS THE DESERT AT THE HOUSE WITH the new roof. She thought about the young couple she had seen working on the house. The extra phone line could only be one thing. They had pulled in a better cable for higher-speed internet. They weren't going to an office anytime soon. It wouldn't take them long to become bored and nose into their neighbor's lives. It had happened before, and it would happen again.

She rolled her eyes closed as she turned. *The desert can only hide so many harvested bodies.* It would force her to move—like last time.

"Dorothy. It's time to go to work."

The woman looked up from the plate on the table. "Is today a garden day?"

Debra took the plate up and placed it in the sink. Running some water on it, she used the scrubber to remove most of the left food. Originally, she had not liked the idea of the garbage disposal, but the landlord said he thought it was okay with the extra-large septic tank. He had shown her the access cover, which is the size of a city manhole cover. She said she didn't believe it was as big as he said, so he opened the cover to show her.

If the new neighbors didn't force her to move, the large man choking the septic tank would eventually force the issue. Either way, it was something she knew would happen before next summer's heat. By then, the neighbors would wonder about the smell of the covered manhole. The houses weren't close, but smells carried across the desert.

26

HITS AND MISSES

JAZZ GENTLY FLEXED her hand open and closed as they walked.

Frank chuckled. "That's what pockets are for."

She peeked over at the man and then down at his hand flexing in his jacket. The burp was more of a stifled laugh. "Rule number one?"

He bobbed his head. "Never let them see you sweat…"

Jazz watched the motorcycle pass. The man looked more like he was trying to sing the YMCA song than control the large bike with the ape hangers. "Or show how much it hurts."

The two had suffered the same megalomaniacal sadistic hand-to-hand combat instructor at the police academy.

Nash leaned forward to see around Jazz. She snickered as Frank's hand stopped moving in the jacket pocket. "Don't feel bad. It took me a few months before I could keep up with her and not watch for bruises."

"I'm right here, you know."

Nash sidestepped and rested her arm on top of the shorter woman's head. "Did someone hear something?"

Muna kept walking but with a slightly larger smile. The taunting between the two was the closest either of them knew of sisterly give and take. For both, she knew they'd take it and dish out more.

Jazz ran her left hand through her spiked hair and snuck a peek at Frank. "Maybe we should dig a basement under Deep Six."

He stared over at the tall woman and then laughed. "You know the small lot behind us?"

"The truck dealer?"

He nodded as they crossed the street. "That's the one. It's almost three acres, and he wants to retire."

Jazz glanced over at Nash. Nash laughed. "I'm not even in the rarefied air of you guys, but even I can figure out it's cheaper to build a new shooting range than dig out a basement."

Muna snickered. "Then sign up memberships and make money. Heck. If it was twenty-four-seven, even I'd want a membership."

Nash stopped with her hand on Jazz's arm. "Don't. Don't do it. It was the only thing stopping her from taking Ming's job offer before."

Jazz's eyebrow rose. "Really? That was all that stopped you?"

Muna shrugged. "Kind of. After all, you have the dorm and better food…"

"Just not a shooting range."

Muna winced. "See, that's where things get squishy."

Jazz narrowed one eye. "If you're shooting your three personal weapons every morning, the ammo has to set you back… what? About eighty a day?"

The smaller woman shrugged. "More like thirty a day. Werner has a reloader set up in the back-office. And from what I save on not renting an apartment or owning a car…"

"Still, it's a major chunk out of a federal paycheck." The implications hung in the air.

Nash squeezed Jazz's arm a little harder. "Until you figure in the Olympics fund."

Jazz frowned. "The what?"

"The guys all did the same math. But every quarter, she takes everyone to task. Her eyesight is seventeen-twenty. After she competes this year at the WIFLE competitions, the guys will also buy her the correct weapons for shooting anything at the Olympics. Meanwhile, we all chip in a bit to the fund, and it picks up the ammo expense. If she keeps shooting, she's happy, which makes us happy."

Frank frowned at Muna. "We can help with the fund..."

Muna held up her hands. "You guys do enough. Heck, you loaned us Chips for a while."

Jazz snorted. "Oh, you still have her for longer. Slug is trying to figure out how to build her an office with a hardware assembly area but also let her help the girls upstairs. She's the first try at a hybrid team member we've ever had."

Muna's forehead furrowed. "But the boys crunch code like nobody's business..."

Jazz nodded. "You're not wrong. They can crunch better than they play games. But with research, they don't have the creativity the girls do. So, they suck."

Muna wove her head around in the air. "But he sure slammed together a sweet blaster castle for her."

Jazz snickered softly as she slowly shook her head. "The boys didn't send anything up. She locally sourced everything up here. She built her own machine. But Slug has seen the specs. And if she didn't qualify to be on his team before, she has now."

Muna's voice was soft with awe. "But it's a monster..."

Nash leaned into Jazz. "Aha... I think my girl just got her first crush."

Jazz pursed her smile as she wiggled her eyebrows. "They fall so hard the first time."

THE COMPUTER ROOM WAS SILENT, EXCEPT FOR THE occasional clicking of a keyboard. Bunny had learned to type on an old manual typewriter. Someone carrying it around without a case had rubbed away the face. There was more silver metal than the word Royal. She had laughed when the pawnshop had sold it to her for a crumpled five dollars she had earned from a weekend of babysitting. Only by trial and error did she get it working. It now sat on a shelf of honor in her small house.

"Hey, Bunny?"

She squinted across the long room. The small young woman could pass for her daughter, but was a foot shorter than her actual daughter. "Yeah, Baby?"

The young woman's choice of seats wasn't lost on anyone's love for irony and poking fun at convention. She turned from her corner desk. "Can you come look at this? This doesn't make sense."

Bunny smiled and indulged her inner child. Digging in her heels, she pushed her rolling chair the length of the room. "What am I looking at?"

Baby pointed both hands at the two monitors on the corner walls. "I'm running a hard check on all of California's records I can get into." She waved her left hand. "This has a ninety-seven percent hit, but it's from like twenty-five years ago. But it's a sealed juvenile record." She dropped her index finger and pointed at the lower screen. "This is an emergency room record I found that would corroborate the scar."

Bunny studied the other top monitor screen. "And this one...?"

"A ninety-four hit, and only seven years ago."

Bunny narrowed her eyes. "Still in San Diego County. So what's the problem?"

Baby turned and gazed at the older woman. "Read the names."

Bunny's eyes bounced from screen to screen. Her voice was small. "Oh, shit." She stared at Baby. "Get out the bigger backhoe. You need to find birth records. Something stinks. But I want live squawking ducks before I call Jazz." She rested her hand on the girl's shoulder. "Great work. Now go for the throat."

Jazz read the text. Frowning, she handed the phone to Frank. While he read, she gazed across the cavernous stretch of the airport. The plastic and chrome of the seating lent nothing of homeyness to the utilitarian combine, churning passengers in and out of the air. The seats seemed designed to fit scrawny butted teenagers. But the full-sized adults squirmed every five minutes as they resisted personal posterior paralysis.

Frank handed the phone back. "What do you want to do?"

She thumbed the phone and sat back. "Bunny? Jazz."

"I figured you'd call. I, for one, never saw it coming."

Jazz sighed. "How certain is Baby about the kid?"

She could hear the exhaustion in the woman's sigh. "She's been at it all day. I got here about five this morning, and she was already in her corner. I didn't think to look at what she was working on. We had tasked her with mapping the Houston channel. So I figured she had come in early to get a jump on it."

Jazz chuckled tiredly. "Baby? Early? Fat chance. It was more like she did the channel last night and then decided to spend a few minutes on this."

"Bingo."

Jazz glanced at Frank, with his arm draped over his eyes. "What do you need from us? We're at the airport, but the plane doesn't drop out of the sky until midnight." Frank raised his arm enough to peek over.

"Probably nothing tonight. I sent Baby up to the dorm about an hour ago. I almost had to threaten to unplug her station. Something's wormed its way into her head, but she won't talk. Maybe you can talk to her in the morning."

Jazz leaned forward and rested her elbows on her knees. "Have you sent this to Chips?"

Bunny blew out her air. "Not yet. I wanted to talk to you first. This shit is way left field for these kids. Even I'm kind of lost here."

"Let me talk to Frank a minute. I'll call you back."

"Okay."

Her hand fell forward with the phone. As she took a deep breath, she gently leaned back into the seat. She watched the somnambulistic movements of the almost brain-dead passengers shuffling toward their gates. The floor-to-ceiling cold glass was black except where the work lights of the gates surreally penetrated the dark.

"What do you want to do?"

Jazz peeked over at the man who had returned his arm to his face. She wasn't sure if he was trying to sleep or just escaping the bright lights enough to think. "Bunny hasn't sent the files up to Chips yet. I think she's close to the edge on this. But the good news is she sent Baby up to the dorm about an hour ago. If Baby needs to talk, Ming is there. But none of these kids are ready for this kind of stuff."

He slowly folded his body back into sitting. He rubbed his hands on his face. "I don't think you give the girls enough credit. They've done some deep research into some exceptionally dark holes…"

"They signed on for dredging and number crunching. And some gaming. I think we forget they're just kids—for the most part. They're just playing at being adults."

He hung one eyelid as he watched her. "Did you watch the video of the last half hour of the games?"

"Yeah…?"

"That's the intensity I've watched on experienced surfers. It's the focus only coming with maturity… and yet Slug is what? Twenty-four?" He glanced out the window. "Some guys on the SEALs, as much as we tried to beat it into them, never got it." He leaned back. "No, they aren't Muna. They didn't sign up for the crazy train she and Nash ride. But they jumped in and did research for those women like nobody else could do for them. Not the FBI or the boys on Nash's team. Our kids are the best, hands down. And they don't have to come up here to any Super Bowl to prove so to me. They just quietly do it every day. Day in and day out. It blows me away every day. I gave Ming and Tree a bit of pocket change out of my trust. I never imagined our team. A five-million-dollar complex they earned—not in my wildest dreams. But being millionaires before they were twenty-one. Those two had it wired before they ever left UCI." He stood. "For my money? I'm going all in on our team. Tell Bunny to send the files to Chips. We can grab some rooms and then go talk to Nash in the morning."

She stood and stretched. "What about the sealed juvenile record?"

He peered into her drained eyes, recognizing a reflection of himself; he knew all too well how bad he felt. "I'll need sleep and a couple of pots of espresso before I can face the thought of reaching out to old acquaintances who now wear the black robes. Especially since I haven't spoken to any of them in the last decade."

She stared down at his Ramone's last tour T-shirt. She had noticed the frayed holes in the shoulder seam the day before. "Do you have a clean shirt left?"

He growled. "If the airport shop doesn't have anything, we can always find something on Polk Street."

She reached down for her bag. "Let's go change our tickets."

27

DIALING FOR DATA

NASH RAISED one eyebrow as Jazz and Frank walked into the restaurant. Muna frowned at Nash's face and then turned around.

"Where's Chips?"

Nash frowned. "She muttered something about a protein bar and cold cereal. She sounded distracted, and we know better than to get close to her wall of solitude."

Frank sluffed off his jacket. "Yeah, Bunny sent up some files last night. There was no way to warn you guys, so we just let it take its course."

Nash eyed the obviously fresh shirt. The rainbow-colored seal wore a set of headphones. The words alluded to the Marine motto but were Summa Fidelitas. "Super fidelity?"

Muna pulled at his sleeve to turn him around. "Great headphones. And I love the seal." She turned toward Nash. "Superior sound. Half of the gamer's edge is hearing everything." She looked at Jazz for confirmation. "I think Slug said he paid over three grand for his Gold Blocks."

Jazz nodded as she sat next to Nash, moving over. "Custombuilt from the ground up. Essentially, they're expensive hearing aids. He has a bit of clipping in a certain range. Those headphones compensate."

Frank snorted. "After what the team brought home this week, I'll never bean-count anything they need."

Jazz choked. "He mentioned he wants a Lamborghini."

Frank and Muna laughed. "He wasn't talking about a car. It's a custom graphics card driver."

Frank finished the line of thought. "I already ordered six of them from the kid at the games."

Muna giggled. "Gee, Santa…"

Jazz rolled her eyes. "Your T-shirt is in the car. He bought every shirt they had. But I think Slug will have to order his triple-extra-large."

Nash coughed and batted her eyelashes.

Frank growled. "We already know you don't game."

She smiled demurely. "But I was a seal."

Jazz ducked her lips as she pointed at Frank. "Point and match."

As the five approached the wall of monitors, the glow on the back wall was static. Muna stopped. "I don't think she's back there."

Jazz poked Frank. "Go look."

He turned and poked Nash. "It's your fault we hired her. You go look."

"Not without armor."

The voice was small from the laboratory doorway. "Four of the most macho people I know. And every single one is afraid of a little girl." Her hallmark smile and bubbles were gone. This was a young woman dipped in the acid bath of strange reality, and survival was subjective.

They turned to see the young woman standing with a large bowl in her hand. She pushed a spoon in and shoveled the heap of cereal into her mouth. The center of the sweatshirt bore a marked football with the letters UCI. Around the football, the sentiments read *Undefeated Since 1966.*

Frank's forehead wrinkled. "I didn't think UCI had a football program."

She swallowed. "They don't. They played one game in sixty-six against the University of California Santa Cruz and won."

Jazz leaned against Muna's desk. "The banana slugs have football?"

Chips took a smaller bite as she shook her head. "They only played a single game. The score was three to two."

Nash laughed. "That's not a football score."

Jazz leveled her hand against Nash's arm. "It is for a bunch of nerds."

Chips fished a small remote out of her hoodie's kangaroo pocket. "But you're not here for football." She pushed the remote, and Muna's wall of screens wiped into completely new screens.

Muna quietly stepped over to look at the remote. Chips handed her the unit. "My system has now slaved to yours. Not the other way around. It was easier than trying to shoehorn you and Nash back in my tiny pocket." She waved her spoon back and forth at Jazz and Frank. "I didn't expect the southern contingency."

Nash stood with her hands on her hips. She pointed at the old file marked sealed. "That's what you came back for?"

Frank stepped over and nodded. "I was hoping you had friends in low places, and I don't have to make phone calls to people I haven't spoken to since my accident. Even one of those phone calls can stick a grenade in a morning."

She could guess what the questions would sound like. She rested her hand on his shoulder. "Let's look at what we have and see how it plays out. But I appreciate you guys opting out last night and sticking around." She pulled her phone out of her pocket and read the text. "I need to go make a call. Grab some coffee and Chips can bring you guys up to speed. I won't be long."

She looked down. "Let's go take a walk, girl."

Grabbing her light jacket, Frank watched the woman and dog

turn left in the hall toward the elevator. He turned back to the files on the screens.

Nash walked down the long ramp to the side of the loading dock. She thumbed the number.

The voice was all business and used to peeling the families off the wall. "She's okay. We're at the hospital, and they're checking her out. She collapsed right after lunch. My guess is those seven-ounce glasses of water were only fours or fives. Her fingers didn't pass my pinch test. So they might want to keep her overnight and hydrate her while they watch her. I suggested a short battery of tests if they do."

Nash watched the blends of light gray shadowed by darker swirls of the thicker clouds. Powder chose the second tree but only squatted for a few seconds. Powder recognized Nash's leaning against the compound's wall. Her walk slowed and became measured as she watched the street and a few people.

"Her insurance is double platinum, so check her in. Don't let her fight. It's just a sham. She knows she can use a tune-up and the rest. But if they say a couple of days…"

Lele chuckled. "I'll bring her laptop back tomorrow. Maybe with her Linus blanket, she'll let them keep her for a few days. We're good, but the extra attention can't hurt."

"Other than falling, how has she been?"

Nash could hear the nurse suck on her upper lip that she chewed on when she was trying to think of how she wanted to explain her patient. "Back home, we would say she's been off her feed. I don't expect her to wolf down a steak and potatoes, but this week, we've been down to a light breakfast of toast and a poached egg with a small cup of coffee. Lunches seem to be mostly a small salad and a bit of fruit. Some days, she finished, but most of the time, she didn't. Dinner is mostly a bowl of light soup. I'm guessing her calorie intake is under eight hundred."

Nash rocked gently. "I've seen her do that before. I've seen her eat like a hummingbird and still put in a long, hard day. And then, too, I've seen her throw down the T-Bone with a large baked potato and wondered why there wasn't any ice cream in the freezer. But usually, it's only for a day or two. So I'm going to say, bring the laptop and anything else she asks for. Give her the solitude, and let's see where it goes."

"Any idea on how much longer you'll be out there?"

Nash rolled along the wall and waved at Powder. "No idea. The case just took a large left turn, which nobody saw coming. We'll probably have to go back down south. I'll let you know. But tell Mina I'll call her tonight. And I'll try to remember you guys are three ahead of us."

"I'll let her know. And take care of yourself and Powder. I know she misses both of you."

Nash started up the ramp. "Trust me. It's mutual." She thumbed the red icon and slipped the phone back into her pocket, only to pull it back out. She found the text address and poked in the three purple hearts.

The tiny vibration responded as she slipped it into her pocket. She'd save it for bedtime.

She thought about who to call as she pushed the button for the third floor. Lower court judges weren't the usual allies for her investigations. And a judge out of the ninth circuit was the sledgehammer she only wanted a screwdriver for.

Jazz looked back at Nash, taking off her jacket. "Jeez, Frank, what the hell were you spending all the time with the sheriff for if you can't call him?"

Frank's eyes danced as he kept studying the files. "Because he is just as likely to tell me to go fuck myself as who I might have success with. Time solving an enormous case and busting for him didn't exactly make us buddies. Sure, he owes me a big one. But just that fact alone can make a man like him resent me even more. Besides, I'd be asking him for a solid for the feds—not me."

Nash pulled out a chair and sat. "Sheriff of which county?"

Frank grumped. "Orange."

Nash pointed at the header on the file. "But the folder is in San Diego...?"

Jazz rocked her chair back. "It doesn't matter. I mean, yeah, it does... but when it's integral to an investigation, crossing county lines is nothing."

"What if the county is more than a few hundred miles away? But still in California?"

Frank tossed his head back and forth and finally stood. "I require more coffee for this. My head is already hurting." He paused at the doorway to the laboratory and turned. He studied the floor as he frowned. "The judge..." He looked up. "The judge would still need to be in San Diego."

"But the request to unseal the file? It could come from the sheriff in... say... Harking County?"

Frank rolled his eyebrows in a single pump. "It's worth a shot. We just need to figure out which courthouse he needs to call and which judge."

The screen flickered, and a yellow sticky note filled half of the screen. Muna spun around and stood. "I require more jet fuel." She pointed at the screen as she followed Frank. "You're welcome. I also texted it to Thomas."

Nash snorted. "Jeez. I hope he's up by now."

Her pocket vibrated. She chuckled. "There he is now." She looked at the screen and laughed even harder. She pushed the green icon under the word *Uncle*. "Hey, Indian. Are you rummaging around your teepee?"

"Funny little rabbit. Sunup was half a day ago. We're shopping for the new freezer." She could hear the wind moaning between his cheek and the phone.

She smiled as she spun around to cross her feet on the desk. "Driving around looking for roadkill?"

"We jerked the roadkill buck last week. I have a friend over on the coast. The fires have driven the deer down to the highway. The highway patrol guys have been dressing out roadkill for two weeks.

He's already vacuum-bagged over a ton of jerky. Tommy and I'll go fishing later this fall when halibut is running." The phone connection was scratchy for a moment. "He said he doesn't know why Muna sent some elephant file he can't open on his little phone."

Nash laughed at the image of an elephant and then frowned. "Where is he? On the toilet?"

Uncle laughed. "No. We're on the east slope of Shasta. Dutch Withers died in July. His daughter gave the kid his old thirty aught six. Dutch dialed in the scope on the football field. He didn't enjoy walking so much. So we thought we'd come up here and see what we could get. Tommy has a doe tag, and I have a buck tag."

"But where is Thomas?"

The chuckle sounded more like a bunch of rocks pouring out of a leather bag. "Tommy bagged a mountain goat. He's downslope field-dressing it. He's going to learn the only thing on a rock goat is hard work and little meat."

Nash rolled her eyes as Muna came back and shoved Nash's feet off the corner of her desk. "Have some respect."

Muna ignored the snickers from the other two as she sat.

Nash groaned. "I have to go take care of some light work. But when Thomas finishes learning his lesson about what to shoot or not shoot. Tell him it's a sealed juvenile record we require a judge to unseal. We need to look at the file. It's down in San Diego, but it only needs a sheriff to make the call. Once the judge signs off, they can redirect it up here to San Francisco and Muna. She's the lead on the research."

"How is Mighty Mouse doing?"

Nash glanced over at the other end of the extended desk. "She needs to go shopping for larger britches."

"She just needs to take Powder for more walks. I'll let Tommy know. He's screaming about all the bones or something. Time to feed the vultures."

28
OLD PAPER

Nash and Muna were used to seeing the upper right monitor, which only displayed information from the dark web. It flickered to an old newspaper. Chips walked around the end of the wall of monitors. "Oh. It's that monitor. Hmm... I thought it was..." She looked at the other four. "Sorry." She pointed at the small article at the bottom. "Page seven news. Says they arrested a troubled boy for poisoning neighborhood cats."

Nash frowned. "When?"

Chips slumped her hip against the desk as she distractedly picked at her thumb. She glanced at the screen and squinted. "August. Eighty-three. It's in a San Diego suburb. Poway."

Frank squinted reflectively. "Poway? In the early eighties? Tough rural area. Mostly marginal middle-class or poorer."

"Does it give a name?"

Frank and Jazz harmonized. "Juvenile."

Jazz rolled her eyes as she continued with caustic disdain. "We don't want to stigmatize the poor children for practicing murder. It's why they seal the juvenile records. And then we must try them as beginners all again when they decide to try their skills on humans as adults."

Nash looked at Jazz with a deadpanned face. "You don't miss it at all. Do you?"

The spiked head rolled to look at Frank. "Only he got to hit the streets. I knew how to type. So, they made me fly a desk."

"Horseshit. You're just the only one who didn't do it with two fingers." He looked over at Nash. "But her organizational skills were miles ahead of the other desk weenies. Imagine their surprise to find out she was going to night school to be a hot-shot lawyer. The office has been walking backward since then."

Chips rolled her eyes as she looked down at Muna. She twitched her head toward her corner and then rolled around and retreated.

Nash watched Muna click her mouse a few places to make it look like she was working. She had done it herself. It was how the system in Washington kept track of whether people were working or not. The system also recognized if you had pulled up a game of solitaire. Nash smiled as Muna quietly stood and wandered over to the distant corner castle.

Muna leaned against the wall. "What did you have in mind?"

The blond turned her chair. Her right leg was bent tight with her barefoot on the seat. Her chin rested on her knee. "How far does my contract with the FBI extend?"

Muna frowned. "Like in working permanently for the FBI?"

The young woman's eyes grew enormous. "Oh, gawd no. I'd get stuck with those guys down on the main floor." She shuddered. "No. I mean ethically."

Muna pointed back toward her desk. "Did you steal some of my pork rinds?"

Chips exploded in stifled laughter as she clapped both hands over her mouth. Her head shook, but her eyes screamed. She couldn't trust her mouth not to laugh out loud.

"Okay. But just so you know, those pork rinds will rip your head off and shit in your neck if you don't eat hot all the time."

Chips held up her right index finger. "I licked one. Once."

When they both stopped snickering, Chips continued. "No.

About doing research. You know what kind of stuff we can dredge up at work..."

Muna wasn't going to let this one go by so easily. "Yeah. Mud, sand, dirt, and rocks. What's your point?"

Chips guffawed. "That is what the boys do. Well, okay, I'm technically on the boys' team, but for the research... I'm all girl."

Muna turned and sat on the corner of the desk. "So, what did you have in mind?"

Chips glared at the corner of the desk hidden by the black leather pants. Her growl was quiet but sharp as a dirk. "Some respect..."

Muna immediately stood.

Chips offered her hand out at the desk corner. "Please. But it goes both ways."

"I'll stand." Muna's voice was as flat and deadpan as her face.

Chips rolled her eyes closed. "I insist."

Muna leaned an inch onto the desk.

"When you're the new kid, people don't really pay attention to you. When you're a quiet kid, the same applies. I learn more about people by listening and watching. I was the youngest of nine kids. My brothers had friends who didn't want to go home. Mom said nothing, but she saw the bruises. One night, they took the neighbor kid to the hospital. It was the first time I ever heard my father lie— he said it was my brother who fell out of a tree. The police came and questioned him because the doctor knew it wasn't a fall. The cops let it go only after my father made a deal with them. They wouldn't report it if my father told them the truth. It took a couple of years, but his father was finally arrested. But the boy spent a long time in the hospital."

Muna waved her finger around the small area, the computer, and finally her butt. "What are we talking about here, Chips?"

"You sitting on my desk? No. But you can't get territorial about your desk and then disrespect someone else's."

Muna frowned. "I refinished all those desks out there..."

Chips flexed her head around in a figure-eight until her neck rattled with a string of cracks. "On company time or in the middle of the night? Oh, wait… you live here. Same as I live at Deep Six. We don't pay rent, but it doesn't make the territory ours. Does it? When you print a figure on the 3-D printer? Is it yours or the company's?" Her head ground for one last large crack. "You see, this isn't about the desk, the figurines, or where we live—or don't live. It's about how we hold things like boundaries."

"Boundaries…"

Chips nodded. "You and Nash are more than sisters. You're like clones. But it's like neither one of you had siblings, so you poke at each other to find where the boundaries are."

"She has a sister."

The young blond laid her head over onto her left shoulder and smiled wanly. "Close?"

Muna held her stare for a minute and admitted defeat. "No."

"But she was a jarhead." She held up her hand. "My brother Jerry is a jarhead. But my point is, she shit where they shit. She slept where they slept. It's the team way. They swam, she swam. They shot, she shot. Everything was them doing the same things." Muna nodded. "But when it was all said and done, she wasn't one of the boys. Not because she was female. But because she was the officer."

"And…?"

"I'm not FBI. And someday, I'll maybe do something and be Deep Six like Bunny or Slug or Petey. But until that time… I'm just the new girl in the corner."

Muna gently vibrated her head. "Nope. Baby is the girl in the corner."

Chips smiled. "Yes. Yes, she is. But Slug is building me a corner office." She let the implication hang in the air.

Muna's eyes slowly narrowed as she thought of the implications.

Chips rocked her chair. "Yeah. Not even Ming has an office. She shares the special room with Tree and Jazz. It's just the adult table."

"So is the special room for you a good thing or…"

She cut her off. "I don't know. We'll see. But it's like here. Mike is in the forensic lab. And Oz's world is the autopsy. I'm guessing you came in at half the size of them, dicked around for a little while, and then staked your claim to this empire. The boys grumbled, but the truth is, they wouldn't have it any other way."

"And Nash?"

Chips snorted. "She's a marine. She's fine wherever she is. I'll bet she can still sleep standing up. Shoot her, and she still insists on driving."

"Flying."

"Flying what?"

Muna smiled. "A few years ago, she got shot during a raid. They called in a helicopter to medevac her and Powder. They had to knock her out, so she didn't get up and fly the helicopter herself because they were flying too slow."

Chips held out her hands. "See. Jarhead. And she probably doesn't remember you knocking her feet off your desk because it didn't matter. Not her being relaxed. Not you polishing your desk, or even you thinking you were being disrespected. None of it. It doesn't matter… or it isn't the important parts. Why do you think she hops a fly out here at the least provocation? Because some weenie told her she had to get out here?" Her head wagged. "She likes it here. She loves her wife, but if her wife could work from here… where do you think they would live?"

"But her job isn't here… really…"

"But her little sister is here."

Muna took a slow breath. She looked at the computer screens. "What does this have to do with ethics and you working for the FBI?"

Chips watched the dark face as she gently leaned forward and clicked on a couple of icons on different screens.

As she leaned back in the squeaking chair, her right hand picked at her left thumb. "The newspaper was the only safe thing I found."

Muna leaned in. "Who is Danial Scalise?"

"I dug around. There were police reports of people finding their cats and dogs poisoned in the neighborhood in Poway. There is sound evidence of serial murderers practicing as children on neighborhood pets." She clicked on another icon. A long list of names appeared. "This was the class roster for Poway middle school the year of the arrest. And…" She clicked again. "This is the next year. Two girls are gone, and three boys. I found the other two. There was no trace of Danial."

Muna swung around deeper on the desk. Chips looked down at the territory now covered by the leather-clad leg. She softly snorted as she clicked on the next icon in her column. "This is the roster of GED recipients for Poway when he turns eighteen and gets released from the system." Another click. "He's on parole, so he must report when he gets a job."

Muna frowned. "He's a groundskeeper for Yes-a-Dew? What kind of…?"

"Gardening. Commercial gardening. The kind paying real money." She clicked on the next icon.

Muna leaned closer and read. "Worker's compensation claim for…"

"A cut finger. But look at the name." She enlarged the document. The two-inch-tall signature was clear and short.

Muna leaned back and looked at Chips. "Dani Scalese." She turned her head toward the larger room.

Chips held her finger to her mouth as she shushed Muna. Clicking. The document was five years later. "And we have what we're looking for."

Muna found the final name. "Debra Scalese."

Chips clicked one icon after another in rapid succession. School records, work records, and even a passport cascaded down the screen.

Muna turned on the young woman. "Okay. What do you want?"

The blond looked at her wrist. "Dinner for starters." She looked out at the larger room. "Without them. Just us." Her cheek pulled back. "Well… maybe Powder too."

Muna chuckled. "They tied her badge to Nash's badge. Without Nash, she's not a legal service dog."

"It won't matter where we're going."

Muna frowned as she cocked her head sideways. "Why?"

WHERE DID SHE GO?

THE TREES LANCED up from the musty earth and spare underbrush. The limbs only sprung from the trunks after they were already well above a two-story house. An arbor of fairy lights softly illuminated the handful of picnic tables, paying homage to the small trailer like an intimate rock concert in the forest. The two panels swung up over the open windows to expose the working kitchen.

Muna stepped out of the SUV. Her mouth hung agape. "What is this magical..." She stepped out in front of the vehicle and joined Chips. She looked at the girl. "I don't even know what to call it. How does something this magical exist?"

Chips passed her sweeping arm and hand across the fairytale tableau of forest and eatery. "All of this is state forest land. No building there—ever. But this... this used to belong to a small restaurant back in the nineteen twenties. Originally, it was a waystation back in the nineteenth century when it was first built. This road ran down to Salinas or something. Now it dead-ends at the highway running from San Jose to Santa Cruz. If you talk to the old folks like Mike and Oz, they can tell you about a song about another restaurant that was down the road. It was called Alice's Restaurant. It was famous, I guess."

Muna took it all in. "But this?"

"The restaurant burned down about the time the hippies were infiltrating from the city. And nobody rebuilt it. But the fireplace was always there. And when Pepe started poking around, he found this little slice of heaven still had power, and they had zoned it for a restaurant only. But he couldn't get a building permit because nobody would sell him fire insurance. If the forest burns, he loses the food cart. But because his cart is all-electric, his business license has no problem getting insurance because the fire risk is low. All catch twenty-twos." She held out her two arms and wiggled her fingers at the trailer. "And so we have Pablo Burritos. The best kind of rocky mountain high. He even has Christmas chili sauce."

As they got closer, Muna laughed and pointed at the gigantic fireplace. The logs and fire were fake, like a seventeen-dollar fireplace at the big box store at Christmastime.

"Hola Chica. Welcome back."

Chips stepped up to the counter. "Hola, Pepe. How's your dad?"

The old man stood from behind the counter. "I'm here. Getting older, but still here." He pointed at her. "Nachos…?"

She giggled. "Chips. But close."

He pointed at his son and the kitchen. "Is okay. We have the nachos for you."

She smiled. "Yes, you do. And we'll start with a basket of nachos and a large bowl of salsa cruda, please." She turned to Muna. "I know you don't eat pork. What else?"

Muna shrugged. "Roadkill?"

"Goat, okay?"

"Sure." Her smile glowed in the kitchen's lights.

She held up her two fingers. "Dos Cabra Pueblo por favor."

"Christmas?"

Chips' eyes were enormous in mock horror. "Oh course."

Muna cut up the last of her burrito. "How did you find this place?"

The tan organic fork wound in the air. "I spend about sixteen hours a day doing research. I focus most on finding the guy. But then something triggers another thought, which leads to something else and then down the rabbit hole."

Muna shoved the mouthful to her cheek. "Welcome to my world."

Chips hung out her hand and finger upside down with the fork, wiggling tenuously. "Right?" She stuck the fork in her burrito. "There are times I'll walk by Baby, who has been diagnosed ADHD and refuses to take her meds, but she'll have things running on all eight of her panels, and she's banging away on four keyboards. She has six mice Slug's guys built for her. They're wound tight, and the wheel is five times faster than a normal person. Nobody can use her station. It's like Mister Toad's crazy ride on steroids. But nobody sees it as abnormal. It's kind of like how all of us work. There will be hours of silence, and then suddenly, someone gives out a war whoop, and we're all tagging into whoever started the game. It's crazy, but you can feel the blood pressure drop, the tension runs away, and you can focus again."

"So, what led you here?"

Chips looked down. "I was homesick. Not for any single place, just Pueblo. I Earthed it. Then I went to the street view. So, I was driving around the old neighborhood. And there was a new food cart near the mall. I wondered what they were serving, but I couldn't read the menu. So, I plugged in what I thought the sign said. But it wasn't." She slumped.

"What did you plug-in?"

She tossed her head and eyebrow. "Pueblo Burritos."

"And?"

Chips snorted. "It asked if I meant Pablo Burritos. And there was an entry below. One stinking entry."

Muna dropped her fork in her tray. "You lie. There're always nine thousand sponsored hits."

Chips held up her single finger. "So, I clicked. I was ready to hire an Uber or even a cab. But I printed off the sheet and went down to the dock and asked Andy where it was. He handed me a set of keys to a minivan and told me to go find out. I think he's been here before."

Muna laughed. "The gold minivan? The one smelling like a million dogs?"

Chips held out her finger. "Fire."

Muna laughed. "It's his personal van. I hope you brought him back a burrito."

"I didn't think about it..." The red raced from her neck to her ears. "He's gone home by now."

Muna swung her head. "I think we might sneak down here for lunch tomorrow."

Chips hummed as she smiled around her last bite.

"But back to Daniel turned Dani and..."

The girl shoved the tray to one side and leaned in. "So, I'm pretty sure we'll never get the surgery records. Nor would I want to. It would seem like something that should be between a person and their maker. Or, in this case—their rebuilder."

"But can we get a progression from Dani to Debra?"

She swung her one leg over the bench and sat along the bench. "I think so. But you also had another name from the fingerprint search."

Muna dipped her head as she crossed her hands. "Yeah. A Jana Zabriskie. It was a ninety-seven hit. But it's an easy fudge to go from a ninety-four for the kid to a ninety-seven for her. I've seen some of Nash's finger rolls. She could make a spread twenty-wide. It's not like it's a true science, just a lot of circumstances."

"Where do you go from here?"

Muna's face drew back to one side. "First, we let the big kids do their thing. Meanwhile, let's start with the passport and see if she traveled at all."

"Why would anyone go to the trouble of getting a passport and then not travel? I mean... Isn't the point of getting a passport traveling?"

Muna shrugged. "I got a passport when I was fourteen. But I never left the country until I joined the FBI."

"Where did you go?"

"Switzerland."

Chips furled one eye. "Why not something romantic like Paris or Rome? I mean… Switzerland is a neutral country. But what was there?"

"Work."

"Like a money exchange?"

"Documents. I was the courier. It was a chain of evidence thing."

"With Nash?"

Muna shook her head as she stood and picked up the trays and trash. "We had worked the case together, but I went solo. It was about cleaning up loose ends."

As they walked toward the black Explorer, Muna stopped and looked up at the stars between the trees. "Colorado had a lot of stars."

Chips laughed. "They're the same ones here."

Muna scowled at her. "But in Colorado, you can see the Milky Way. You had way more stars than here."

Chips shook her head as she pointed up. "This, this is like looking through a weak telescope. But the trees and the distance from the city give you the effect of a darker sky. In Pueblo, I mean downtown, you can't see this many stars. But you folks were out on a mesa. You were away from the city lights." She waved her hand wildly at the sky. "When you were growing up, did you ever get away to those mountains in upper New York?"

"The Adirondacks? No. We were the people who took a vacation and went to the museum. My dad drives a city bus."

Chips grimaced. "Someday, you need to get way out in a desert or out to sea. Somewhere, there is no light fogging the night sky. Then, you will see the Milky Way. It's all the same sky, just perspective."

Muna clicked her seat belt, and her finger rested on the key. Her hand fell to her knee. She turned and quietly studied Chips.

"What?"

Muna looked back out at the magical trailer parked in the most unlikely spot. The tree trunks were lightly lit as they reached up into the dark high overhead. The tiny fairy light swayed gently over the heads of the couple who arrived on the motorcycle. Pepe cleaned as he murmured to his father. Muna turned back. "Thank you for the best date I've ever had. It was as magical as it was... um..."

Chips smiled at the scene. "Illuminating?"

Muna softly bobbed her head. "In a lot of ways." She started the truck.

Chips leaned her head against her window and looked up. "Computers aren't everything."

"Hola Debra y Dorthia. ¿Como estas?"

Debra looked up from getting her mother out of the car. "Oh. Good morning, Tito. How's the arm?"

The man held the bandaged arm up. "Es bueno. That stuff you make. It help muchos. Poco pain."

She nodded. "Si. There are many plants that help with a lot we suffer from."

He nodded toward the older woman standing as she held onto the door handle. "No, all."

Debra rolled her lips. "No. Not everything is curable. But some can help."

"Is Dorthia working in casa cinco today?"

Debra thought about the long walk to the distant greenhouse. "If you can give us a ride out there. Sure. We can have her work out there." She guided the woman over to sit on the back bed of the golfcart converted to a small electric work truck. "Hold on to the chain, here." She guided her hand and then sat next to her.

The cart slowly made its way down between the two long greenhouses lined by large stacks of crates and pallets. The harvesters put the small cherry tomatoes onto a conveyor belt. Two sorters watched for any questionable fruit. The fruit fell into a hopper that was constantly fed by another belt with little walls dividing portions. The belt twisted, and the fruit fell into a plastic clamshell, which was automatically closed and stacked in the larger boxes. Within hours, the boxes would cross the border and arrive at stores. Organic and freshly picked.

Debra liked the orderliness of the farm. Even the dirt stayed where it was the most useful.

30
OPEN IT

THOMAS KICKED the boot-sized rock over the narrow cliff. The stone rattled against stone, gravel, and an occasional small bush on its way to the valley floor. He sighed as he listened to the man talk to his marshal.

"Can I call you back? What's your office number?"

Thomas winced. He knew he needed this man to help him, but was about to piss him off. "No sir, you can't. I barely have two bars on my phone with a low battery. While you're in your nicely paneled office and your uniform of the day is custom-sewn to hide your vest, weapon, and access card, I'm perched on the side of a mountain. My uniform is from the cheap section in Target, and I'm trying to stick something in the freezer so we don't starve this winter."

"Where are you at? I don't even... where is Harding?"

"Harkin, sir. If you look at the completely opposite corner of the state from you, I'm just left of Nevada. From this skinny, rugged cliff, I stand at the threshold of Oregon. My hands and clothes are smeared with a mountain goat's blood. I got more fur than meat from this kill. But my family and friends in this poverty-stricken county don't have many other options. They pay me half of what they pay your bailiff—but I would rather take on these wilds than tackle your freeways any day. All I'm asking from you is two inches of ink. With that, I can go back to finding something worth eating instead of thinking about those FBI agents that keep hounding me about some crap I want nothing to do with. Then maybe my life will have a few days of peace until the city folk come up here again and wreck it all, sir."

"Son, you have a mouth on you."

"That's what my commander told me when they stuffed me in the body bag and shipped me out of Fallujah, sir."

"You served?"

"Helicopters. Army. Until they shot me out of the air, sir."

Uncle harrumphed quietly. "If that don't put the nail in the coffin…"

"Why the body bag?"

"It was the only way to get me lifted out of the desert. They didn't have any shrink-wrap to hold me all together, sir."

"But now you're a sheriff…"

Thomas gazed toward Oregon. "As long as the voters don't give me any other choice."

"Shit. Okay. Tell your FBI to send the forms, and I'll sign off on them. This case is how old?"

"The juvenile record is about twenty. But this case is still on your news down there. We clear this up, and your reporters will eat crow about that mass suicide."

"Oh hell, son. Why didn't you lead with that?"

Thomas closed his eyes as he hung his head. *God, I hate city folk.* "Because everyone likes a little dessert sometimes, sir. And thank you. I'll call the FBI in San Francisco before my battery dies."

"Good hunting, son."

Thomas thumbed him off. "Prick." He eyed Uncle. "Can we get off this cliff?"

Uncle leaned back against the large rock and closed his eyes as he turned his face to the late afternoon sunshine. "Pack your meat."

Thomas glanced over at the half-field-dressed carcass. "I think I'll feed the vultures and marmots. I can buy better jerky for twenty bucks at the Gas-n-Go."

Uncle smirked with the other side of his mouth. "Twice as much meat too. I warned you about those goats."

Thomas looked at the sun, barely above the distant mountains. "What's the fishing like in Eureka right now?"

Uncle stretched his face. "Probably not as good as bringing back a large cooler or two of frozen deer." He smiled across the cliff. "We can take the bus… but then the boys will want to come along."

Thomas cleaned his knife and stuffed the plastic bags back into his rucksack. He pushed his lower lip out as he tossed his head. "That gives us a foursome for gin or hearts."

Uncle held up his finger. "That reminds me. Felix still owes me that thirty-seven bucks."

Thomas shouldered his rucksack. "That kid needs to learn how to cheat better."

Uncle watched as Thomas poked at his phone. "Texting Nash?"

Thomas shook his head. "Muna."

Uncle turned toward the narrow path down as he snorted. "Safer that way."

"Amen."

Muna held up her phone to Nash.

Nash laughed. "Chickenshit." She leaned her head back and studied the ceiling. "Send it, Chips."

"Gone." The voice sounded more distracted from the corner.

Nash frowned at Muna and Jazz. "What's…"

Jazz pointed at the corner of the upper right screen. Nash frowned and squinted. Muna clicked on the window, and the multi-player video game grew to fill all six of Muna's monitors.

Nash laughed. "I should have known. Who is she playing against?"

Jazz glanced at her large dive watch. "It's after three. This would be team Slug against the girls."

Nash frowned gently. "Not team Herra?"

Frank walked up with a fresh mug of coffee. "Not when Chips is leading the girl team. We need to produce a better name for them."

Jazz snickered. "You're just squirmy about seeing them print shirts with Team V on them."

———

THE SMALL LAMP ON THE NIGHTSTAND CAST A SMALL pool of warm light spilling onto the edge of the bed. The sheets were a cheery powder blue that Dorothy had always favored. Debra knew they made her happy to climb in and sleep through the night.

"I had a boyfriend once."

Debra had heard the same story of her conception a thousand times. Its repeating was the first indication of the illness that had removed almost everything else from her mother. She also knew the indications were there in her as well—and it wouldn't be long. She hummed acknowledgment.

"Peter was a very handsome upperclassman. He was a teacher's assistant. All the girls were in love with him."

"Okay. Second diaper now. Legs up."

Dorothy straightened her legs out from the bed where she sat. Her breasts sagged almost flat. Dressing her in a brassiere had proved useless to Debra years before. She fed the diaper over the two feet and above the knees. Picking the feet up, Debra rested them on her shoulders and rolled the woman back on her back as she pulled the diaper over the smaller one. Neither one of them had liked the feel of the rubber over panty. They both relaxed, and the older woman returned to a sitting position.

Debra picked up the tiny white pill from the nightstand, along with the glass and a small amount of water. "Okay, here is your night-night."

The woman mechanically took the pill. Sticking it on her tongue, she took the glass and drank a sip of the water. "I liked

Peter, but he did things to me. They weren't nice. So, he had to go away. It was before my boy came to live with me." She looked up at her friend, who took care of her. "I was an excellent student."

Debra held the light blanket and sheet up. "Yes, dear. Tuck your feet under the covers. It's time for night-night."

"Night-night time." The woman's sing-song voice was flatter than it had been all of Debra's growing up. All the night's little messages, now returned only to be parroted back to the original mother.

Debra reached for the tiny lamp. She pulled the chain once, leaving only the small night-light to glow dully from the glass base. "And a tiny light in the gloom to remind you there are angels looking out for you."

The woman smiled. "A small light to guide their tiny wings."

Debra patted her softly on the shoulder. "Sleep tight, Dorothy."

———————

AS THEY WAITED FOR THEIR COFFEE, CHIPS PASSED A folded piece of paper under the table to Muna.

Muna opened the paper and read the document. When she got to the name, she smiled at Chips. She pulled it above the table and passed it to Nash.

"What's this?"

Muna leaned back as the coffee arrived. "Your sealed record."

Nash handed the paper to Frank. "Who is Danial Scalese?"

Muna happily smirked as she held out both of her hands in presenting Chips. "May I present Chips? Leader and founder of Team Hybrid, research digger extraordinaire."

Chips pointed at the sheet of paper Frank was slowly lowering. "That boy went away because he poisoned a lot of neighborhood pets. After juvenile hall was done with him, he assumed the name Dani with an *I*. Then he got a job as a groundskeeper for golf cour-ses. There was an industrial accident with a mower blade. He went to the emergency room where his finger received four stitches…" She glanced over at Nash, who was frowning. "Where did I lose you?"

Nash's face shifted from frowning to narrowed eyes as she sipped her coffee. "You didn't. But either you are rattling off a supposition, or you have done a lot deeper diving in the dumpster than…" She nodded her head at the paper. "That single piece of paper."

Chips' smirk tugged tightly at her right cheek as she plucked the paper off the table. "This is just the cover page of a sixty-seven-page record on him. He wasn't exactly the nicest kid in his dormitory. In fact, there were a few other kids who suffered strange, unexplained maladies while he was being tormented during his imprisonment."

Frank grumbled. "But once they bounced him, his record got sealed. But you knew who he worked for and the injury? You knew who he was before we got the record unsealed…"

Muna smiled and held her hands up again to present the young woman. "And she found the name change and passport of the new identity. Every bit legally through public records. These are records I would have never thought to connect. She knew all of this when we ran away for dinner the other night. But I wanted to go through it and make sure she had worked clean enough to merit getting a warrant."

Nash frowned at the young blonde. "Clean?"

Chips sighed as she dropped her hands where she was picking at the side of her thumb. "Sometimes, when you're dancing on the fence between the light side of the internet and the other…" She winced with one eye. "If I had accidentally crossed a line in opening certain records… I wasn't sure of my standing with working for the FBI. I didn't want there to be any chance of blow-back on you guys or Deep Six. I like my new job." She stared at Jazz and Frank. "No. Scratch that. I love my dream life at Deep Six. And I didn't want to put any of it at risk. Not for me, and definitely not for Deep Six or the FBI. Especially Muna."

Muna grabbed and squeezed her hand.

Nash smiled. "Awe... Muna has a new little sister."

Chips's face changed to horror as she eyed Muna. "I thought you were an only child."

Muna laughed as she pointed at the multicolored face of Powder at the head of the table. "I was... Until Powder came along."

Jazz chuckled. "Oh yes. I can see the resemblance."

Frank cleared his throat. "You mentioned a name change and passport...?"

She held her shrug for a moment and then released it. "It's back at the office. He was Dani, but still a Danial. So, the name change made her a Debra—no *h*. Afterward, she got a passport a few months later."

Nash picked up her fork and pointed the back end at the young blond. "But there was another woman."

"I'm working on it. She got fingerprinted for DUI in Imperial County. A place called Centro."

"El Centro." Frank glanced up and smiled at her. "Pinche town, enormous hat, no cattle, but they like to think they are the center of the universe. So, it has an El in the name."

Jazz laughed. "There are three bars. You'd have to be very drunk to get the attention of anybody in that town. I think I'd stay stewed just living there."

Chips nodded as she chewed. Swallowing, she took a sip of coffee and looked at Nash. "Not being rushed or having much else to do is what probably led to a better set of fingerprints."

Nash shrugged her lower lip. "Now you just have to find her."

The young woman held up both palms and then crossed her index finger over the other. "Not my problem. Tree has me on a crash assault of the lower Houston Shipping Channel. I guess they don't want any more of the flooding they've been getting every year."

31

GAMES WITHIN GAMES

THE ROOM full of hunched-over young women had its own music. The clacking of keyboards. Only three of them wore headphones. Two were esoteric music choices, but Betty had long ago eschewed the psychotropic drugs for listening to brown noise. It calmed her as it reminded her of the moment before a rainstorm on the homestead's tin roof. It was the last joyful moment she had as a child. As the storm brewed, her father had gathered them on the summer bed on the deep front porch. Her big sister and little brother, mother and father, Betty and her mutt dog, Stinker. All gathered up on the bed, waiting for the rain. It was a magical moment. And the hours of brown noise extended those few minutes into long days of work. With the brown noise, the magic moment never ended with a tornado nobody saw coming from the other side of the house.

The overhead crackled, and everyone looked up at the hidden speakers.

They rarely heard Tree's voice on the overhead. If she was talking to all of them, it was important. "I am suspending all projects for the next six hours." The screens in the entire room turned a black charcoal. "They are all in stasis. For the next six hours, Chips and Muna need our help. Each of your main screens will have your division of the work and an outline of the overall project. You can work with your neighbor or buddy up once you understand where you're going. This will have no trackers on it. So there are no guardrails or boundary lines you need to worry about. If there's an area you're uncomfortable doing research in, tag me or someone you think might take it over for you. This is not a drill. The work clock is in your upper left corner. In six hours, we will have an all-deck meeting to compare notes. Happy hunting."

The heads dropped, and the silence was complete as they read the assignment.

Thousands of clicks later, Chef silently wheeled in his cart. With the whispers of an owl's wings on Halloween night air, he placed their preferred snack of choice next to each woman. As if they were his own children, he knew which preferred chunky peanut butter on her untoasted English muffin, which liked her cheesy Pringles in a red bowl instead of white, who drank which tea, and which got the hydro flask with the quad shot tempered with goat's milk and the chunky powdered cocoa mix. He gave no one any service that would produce a distracting noise. No noisy plastic or foil bags, no metal utensils, no noisemakers of any kind. He nodded and silently retreated, leaving only the constant resonance of the eleven keyboards and mice.

The tinny click was followed by the sound of Tree's voice. "Table in fifteen minutes."

Some retreated to the bathrooms. Others finished the last detail and then ran. The printers whirred into a full-throated awakening as Tree and Ming entered. They took the north end of the long oval table. Few knew the design was a homage to the founder's extra-long surfboard. Few had seen a long board, much less the twelve feet of a long gun Frank had used since he was in high school.

Mugs, glasses, flasks, and papers hit the table. The team assembled as Tree glanced at her watch. She nodded to Betty, the youngest. "Take us out."

The girl glanced at her single sheet. "From the name change, we have Debra Scalese. Her only provable relative is her mother, Dorothy Scalese. If she's still alive, she would be sixty-seven. I tracked her to her last known residence. They admitted her into a care facility for memory care. That was six years ago. The facility released Dorothy to her daughter three years ago. The address given at the time is now a defunct liquor store being used as a shooting gallery for junkies." She glanced up. "Current location wasn't on my list."

Tree peeked at her phone. "Bunny?"

"When Dorothy left the North University Memory Care, Debra had, according to the stamps on her passport, been out of the country seven times. All to Mexico. Exits were El Chaparral, San Ysidro, Otay Mesa, and Tecate. But all the returns were through San Ysidro." She looked up from her notes. "Tijuana to San Diego." She nodded at Baby.

Ming nodded. "Baby?"

"I've got seventeen growers in Baja and mainland. Most are small and or grow the wrong products. Two are growing a cover for coca. I don't think she would risk a raid by the Federales."

"Leaving us with…?"

She held up her thumb and two fingers. "Three. All are large-scale produce hot houses. Or, with Mexico—shade houses." She looked across the table. "Squeak?"

The girl with the black-tipped green mohawk turned, shaking her head. "All three fit the profile. Tomatoes, cucumbers, kiwi, guava, broccoli, squash, carrots, lettuce, cabbage, and more. Huge sprawling collections of giant growing houses and lots of turnover of workers. Many are day or contract labor."

Tree nodded. "Tina. What did we learn about Jana Zabriskie?"

The blonde with the washed-out pale blue eyes sat back. "Ghost. Until three years ago, she didn't exist—until she rented a post office box in Tecate. The American side. It's a tiny, nothing town, but people rent mailboxes when they live across the border. That way, they still have a United States address. My guess is she was living across the border."

Tree frowned. "Don't you need to show some identification to rent a box?" She focused on the oldest person at the table.

Bunny raised her eyebrows and nodded. "Absolutely. And if you're not in and out of there getting packages and making friends with the staff, they'll want to see your ID every time."

Tina checked her notes and turned to the second page. "Identification was a passport."

Ming smiled. "So she got a passport... Trace?"

The brunette with the single, drooping eye stared blankly ahead as she shook her head. "Nada. It was bogus." She held her hands to her cheeks in a caricature of a famous painting while rocking her head in disbelief. Her voice was raw and unfiltered. "I'm shocked—shocked, I tell ya!" Rolling her eyes, she resumed her usual deadpan delivery. "My guess is she would have to get fingerprinted to get a passport from the government—if she wanted one. But... out there on the mean streets from San Francisco to San Diego... if you've got the know-how and a few hundred bucks? You can get a passable document within an hour or two. The passport will pass a visual test. Just don't try to scan it."

Tree rocked. "So we're back to Debra Scalese."

Trace slowly bobbed her head as her drooping eye closed. "Back to the passport that can get scanned."

Ming pulled her hands down, stroking her long black hair. "I'm going to spitball here. Debra has her mother with her. And they're in Mexico hiding out or hiding out in plain sight. My question is, how did she get her mother across? Does Dorothy have a passport?"

The small hand rose near the other end of the table.

"Terry?"

The girl held up her paper. "Passport number seven, six, eight, zero..." She lowered the paper. "To answer your question, yes. But because it's the nine numbers instead of a letter first, she has the old generation passport, which means she got it before twenty-twenty-one. Which would fit in with getting her released from the care facility three years ago."

Ming sighed. "Damn."

Tree snapped her fingers and pointed at Tina. "Does Jana still have the post office box?"

The girl scanned down her pages. She held her finger on the passage on the third page. "She paid the rental until twenty-thirty-one. Probably a ten-year rental." Glancing up. "I couldn't access any records of frequency or last known access. And even if that existed... that would just be too creepy, Big Brother."

"Agreed."

Tree glanced around. "But nobody found another apartment or any kind of rental?"

Baby shook her head. "Only the original apartment in North Park. Either under Debra or Jana."

Ming peered around. "Anybody else?" The faces were deadpan or shaking. "Okay. Great work girls. Chef has dinner ready, so make your way down." She held up her one finger to the rising group. "But! Early night tonight, so I don't want to catch anyone sneaking back up here to squeeze in any more work. Hang out with the boys, play videos, watch TV, or go home. But go eat and relax. Tomorrow is pajama day. You guys earned it."

Tree stepped over to the doorway and stopped Chips. "We need to see you for a couple of minutes in the office."

"Sure."

The three settled into the lounge chairs next to the small desk.

Ming glanced at Tree, who nodded. Turning back to Chips, she smiled. "So you really... how did Jazz put it? Love your dream life?"

Chips nodded nervously.

Tree jumped in as she sensed the apprehension. "Good. Because you're kind of our dream team member, and we want to encourage that going forward."

Ming coughed in her fist. "We never spied on our teams before. And we don't have any reason to now."

The blond hair swung forward as Tree leaned in. "But I had you doing a kind of over-watch today. Your research skills are off the charts." Tree looked at Ming, who nodded. "What you did up in San Francisco for Muna and Nash... well, we'd like you to keep doing that even more. But today, I gave you access to everyone else's terminals to watch how they search and dive."

Chips leaned her head over. "And you want to know who can use improvement...?"

"Essentially, yes and no." Ming winced at Tree, who shrugged.

Tree held up her hands. "We're clueless. The team does research, but we've told no one how to do it. We hired them all because they exhibited superior skills. They know what we need, and they produce it. But? Is it being produced through brutalist means, or can there be a better way?"

Ming jumped up and held out her hand. "I just saw it in your face. Don't! *That* was not a question we wanted answered right now."

Tree stood laughing. "Only thing right now is dinner. But we'd like you to think about what you saw today. We spooled everything from everybody's terminals so you can review them when you want. And if you want to go over anything with anybody, it's there. It's behind your command wall so only you can view it. When you don't need it or want it anymore, we'll shred it. But we think you can mentor some of the young ones and probably us."

Ming held out her hand. "Are you okay with this?"

Chips shrugged. "Tina's comment about Big Brother... but yeah. I understand what it was about. We're good."

Tree wiggled her eyebrows. "Good. Because I hear Chef has been working all day on something called Pueblo burritos."

Chips licked her lips and tilted her head. "Only if he made it from jerky, and it comes with Christmas salsa."

Ming slapped her on the back as they walked out. "I think those were his words exactly."

Tree stopped at the large table and eyed the notes left where the girls had been sitting. They all knew from habit that the notes would be there when they got back—if they needed them. Each girl handled her own research. "Hey Chips?"

"Yeah?"

Tree pointed at the notes. "Tomorrow morning, get with Bunny and whoever you need. But this all needs to be boiled down to a couple of pages and sent up north."

Chips smiled. "Already done. Well… mostly. I just need to clean up the last ideas we produced here."

Ming snickered as she turned the taller girl around and headed her out the door. She put her arm up over Chips' shoulder. "Dinner, superstar. Burritos the size of your head."

WHO DO YOU KNOW?

THE CALM FALL weather washed gently warm over the seven surfers dozing on their long surfboards. The gentle swells could raise one end six inches above the other end as it slides silently under the board and human. Some surfers had taken to wearing a small wet towel over their heads and necks. Others were old and cantankerous enough to not give a shit. Granite was squarely in the latter's camp. He turned his head to the other side at the small sound. His eye, closest to the board that was adorned with ice-blue flames, squeezed open.

"Frank?"

The board nearby hummed.

"Frank?"

"What?"

"Your redheaded skeleton wants you."

Frank shifted till his metal spinal centipede rested better as the weight distributed to his right shoulder. "Fuck you. He's working."

The air horn was a short blast followed by a longer one.

Granite held up his only complete hand and then clenched it into a bird. "He's getting obnoxious."

"Fuck him. If he wants me so bad, he can swim out here and get me." He shrugged his shoulder against his head to adjust his cheap wraparound blackout glasses.

The air horn sounded for the count of three. Neither surfer moved. Two of the younger guys sat up on their boards. One rolled his eyes. "Oh shit. I'm leaving." He laid down and started paddling north.

Granite didn't move but opened both eyes. "Oh shit. It's Berni, and she has her bullhorn."

The older lawyer's voice carried clear across the water. Everyone in Crystal Cove now knew exactly what the commotion was about and for whom. "Frank Pounds. If you don't come deal with your man-child this moment, I am going to go grab Kalani's board and come out there and harvest your balls."

Shit. Frank sat up and waved one hand.

"Now, Frank. Not next week or when the surf comes in from Hawaii."

Frank lifted his legs and swung around. Lying forward, he began paddling. The long gun responded sluggishly.

The woman poked the tall, skinny redhead with her bullhorn. "Get a fucking mouthpiece, Danny. The fucking horn just irritates people and means nothing."

He smiled. "Yes, Maddie. Duly noted."

She looked at him with a narrowed eye. "What has your cook excited today for lunch? I might walk up there today."

Danny's smile grew on one side. "Anything you want. Come in the back way and sweet talk him into showing his drawers."

She poked him in the chest with her middle finger. "Don't try to dance salacious words with me, young man. I gave up talking obtuse nasty when you were still in diapers."

The young man smiled. If he needed another mother, he'd adopt her.

She waved the back of her hand at the bay. "Your boss is here. Take care of business and then go warn the cook that I'll be up in an hour. I expect something other than raw meat. I get enough of that in court."

Danny gave her a two-finger salute and turned to watch Frank leaning his long-gun board against the raised porch of Beachcombers.

Fishing his cell phone out of his pants, he handed it to Frank. "Jazz is hot to trot. And almost as burning the barn as Tree was. At least Ming asked how I was." He slouched with the weight on one hip. "And make it snappy. I left some hipsters reading the menus. They drove in with one of those stupid Mercedes boxy jeepy things."

Frank rolled his eyes. "So, who do I call back?"

Danny dramatically threw his head back as he waved his hand in the air at his side. "Who the heck cares? All your harem has an agenda. And it's probably the same one."

Frank rolled his eyes and just hit redial as he turned to look out across the flattened bay. The tiny black tip of Santa Catalina smudged the horizon.

"Did you find him?"

He snorted. "Yes, Ming. Danny found me. What's happening, and is everyone safe?"

The tinkling voice paused. "Safe?"

Frank closed his eyes. "Is the building on fire?"

"No—"

"Then who died?"

"No—"

"Then why are the cops breaking down the door?"

"No... That's not... Fuck you! Stop that!"

Frank counted to five as his smile grew. "Hello, dear. How can I be of service?"

"Shit."

His voice calmed. "You know you get me all excited when you talk nasty. And then I have to turn my pacemaker down."

She giggled. "Stop that. You don't play fair."

"Then tell me what is fair about taking Danny away from his important work keeping my restaurant afloat. And then he brings a damn air horn and starts waking up all the degenerate residents…"

"Call Nash. We found her. We think. They're in Mexico."

He frowned and turned. He waved the back of his hand at Danny.

Danny shook his head. "No way, Jose. That is my phone."

Frank pulled the phone away from his ear and looked at the rhinestone-encrusted pink case. He growled. "Let me put my board away, and I'll be right up."

Ming coughed in his ear. "Why are you coming here?"

"I was talking to Danny."

"Where are you?"

He walked to retrieve his board. "Until I was so rudely interrupted, I was surfing."

The raspberry was juicy. "Bullshit. The surf is running three to five *INCHES*, asshole. You were sleeping."

"I warned you about that swearing. It gives you wrinkles at an early age."

"Fuck you. Call Nash. She needs help in your old backyard." The tiny tin snick was as definitive as if she had slammed down an old cast-iron phone. *God, I miss those old phones.* He looked up the cliff where his shack and restaurant only existed until his death.

Frank hung his board in his garage cum shrine to past surfing friends. Kissing his fingertips, he touched the board above his—his ex-partner's Hawaiian special.

He held up the phone and then realized it wasn't his. Nash's number wasn't in it. He hit the redial.

Ming growled cartoonishly. "What now? I'm flogging the crew."

He walked with his eyes on the road. He didn't want to catch the eye of anyone who might rub in any salt about Danny and the horn. "I have Danny's phone. Patch me through to Nash."

There was silence.

"Ming?"

"I'm waiting for the please."

"Do I need to come up there and turn you over my knee?"

"If you do, I won't paint your toenails."

He stopped and looked at his feet. The pink polish was cracked, chipped, and half worn away. He realized the real butt hurt was he hadn't been around lately. "Please. And I'll be up this evening. Is Tree joining us?"

"I'll ask her. Here's Nash."

The voice was husky and distracted. "Hey, Ming. What's up?"

Frank resumed walking up the path to his side of the headlands. "Nope. It's Frank. Ming patched me through. I have Danny's phone."

"What happened to your phone?"

"It went surfing. What's up?"

"The girls did us a huge solid. They found Debra. Well, kind of. They think she's at one of four large greenhouse growers of produce down in Mexico in the Tijuana area."

Frank got to his shack and sat on the low deck. He could now see almost half of Catalina Island. "So go on down. You can't arrest her, but at least you can..." He buzzed his lips. "Shit. I don't know. It's been so long since I was down there..."

"So, do you know anyone in the Federales who can help us?"

He looked down at his Thumb Island Beach Boys Concert T-shirt. The hole above his bellybutton was the size of his palm. "Yeah. I'll need to make a few calls. But I need a fresh T-shirt. Where are you at?"

"San Francisco."

He stood and smiled. Peeper, the young coyote, was peeking around the corner of his door. He rubbed his thumb and fingers together. "And I need to talk to my granddaughter. When are you coming down?" His hand grabbed the side of her neck, and his finger raked the fur. She rolled over and offered her belly.

"We're just waiting on you."

"Don't wait on me. Just get here. The girls can pick you up at

John Wayne airport. We can lend you one of the Explorers. Just push the dredging crap to one side."

Nash chuckled. "Yeah, more like computer stuff. BTW, Chips castle of a computer empire is still here. Do we ship it...?"

Frank pulled his T-shirt off and rubbed it on the wild coyote in gentle roughhousing. "I think she left it there for when you have her fill in for you again."

"Okay. I'll talk with Muna. See you as soon as we can."

"Tink gets off at six. And she was thinking about the sea bass down in the cove. We could make it a foursome and a dog about eight. I'm sure they can rustle up something Powder would like."

Nash snorted softly. "Let's see how fast we can get a flight."

———

DOROTHY'S FACE DARKENED. THE FROWN WAS AS CLOSE as she ever got to anger. "Who are you?"

Her daughter sat on the bed. "I'm Debra. We're going to have fun today. How about we get you cleaned up and put into a fresh, clean shirt and pants so I can make us some yummy breakfast? How does that sound?" The days hardly ever changed anymore. Debra gently pulled back the sheet and thin blanket so as not to startle the woman. "I'll bet you'll be happy to get out of those diapers. Maybe sit on the toilet for a bit, and then we can freshen you up."

She left her purple gloves on from cleaning her mother. While the woman sipped on her morning coffee, Debra pulled the flowers out of the plastic bag. Working on the polyethylene cutting board that she only used for the poisons, she began finely chopping the Fox Glove flowers. She glanced over at the other four bags of flowers and plant material. Behind stood the box of brownie mix.

She had never been a pessimist. Nor was she ever an optimist. If she ever thought about it, she would think of herself as a realist. Nothing was ever good or bad. It just existed. To be anything other than practical would have meant she had feelings about how things should turn out or the way the world worked. As a young girl, she couldn't understand why some people seemed to be in a constant emotional state; it seemed like such an ineffective use of their energy.

The woman who had raised her the best she knew how was wasting away in what was left of her shell. The body would long outlive any part of the mind. It was neither good nor bad. It was just the nature of the woman's genetics. And Debra knew she shared those same genetics.

She glanced down at the finely chopped flowers. Someone else might have smiled at the job well done. But Debra was just satisfied with the fineness that would cook easily into the brownies, the brownies that would allow them to end those genetics together.

She scooped the half cupful of Foxglove back into the bag. Putting the cutting board and poison aside, he pulled the bowl with the four eggs toward her. Turning, she set the skillet on the stove and turned on the burner to heat. Next would come the butter.

DIEGO D. WINTER

33

SEARCH AND PROCEDURES

THE BORDER WAS LARGER, and the line to cross into Mexico was longer than Nash ever remembered. But it had been over fifteen years since she had last crossed any southern border without an airplane. Even if you could consider November as late fall, the heat was obnoxious. Even with the windows up and the air conditioning set to sixty-eight, Nash could feel the heat radiating through the window.

She glanced over at Frank, resting his head against the passenger window. "Are you even awake?"

He never moved. Not even a twitch. "Even if we had left Deep Six at four this morning, this line would still be only half this long."

Muna's head was back as she sat slumped in the back with Powder's head on her lap. "But it's Tuesday. Don't people work?"

Frank snorted and looked back at the girl and her dog. "About as much as you are now."

"Hey. I'm on the clock. So is Powder."

He smirked as he looked at Nash. "This morning at breakfast. Who dressed in street clothes?"

Nash snapped a glance. "We did."

Frank rocked. "Even Chef was in his Day of the Dead pajama

bottoms. Well... sweats. It's pajama week. If anything serious gets done, it'll be between rounds of games." He pulled his feet out of his huarache sandals. He pulled his left foot up onto his right leg to admire his pearlescent pink toenails. "While you two were working, I got touched up."

He laughed at Nash's frown. "Don't be a grouch. It's a holiday. Flow with the go."

Nash scanned the mirrors for the hundredth time. She hated being boxed in, sitting stationary, with no escape. "Taco Tuesday isn't a holiday."

Frank wrinkled his forehead as he scanned Nash's and then Muna's deadpan faces. "Let me guess. You work on your birthdays and Christmas."

Neither one looked at him.

"Oh, fuck me. You do." He rolled his head to the window. "You seriously work for the wrong fucking company."

He caught Muna's slight movement out of the side of his eye. The tiniest of clicks came from the phone opening. Nash's next move confirmed their connection went beyond the badge or their outfits.

Nash looked at the rearview mirror. "Muna?"

The groan was quiet but crushing. "It's not Rosh Hashana or Kwanzaa."

Nash glanced over as the car in front of her pulled forward thirty feet. "Turkey."

Frank nodded with a smirk.

Nash snorted. "White man day."

Frank pulled back with a snort. "I call bullshit. You just forgot."

She looked at the mirror. "Muna, what is your mother making Thursday?"

Muna's phone was at her ear. "Mama..." She smiled and bowed her head. Her voice became quiet. "Yes, Mama. I'm behaving. No. I'm not in trouble. Mama! Stop! I'm not dating. No. Mama, I'm working." She looked out the window. "Yes, I know I didn't come home for Ramadan. Mama, I have a job. It's a very important job. It is no less important than daddy driving people to their jobs and home every day."

She dropped her hand and phone into her lap as she rolled her eyes. The eyes in the rearview mirror nodded softly.

Muna put the phone back to her ear. "Yes, Mama. I'm here. But listen, I'm at work. But my boss has asked me a very important question." She nodded quietly. Her rock was as practiced as an old habit. "Mama? Please. Another time. Please." She dropped the phone again. "This may take a minute or two…"

Nash glanced back. "And we were going… where?"

Muna growled. She picked up the phone. "Mama. I've got to go." She hung up and held the phone in front of her. "Three, two…" The phone vibrated. "What are you cooking for Thursday dinner?" She smiled. "Thank you. I love you." She looked at the mirror. "Goat stew. Your turn."

Nash laughed and scrolled her contacts. She chuckled as she poked the number.

"Hey, Indian. We were talking about you."

Nash growled. "Define we."

"Tommy and me. Well, and the boys."

Nash smirked. "Tell Felix he needs to call his girlfriend. He missed the big game."

Nash could hear the click, and the volume of the phone told her it was hands-free to hand-free speaker phones.

The young man's voice tinkled with humor. "Nope. I was streaming the entire Super Bowl. Who shut the lights down and took over control of their system?"

Muna leaned forward. "Petey."

"I knew the kid had potential. Now, when he turns sixteen, he can buy a car and stop driving the suicide board."

Nash glanced back before she pulled forward twelve feet. "Where are you guys taking the bus?"

Alex growled. "Supply run."

Nash rolled her eyes as she checked all the mirrors and gauges. "What supplies?"

The older voice rumbled. "Freezer ammo."

"I thought you went hunting already."

"Tommy bagged a mountain goat."

Nash snorted. "So he got vulture bait. What now?"

"Roadkill. Puddy says he's saving about four hundred frozen if we help him stake out a ton of jerky."

Frank's eyebrows rose. "Is the ton wet or a ton dry?"

Nash laughed. "It's the Frank Pounds you never got to meet. Ming and Tree's sugar uncle."

"Ah. The man who lives with wolves."

Frank chuckled. "Not so much. This is southern California. We only have coyotes and cougars."

"Oh, so you live with coyotes too."

The men laughed. Uncle coughed. "Puddy was intimating more like a ton plus of dry and bagged. We'll probably be in Eureka Crescent City for a couple of weeks."

Nash glanced at the rearview mirror. "So, what are you cooking for Thursday night?"

She could hear Alex looking over his shoulder as he drove the bus. "We'll be in Crescent City by then."

"What's that mean?"

"Halibut."

Nash put the SUV in gear and edged forward another forty feet until the taillights of the overloaded Subaru flared. "Okay. You boys have fun at the coast."

Uncle growled. "What did you call for?"

Nash smirked at Frank. "We were wondering what you were cooking for Thanksgiving."

"White man holiday."

Nash laughed. "Check your wagon Indian. They've got you surrounded." She poked the button on the steering wheel.

Frank opened his mouth, but Nash stopped him with her finger in the air. The border was only nine cars ahead. She scrolled and poked the number.

"Mon Dieu, what can I get you, agent?"

"Chef, what is on the menu for Thursday night dinner?"

They could sense the man leaning back against some table or counter. This was where he lived. "We'll be starting with a bib lettuce salad with baby bay shrimps for those who can and hearts of palm for those who cannot. The soups are Boston creamed clam chowder and French onion. For entrée, I am flying in the North Sea Turbot or a vegetarian Biryani. Dessert, I haven't decided yet. But most likely, baby beignets with three dipping sauces of chocolate, strawberry preserves, and maybe I make pineapple compote. Why? Are you coming? I'll make something special for my furry friend."

Nash's smile was as large as she could make it as she turned on Frank. "No. We'll still be in Mexico. But I'm surprised. No turkey with all the trimmings?"

"For what?"

"Just a thought, Chef. Just a thought. Got to go to work. We'll talk later." She slid down her window as she eased up to the checkpoint.

The US Border Guard looked past her two badge wallets. "Hey Pounds. You got a surfboard in the back?"

Frank smiled at the guard. "Hey Henry. No time for surfing. Maybe some bugs later, but I'm just here to show the feds around."

The man smiled at Nash, still holding her badges. He vibrated his head. "Happy hunting, but those hunting licenses aren't valid south of here."

"We're just coming to talk."

He waved them forward. "Just don't drink the water." He waved at his counterpart on the other side of the border. The Mexican guard waved them through.

Frank pointed at the low building on the right. "Anywhere out front. We need to check in."

Nash nodded at the collection of SUVs angled into the curb. "It looks like a team mustering to go downtown." She nosed in and turned off the Explorer.

Frank opened his door. "Not hardly. These are more uptown guys. Not enough armor plate for downtown."

Muna stepped out with Powder. The dog at once started sniffing. Muna leaned to look at the markings on the tire. "Powder. No sniffing. So play nice."

Nash turned with a frown.

Muna stepped up onto the sidewalk and waved her hand back at the tires. "Extremely expensive armored run-flat tires. On the dark sites, they range from two grand up to four." She glanced back. "Probably in the three range."

Nash nodded at the hood. The blister nostrils sported baffle plates. "It's probably turbocharged as well."

Frank snorted. "Turbocharge, and you lose your braking back pressure. It's more like a pumped thousand raw. No more shopping. These people get twitchy about snoopers."

The thick man with chestnut hair going gray stood. His white shirt was a relaxed short-sleeved shirt with a braided pattern down both sides. Nash always associated the shirts with waiters in Mexican restaurants. She recognized the white Panama in his hand as the very expensive kind woven from fine staves of seagrass. This was no waiter.

"Your taste in compadres is improving, Frank." He stuck his fist out.

Frank bumped the fist and turned. "Ralph, this is Nash, Muna, and their furry friend, Powder."

Ralph stuck his hand out. "Mucho gusto. So you are the FBI."

Nash smirked at the reduction of introductions to just first names. "Only a small part of it. We left the rest at the border."

He turned slightly to hold out his hand toward the woman dressed in a dark blue uniform. "This is your guide and guardian, Frederica."

The woman extended her hand. "Mucho gusto. Welcome to

Mexico." Her English had no accent. It was as if she had grown up in the backwoods of Washington state. Far from any ethnic influences.

"Thank you." Nash noted the name tag sewn to her uniform shirt covering the light armor. Guzman. "Do we have any idea where we're going?"

Ralph held up his hands. "This is where I stick my fingers in my ears and back out. If you need dinner, it's not that far of a drive out to Rosey." He stuck his fist out. "Flaco?"

Frank bumped the fist. "We'll see how things go. It was two hours getting across the border."

"Si. Many tourists come for Taco Tuesday to escape the wild turkey nonsense." He raised his hat to his head but tipped it to the Federales. "Frederica. Give your mother a hug for me and we'll see you and your boy out for surfing this Sunday."

She nodded minutely. "Sunday, Tio. We'll bring Mama."

They watched the man leave. As the door closed, Frederica turned back. "As the mayor of Rosarita Beach, he walks a fine knife's edge. His world is a mix of the law and the tourists."

Frank coughed in his fist with his one raised eye and eyebrow. "That's putting it mildly. So what did you find?"

"There are two growers. Both produce crops for export that are in demand north of the border. And both employ a Norte Americana named Debra."

Nash shifted. "Where?"

NOT WHAT YOU THINK

FREDERICA HAD POINTED out the two locations on the map. Nash had chosen the more distant first. "If she's here, we're golden. But if not, we're headed back this way, anyway."

The blonde stared at the two FBI agents and the dog. She blinked as she pulled at her pink-tipped hair. "I don't know what to tell you, but my name is Deborah Schwartz. I grew up in Redwood City, and I wanted to be as far away from my drunk mother and creeper stepfather as I could get. You're not going to tell them you found me, are you?"

Muna looked her up and down. "Are you even eighteen yet?"

The girl turned on her as her eyes flared. "I've got a passport, don't I?"

"So does a two-year-old. But that's not what I asked."

Nash touched Muna's arm. "Nah. We're good. We're looking for a different Debra. Where you want to hide is up to you. Besides, there's no extradition for someone hiding from an abusive home. I hope you find what you're looking for."

The girl looked at the farmer. "Can I go back to work now?"

The man nodded. "Si."

She turned and disappeared into the back of the building. Nash looked at Frank. He shrugged. "Her life." He looked at the farmer and didn't have to say anything about the pay scale or the possibility of her ever getting free of the prison she had stepped into.

As they came out, Frederica bumped her back off the front of the front of the truck. "Wrong one I guess."

Nash glanced up at the sun. "No. No problemos. We still have plenty of daylight."

THE MAN SLOWED THE GOLF CART AS HE ENTERED THE large doors at the end of the gigantic building. He turned in and slowly made his way up the middle aisle between the rows of tall tomato plants. What everywhere else saw as a seasonal plant, the greenhouse knew how to make the plant thrive and produce continuously for up to five years. The result was many jobs that didn't require sizable sums of money paid to coyotes to cross a border, which resulted in too many deaths in the desert. The pay wasn't what they would pay in the United States, but working here and being home with family every night made up for the smaller money.

The small woman standing back up caught his eye. "Ai, Dorothea. ¿Dónde estás Débora?"

The woman turned and stared at him. Then, recognizing the last name, she looked to her right, up the aisle. Her arm and hand raised.

The man moved the golf cart forward until he saw the woman watching him. "Debora, there be Federales to see you."

The woman frowned. "Federales, Phillipe?"

"Si. Tres mujeres y un perro. They are asking for you. In the office."

"A dog?"

The man scratched at his chest. "Si. It has a badge… here."

Her head and face jerked her short blond hair in a violent twitch as her tongue stuck out in a fat sausage to lick her lips. "That isn't a Federales."

He shook his head. "No. Si. Un Federales. The other two women..." He waffled his hand in the air. "Maybe Norte Americana."

She pointed back down the aisle past her mother. "Bring the cart down to the end."

"Si." He jockeyed the cart back around toward the other direction and shot down the wider aisle as the woman rapidly walked back to her mother.

Debra gripped her mother's arm. "We need to go to lunch."

The woman raised her eyebrows in surprise. "Lunch? Now?"

She got the woman walking. "It's a special day. We have brownies for dessert and a nap."

"A nap?"

"Yes. It's a special day."

They approached the man and the cart. "Phillipe, I need you to do me a big favor. I need you to walk over and check the water flow at greenhouse four. And then take your time getting back to the office. But then walk the police down to the picnic tables at the end of building five." She waved in the air to show the distant spot. "No hurry. I need to feed Dorothy her lunch before they get there. Please."

He winced at giving up his golf cart but then nodded. "Si. The water, and then office." He pointed at his chest and then at her. "This I do for you."

Debra seated her mother in the cart and then moved to the other side. "Thank you."

As the man walked out of the door and turned right, she drove across the space and through the next building where she had left her bag.

Dorothy was down to the last few bites of her brownie by the time the people rounded the end of the extremely long greenhouse. Debra looked up and waved.

Dorothy picked up the last bite of brownie. Debra stood and grabbed under her mother's arm. "Here Dorothy. I need to talk to these nice people for a bit. So why don't you lay over here and take your afternoon nap."

The woman looked up at her, confused. "Nap?"

"Yes. You always take a nap after your lunch. And when you wake up, you can have another brownie."

The woman stood and allowed herself to be guided. "The brownie... I like brownies."

"Yes dear. Here, lay down on the chaise here in the shade."

The woman stretched out as Debra straightened the front lock of her hair. "Close your eyes and drift off to dreamland. That's a good girl." She pointed at the picnic table. "I'll be right here."

The woman's voice was already half asleep. "Okay..."

Debra patted the crossed hands on the woman's stomach. Standing, she walked back to the table as she held out her hand toward the other side of the table. "Please. You have questions, and I have my lunch."

Nash took the middle of the bench. "You are Debra Scalese?"

"Yes."

Muna sat. "Formally Daniel Scalese?"

She nodded. "Yes."

Frank slid in from the end. "Also known as Jana Zabriskie?"

Debra took a large bite of the rolled food. She nodded as she chewed.

Nash waited until she swallowed. "Did you poison the people at the compound in Fort Mojave?"

"Yes."

Muna frowned. "Why are you answering?"

The woman put down the roll and took a sip from her thermos. "This is Mexico. I'm assuming you are police from the United States."

Nash and Muna pulled their ID wallets. "FBI."

Debra pointed at Powder's badge on her chest. "Ah. So the dog is yours."

Nash nodded. "She is also an agent."

Debra nodded as she took a smaller bite of the food wrap and chewed. "How did you find me?"

Muna sighed. "It wasn't easy."

"But you're here. And you want answers to some troublesome questions."

Nash's one eyebrow raised as she looked at the elderly woman lying on the wooden chaise lounge.

Debra glanced for a second behind her. "Ah yes. My mother. Dorothy Scalese. Once a promising student who dreamed of being an engineer."

Nash's eyes shifted to the woman chewing on the rolled lunch. "And you're willing to tell us about her and you. Why?"

"This is Mexico. Your Maranda rights don't apply. You have no jurisdiction here. And I have no intention of returning to the United States. So..." She held out her palms and spread them to her sides. "Here we are. Where do you want to start?"

Frank cleared his throat. "How about wherever you want to begin?"

Debra's smile was only about half, and it was just on the left side. She nodded as she unwrapped the brownie. Folding her hands over the condiment, she glanced back at her mother. "Like I said, my mother was smart and wanted to be an engineer. But my father took it all away."

Nash cocked her head to one side. "How so?"

"She was an undergraduate student, and he was a graduate student who was the teacher's assistant for one of the math classes. Several girls, I'm sure, were smitten with him. I think that's the word back then. And he took advantage of the carnal lust."

Nash nodded. "They had an affair."

Debra's eyes closed as she wagged her head softly. "Not exactly." Her eyes opened. "You see, my mother was from a strict family and would have saved herself for her husband. But he didn't see it her way, and one night... I can only assume from her stories—that he somehow took advantage of her." She wobbled her hand back and forth. "Whether there were drugs or alcohol involved, we'll never know. But needless to say, she was pregnant."

Frank pointed at her. "You."

She nodded as she broke off a small piece of the brownie and stuck it in her mouth. "Me." Her mouth firmed, and she tilted her head to one side. "When she told him, he denied he was the father. So, she went home and had her child. Quietly accepting her fate. Except on the birth certificate." She quietly opened the leather-bound book and withdrew a photocopy of a birth certificate. She turned it and pushed it across to Nash.

Nash studied the paper and then looked up with a frown. "Peter Lambert was your father?"

She nodded. "The term you're looking for is patricide."

Muna growled. "Along with eighteen others."

Debra looked at the diminutive black woman. "All with dirt on their hands. Several had also been teacher's assistants at the same time. They were all friends from their college years, except for a few of the younger ones."

"But why?"

She looked at Muna and blinked twice. "Do you kill bad guys?"

Muna cringed.

"Do you?"

Nash cleared her throat. "Yes. Yes, we do."

Nash watched the woman's eyes. There was no accusation, no compassion, no emotion, only observation. "Well, there are bad people who never get your attention. And I've taken care of that."

Frank rumbled. "That's called vigilantism."

She picked up the last crumbs of the brownie and licked her fingers. Wiping her hands on the napkin, she shrugged. "Some call it justice."

Nash pushed her finger out on the table and tapped it for effect. "And do you see yourself as being above justice?"

The woman smiled wanly. "No. Certainly not."

"But you are down here in Mexico. You're talking to us about everything because you know we are out of jurisdiction, and the Maranda code doesn't apply…"

Debra pushed the wax paper into the paper sack. "You're wasting time. What else do you want to know?"

Muna pulled out her phone and found the document. "Foxglove, deadly nightshade, castor bean, and a few more." She looked up. "What am I missing here? Each one wasn't enough to kill anyone."

"You're missing the arsenic in the water. Hollyhock and water chestnut, also known as hemlock, I ground with rosemary and fennel to put in the crust on the turkey. The hemlock enhances the tryptophan in the turkey. Hollyhock gives the body a boost to the tryptophan to produce serotonin, melatonin, and niacin. So it helps put them to sleep, and the niacin opens the blood vessels to distribute the rest through the body. The hemlock, which was in our brownies, shuts down the kidneys and liver first. The rest cascades from there. A few other compounds dull the responses, to reduce the spasms and let the person drift off to sleep." She waved her hand back at the woman lying on the chaise. "Like my mother."

Nash jerked and pointed at the woman. "She's—"

Debra raised her hand to cut her off. "For the last twenty minutes. Dorothy had Alzheimer's. She didn't suffer, but it was very inconvenient for me. It had reached a point where she needed to be institutionalized or euthanized. You coming here decided for me. I've been ready for a couple of weeks now."

Frank pointed at the paper sack. "But you had a brownie as well."

The woman nodded precisely. "Yes. Our lunches were the same. In a few minutes, I, too, will be asleep." She looked at Nash and Muna. "Who did the research to find me?"

Nash pointed at Muna.

Debra pushed the thin binder over to Muna. "You will need my journal. It will answer a lot more questions. Ones you don't know and now don't have the time to think about."

She turned on the bench. "Now, if you don't mind. We've run out of time. I should go lay with my mother."

She stood but sank to the concrete of the patio.

Frank slid off the bench and rushed to the woman. Kneeling, he felt for a pulse at the neck. Turning, he shook his head at Nash standing. Muna's mouth gaped open. "Just like that?"

Frank rolled back to sit on the patio next to the body. He glanced at the body of the older woman. "She probably misjudged the timing for her, too."

Nash sat on the edge of the table. Her head ground around to look at Muna, who was already reading the notes in the binder.

Muna's gaze fixed on the journal before her. "These pages are from when she was just a child in Poway. She learned about poison at a very early age." She swallowed, fighting the frog in her throat. "I don't think I'll be able to sleep for a while."

SNEAK PEEK

FLAT SURF

Have you wondered about where Frank Pounds, the coyotes, and the ladies of Deep Six started? Here is a sneak peek at their origin story.

BAER CHARLTON

FLAT SURF

A FRANK POUNDS NOVEL

FLAT SURF

CHAPTER 1 — RED SAND

BAER CHARLTON

THE ONE HALF-OPENED eye was blind with sleep. The two eyes of the coyote, a foot away, watched the man twitch in his nightmare.

The heat was always the same—intense and rising. The door never opened—until it was too late. The window continued to crack —a hundred pieces became a thousand that became a million. The dashboard would always balloon from the engine toward the two detectives. The unused radio would become a missile. Darkness became yellow-white heat as the small bomb expanded from the firewall's engine side, turning the moonless night into the sun itself. The freeway overpass loomed as the undercover car now turned fireball followed its given track to destruction...

The twitch always saved him. His shoulder was violent. But his naked butt cheeks told him he was already sitting up. The sweat needled his skin as his hands hung between his knees. He waited as his breathing returned to his slowed rhythm—his heart would follow a minute later.

The fangs of the coyote were still bright white. The pink and black of its tongue curled at the back of the lower fangs. The canine stood just inside the door. Frank was never sure if the coyote was sizing him up for breakfast or just checking in. The bowl of food was sometimes eaten and sometimes went weeks with only a biscuit or two consumed. The water bowl was under a constant drip, refilling the bowl in a couple of hours. The dog turned and stepped outside the open door. It was their arrangement. The door was open. Frank would roll over some nights in the winter, and the pup would be curled in a ball behind his knees like he had the first winter—*five hundred eighty-seven days before*. Frank didn't keep track, but something in his mind had turned on with the accident. He didn't care, but he now knew how long ago.

Two thousand five hundred and fifty-two mornings since the night his life changed. *Two thousand five hundred and twenty-seven* mornings since they told him he would live—they just never told him how. *Two thousand five hundred and forty-five* mornings since they had buried his best friend from second grade on. *Two thousand four hundred and two mornings* since they told him he would walk again—they just didn't tell him what it would take to do it without a walker or cane.

Two thousand mornings since he had sat on the edge of his bed and rubbed the nightmare from his face—again.

He slid from the side of the bed. His toes bent as the heels rose to touch his butt cheeks. He rested until he felt the muscles in his legs relax and soften with the stretch. With his hands on the edge of the mattress, he gently pushed as he unfolded and sat back on the bed. He gently eased his body forward to lie along the faces of his quadriceps. His nipples hung suspended an inch above his knees. Slowly releasing a breath, they touched and then lay squished. As the crosshatching of scars on his back gently stretched, he allowed himself a dozen slow breaths.

He opened his eyes. The pattern of the ancient Persian rug, bracketed by his feet, was always the same. He noted the pale-pink nail polish on his right big toe needed to be touched up. Maybe it was time to get a complete pedicure. But for now, a cool shower on the porch would have to be enough.

Frank rose and padded his way out the open door. Turning left, he pulled the lever for the shower.

As his friends called his house, the *shack* was the last building at the end of homes built long before building codes came to the bohemian enclave of Crystal Cove. Before he insulated the walls, the shack had been nothing more than a cover from the cruel winter winds raking the point and shelter from the hot sun of Southern California.

Frank glanced at his closest neighbor. The yellow house—six hundred twenty-seven feet away. Three hundred and twelve of which was now State Park. The rest would come when he was finally gone.

Frank stepped into the stream of the cool shower. The warmth came from a looping of black hoses lying on the roof. In less than three minutes, the water would be pure cold county water.

Taking a shower in the afternoon was an act of desperation. There was no way to mix cold water to temper the scalding heat from the sunbaked hoses.

Frank rinsed his hair in the now-cold water and turned off the shower. The cold finish was always refreshing. Frank thought of it as the same as the stinging brace of aftershave lotion he no longer needed.

He sat on the wooden office desk chair to dry off. He waved at the woman standing on the deck of the neighboring house. She didn't wave back. Frank figured she would complain about the naked man, and the long-suffering park employee would have to explain the facts of life. The lone building sat in the middle of one of the last clothing-optional parts of the California coast. There was nothing the state or the park could do about the man who showered on his deck overlooking the spectacular coastline he also surfed.

His stomach growled.

He pulled on the next T-shirt on the three-foot pile. The florid image of a buxom bikinied surfer on a fourteen-foot old-school board bracketed between the words *Surf or Die*. It was one of his favorite shirts and the oldest. His physical therapist had given it to him *one thousand six hundred and seventy-two* days before. He fluffed it out over his weathered board shorts.

After slipping his feet into the rainbow-painted huaraches, he lifted his right foot and checked the remaining tread. Most of three tires had basically survived the explosion. He had asked the watch commander to secure the tires for him. Why waste good tire tread? One of the precinct's finest had made him a fresh pair of huaraches from the tire tread. Since they knew how he felt about his longtime friend and partner, and to show him that they were okay with the man's sexual nature, they had dyed the leather in a rainbow. The pink toenails were Frank's idea and contribution. At six-foot-four and still built like a running back, nobody ever questioned his clothes or toes.

The old beater of a Bentley convertible still rode solidly over the gravel road. The old track led almost directly to the shack's side of the café, but Frank wanted it to grow over to discourage any tourists from taking a back route to the headlands. The new road wandered across the fourteen hundred acres he had inherited on his twenty-first birthday. He signed a promise with the state to never develop the land and to leave it as a nature refuge in exchange for access to his house, his café—also called 'The Shack,' free power, water, and no taxes. On his death, the entire refuge would escheat to their control and remain a reserve. Everyone else just thought he was a squatter or a surf bum.

He pulled the Bentley behind the Shack. The screen door squealed—daily routines.

The light through the south-facing window was warm on his right foot. Without checking his watch, he knew it was close to eight. The kids would be clustered off the point. The weather last night would have brought in swells from Alaska. The short boards would be carving up the four-to-six-foot rollers.

HE SCANNED THROUGH THE DOW JONES AS HE REACHED for his mug. A thin finger and thumb gently stopped him at his wrist. He looked up at the tall, emaciated waiter.

"I figure you're going to need this instead."

Frank looked down at the steaming cup of espresso, and then down the small restaurant to the only windows looking out at the large parking lot.

The golden-brown Taurus with the hubcap-free black tire was obvious. There was only one detective left in Orange County who insisted on driving the old Taurus.

Frank growled. "Just go lock the door."

Danny mocked shock. "That is no way to treat your only son. Besides, it's too late."

The tall man sashayed his six and a half feet of what looked like only a skeleton through the restaurant. "Good morning, Mickey. Did you want chai while you beat the old man?"

The young Italian slicked back his hair with one hand. "Morning, Danny. Um, to go… for both of us, please."

Danny turned at the pass-thru between the coffee station and the counter. He backhand-snapped his towel in the air. "Grumpy has already had breakfast, so you don't have to treat him to steak and eggs at the leather bar."

The detective rolled his eyes. "I've seen him eat before. Trust me —I don't want to see it again."

"Just sayin', sweetie. Save your money for new shoes."

The young detective adjusted his tailored suit as he sat in the chair that Frank had pushed out with his foot. His middle finger and thumb pinched the button through the hole.

"You're out of your district."

The one fleek eyebrow rose. "Danny was right. You are grumpy this morning."

Frank glowered at the young detective for the pace of three slow breaths. "Welcome to Happy Tuesday."

"It's Thursday. The Alzheimer's is making you forget days."

Frank leaned back in his chair with a deep sigh. "I should have run you over when I had the chance."

The young man grumped back. "The tricycle would have dented your cruiser, and you would have had to explain it to Dad. Besides, Mom wouldn't have liked it."

"Your mother's lasagna was the only thing saving your sorry ass."

"That and Dad having a habit of losing at your Wednesday night poker games."

Danny placed a tall paper cup with a lid and a pink-sequined thermal tumbler mug in front of the two men. "Have him home in time for his nap, or he's going to be cranky."

The young detective pointed at the bright-pink mug. His face was a sour question mark.

"It's your chai tea. Don't be a dick."

"Pink?"

The tall waiter threw his hip out and rested the back of his hand on it. "Your tea doesn't come in condensed espresso shots like his double quad-shots." He waved his right hand at the tall paper cup. "Besides, I lent you a perfectly fine aluminum—"

"It got a bullet through it."

"And you didn't replace it. So I lent you Frankie's personal undercover brown—"

"A bus ran over it..." The young detective was now growling. Frank was leaning back with only a hint of an amused smile.

Danny was nicely wound up. "I think we're starting to see a trend here. I loan you nice things, and you treat them like shit. I'd beat you with a stick, but I can't trust you to take off that Goosy belt and reciprocate. You just can't be trusted with nice things. So you get the one even I wouldn't be caught dead with."

"It's Gucci."

"Just what I said—Goosy. And you don't." He turned to Frank. "Don't bring him back. He's dead to me." He passed his palm down the air, spun on his heel, and stormed off.

"Who said I was leaving with him, anyway?"

Frank watched the waiter disappear into the back. A moment later, he came out with a tray loaded with a food order and backed his way out the front door to the deck. He frowned and turned his attention to the young man sipping on the pink tumbler. "What are you doing down here anyway?"

"We have a body."

"Tough shit. I don't work for you guys anymore. Do I have to show you the fourteen-inch scar up my spine to convince you?"

"Is that the one crossing the twenty-two-inch scar where you got skegged on Redondo Beach?"

Frank growled. "I deserved that one. I was on his beach and jumped the wave ahead of him. I was trespassing."

"What about the three-inch knife wound?"

"Left or right side?" He smiled as he sipped the last of his espresso in the porcelain cup.

"Left."

"Your mother apologized for it years ago."

"God... you *are* getting old. She dorked you on the right side. The left was the dope dealer."

"He apologized with his dying breath. What's your point?"

"Well, Mr. Zipper, this one is on your beach."

Frank glanced over his shoulder out the window. His frown was superior instead of drama.

"No, Newport. Out on the point. An elderly couple and their little dog found it this morning."

Frank squinted one eye. "That's not your jurisdiction, either."

"No, but we think the victim might live up in my district."

"Why me?" Frank pushed the handle on the small cup.

"Because you have enough special insight that we can justify a consulting fee."

"How big a fee?"

"Your five hundred a day started an hour ago."

"I don't need it." His face was stone. He knew the negotiations and what was a reality in the big cities of Orange County.

"Okay, eight Frankos, but you're paying for lunch." Mickey stood and buttoned his center button.

Frank remained seated and then turned to face out the window at the ocean. "It's gonna be a great day on the water."

"Jeezus. Okay, I'll spring for my own lunch."

Frank turned back. Sipping on the empty cup, he eyed the younger man. He put down the cup and stood. Sliding his feet into the huaraches, he looked up. "A full large, and I choose the choke-and-puke."

The right lip of the younger man curled. "Slut. I told the sheriff you wouldn't come for under twelve hundred."

Frank smiled a toothy smile. "Done." He put his hand out toward the door. "Fifteen big it is. But I'm not changing my clothes, and we're taking your car. I don't want to get mine dirty in the city."

The kid smiled and picked up the pink tumbler.

"And make sure you get Pinkie back to Danny. It's the one your dad gave Kahuna when he made detective."

Mickey held the newish tumbler up. "You're so full of shit."

Frank growled. "Just make sure Danny gets it back. It's his favorite, but I think he's sweet on you."

As they climbed into the sushi-smelling undercover car, Mickey snickered. "Danny isn't sweet on me. I don't wear enough leather."

"Your belt's as close as he'll ever get to his fantasy of going to a leather bar."

Mickey pumped the pedal twice and turned the key. "Why?"

"He's afraid they'll hurt him."

Mickey frowned as he backed the car. "Have you ever watched him compete in tae kwon do?"

Frank nodded. "I was also there when he got his third-degree black belt in karate."

ALSO BY BAER CHARLTON

The Very Littlest Dragon: NEW Editions
(All-new full-color ebook, a paperback with
coloring pages, and a full-color Collector's Edition hardback)

Stoneheart — Pulitzer Nominee 2015
Angel Flights
What About Marsha?
Pirate's Patch
Flat Surf

I Drink Coffee and Make Shit Up
One Writer's Journey Without Signposts

JOLIE "ROCKET" ROBERTS SERIES
Dry Bridge of Vengeance – Book One
Dry Ridge of Redemption – Book Two

THORNY WALLACE SERIES
Death in the Valley – Book One
Light to Light – Book Two

SOUTHSIDE HOOKER SERIES
Death on a Dime – Book One
Night Vision – Book Two
Unbidden Garden – Book Three
Boomtown – Book Four
One Day Under the Grass – Book Five
Southside Hooker Series: Books 1–5 Box Set
(Collector's Edition hardback & ebook available)

ABOUT THE AUTHOR

Bestselling author Baer Charlton graduated from UC Irvine with a degree in Social Anthropology, monkeyed around for a while, and then proceeded onward with a life of global travel, multi-disciplinary adventure, and meeting the memorable array of characters he would come to describe in his writing. He has ridden things with gears, engines, and sails, and made things with wood, leather, and metal. He has been stitched back together more times than the average hockey team; his long-suffering wife and an assortment of cats and dogs have nursed him back to health after each surgery.

Baer knows a lot about many things in this world. History flows through his veins and pours out of him at the slightest provocation. Do not ask him what you may think is a simple question unless you have the time to hear a fascinating story.

You can find more at
www.mordantmedia.com